THE ENCHA...
Ann...

"ENTERTAINING . . . plen...

"HIGHLY RECOMMENDED. Playfulness and pathos blend to form an entertaining and thought-provoking story."
—*Starlog*

SHADOW
The original! Introducing Shadow, a master thief as elusive as her name . . .

SHADOW HUNT
Shadow returns, on a quest to recover a stolen jewel—but her guide is an assassin who could take her life as easily as she takes a breath . . .

SHADOW DANCE
Shadow must lead a band of warriors into a horror-laden swamp to find the cure for the Crimson Plague—a deadly disease sweeping through the streets of Allanmere . . .

GREENDAUGHTER
Generations before Shadow was born, the elves of the Mother Forest had to do the unthinkable—join forces with humans to defeat the barbarian invaders who sought to destroy them . . .

DAGGER'S EDGE
Jaellyn's feisty Aunt Shadow knows what a woman born of royal *and* elvan blood needs to survive when a demon comes to call—a little dagger, and a lotta luck . . .

DAGGER'S POINT
Jaellyn bravely sets out on a journey to the vast uncharted West, determined to find her lost father . . . and a way to make herself whole . . .

And now . . .
The stunning conclusion to the acclaimed series which has swept readers into a rich, sensual world of magic and menace . . .

WILD BLOOD

Ace Books by Anne Logston

Wild Blood

ANNE LOGSTON

ACE BOOKS, NEW YORK

This book is an Ace original edition,
and has never been previously published.

WILD BLOOD

An Ace Book / published by arrangement with
the author

PRINTING HISTORY
Ace edition / September 1995

All rights reserved.
Copyright © 1995 by Anne Logston.
Cover art by Matt Zumbo.
This book may not be reproduced in whole or in part,
by mimeograph or any other means, without permission.
For information address: The Berkley Publishing Group,
200 Madison Avenue, New York, New York 10016.

ISBN: 0-441-00243-9

ACE®
Ace Books are published by The Berkley Publishing Group,
200 Madison Avenue, New York, New York 10016.
ACE and the "A" design are trademarks
belonging to Charter Communications, Inc.

PRINTED IN THE UNITED STATES OF AMERICA

10 9 8 7 6 5 4 3 2 1

To my editor, Laura Anne Gilman,
and my agent, Laura Cifelli,
who put up with me

PROLOGUE

Excerpt from High Lady Rivkah's written history of the attempted invasion of Allanmere:

". . . rumors of an invasion force of barbarians sweeping down from the north, looting and destroying every settlement in its path. High Lord Sharl, then in Cielman at the time, arranged for additional shipments of supplies and negotiated for additional troops, the hiring of mercenary soldiers and mages, and other defensive measures for the city. He arranged also for the manufacture and shipment to Allanmere of a wagon full of trade goods in the hope of entering into a treaty with the elvan clans in the forest known as the Heartwood near Allanmere, although these elves had previously reacted with hostility to any approach of the forest.

"High Lord Sharl, Rivkah, and High Lord Sharl's personal guard then departed for Allanmere with all possible speed to warn the city, to increase the city's fortifications, and to attempt to negotiate an alliance with the elves of the Heartwood. As High Lord Sharl's party rounded the northern edge of the Heartwood, however, they were attacked by a small band of fur-clad barbarians armed with only the most primitive of weapons yet ferocious in battle, likely an advance scouting party for the invading force. High Lord Sharl and his guards fought off the attackers bravely, although only two of his guards survived, and the three surviving barbarians fled into the forest. High Lord Sharl and his folk bravely pursued the barbarians into the forest.

"At length High Lord Sharl and his people came upon their attackers near the center of the forest, where they found the barbarians attacking two elves, a male and a female. High Lord Sharl and his guards killed the barbarians and rescued the elves Valann and Chyrie, persuading the elves to guide them through the forest to the city. During their journey they met and spoke with Rowan, ruler of most of the elvan clans of the Heartwood, who eagerly assented to High Lord Sharl's plan for an alliance between human and elf, and as a gesture of her good faith sent the elves Valann and Chyrie with High Lord Sharl and his people to the city of Allanmere, there to learn the ways of humans and to teach their own customs. High Lord Sharl in his great kindness suggested that when the army should reach the lands near the forest, the elvan clans should send those unfit to fight to the city to shelter in the greater safety there.

"High Lord Sharl conveyed both the elves to Allanmere, although an attack by hostile elves near the edge of the forest cost him the life of his guardswoman Doria. High Lord Sharl made the elves welcome in his home and began the fortification of Allanmere in preparation for battle. He received into his house and protection those elves coming from the forest begging for food and shelter. High Lord Sharl took to wife his companion Rivkah and pledged that she would bear the people of Allanmere an heir.

"At length the barbarian army approached Allanmere, wielding mighty weapons and potent fire magic. High Lord

Sharl sought to focus the brunt of the barbarian attack against the city, hoping that the elves in the forest would be left in peace, and to that end ordered a mighty storm to counter the barbarians' fire. High Lord Sharl's mages conjured the image of a great fire god, the enemy of the barbarians' ice god, and a great earthquake, which caused the barbarians to flee the city. In due course the mighty magics and bold warriors of the city were able to repel the attack and send the barbarians forth, though at a cost of considerable damage to the city.

"When it became apparent that the city had been rendered unfit for habitation by the damage during the attack, High Lord Sharl resolved to return to Cielman to raise money to rebuild the city. He first visited the forest to learn how the elves had fared and was told by Rowan that there was no longer any unity among the elvan peoples. The elf Chyrie, who had been with child and whose husband had perished in the battle, had borne twins, a boy and a girl. She gave the girl-child, Ria, to High Lord Sharl and High Lady Rivkah to foster in the hope that one day the elves of the Heartwood and the people of Allanmere could again stand together in peace and unity.

"To understand these events surrounding the founding of the great trade city of Allanmere, it is first necessary to understand the proposed economic base of the city and High Lord Sharl's expectations . . ."

From the oral clan history as told by Rowan, Eldest of the Inner Heart Clan:

". . . so it was that Rowan of Inner Heart had joined the clans of Inner Heart, Moon Lake, Redoak, and Owl Clan until they lived as one clan, and the women who had ripened danced the High Circle together, and fruit was brought to loins thought barren. And it was Rowan's desire that other clans be brought to deal in friendship with Inner Heart and with each other, so that all in the Heartwood should prosper together.

"It was in that time that Valann and Chyrie of the Wilding Clan, who were mates, Valann gifted as a healer and Chyrie as a beast-speaker, journeyed to the Forest Altars upon Chyrie's ripening, to seek the Mother Forest's blessing of their coupling that they might conceive a child. Thus they came together at the Altars that Valann might plant seed in Chyrie's womb, but were most foully attacked by fur-clad humans who, despite Valann and Chyrie's fiercest struggles, rendered Valann insensible and took Chyrie's body by force. They were in turn attacked by the humans Sharl, Rivkah, Romuel, and Doria, who dared to draw their weapons and spill blood on the most sacred earth of the Forest Altars, but did thereafter somewhat heal Valann and Chyrie by use of their outland magic.

"Thereafter the humans professed friendship to Valann and Chyrie and in the guise of food and fire cast a geas upon them, binding them to guide the humans through hostile territories despite Valann and Chyrie's injuries and despite Chyrie's ripeness and possible pregnancy. Through great guile Valann and Chyrie managed to lure their abductors into a trap laid by Inner Heart, and the humans were captured successfully.

"Our Gifted One, Dusk, completed Chyrie's healing and so learned that Chyrie was with child, but that she bore two sparks of life in her womb, a great and unknown blessing of the Mother Forest portending events of the greatest import.

"Under truthspell the humans were forced to admit that they had knowledge of a great barbarian army approaching the forest from the north, posing a threat to both the forest and the human city. They had deliberately sought to conceal this knowledge and had abducted Valann and Chyrie with the intention of holding them hostage to force the elvan clans to grant trade favors to the city.

"In punishment for their crimes against Valann and Chyrie, Rowan placed a geas on the humans to grant asylum to those most precious to the elvan clans, the children, pregnant and ripe females, and those too sick to fight in defense of their land, within the city during the battle, and to render unto the forest clans such weapons and aid as the human city possessed. Rowan bound the humans to say nothing of the geas laid upon them or of the crimes they had perpetrated, that those who looked to the human Sharl for leadership should obey him more willingly. Rowan sent Valann and Chyrie to watch and assure the humans' fulfillment of their obligations to the forest, and to shield Chyrie and the lives she bore from harm. Rowan sent messages of goodwill to all the clans of the Heartwood, bringing together many clans to raise their magics and fight as one against the enemies approaching, and inviting them also to send some of their people to the city to shelter.

"So it was that Valann and Chyrie journeyed from the forest into the human city, where they gave welcome and comfort to those of our clans who came to the city for shelter, and shielded them against the taunts and abuse of the humans of the city. Valann and Chyrie and the elves who came to the city worked together to help the humans, to teach them in the ways of preparing and preserving food and in the magic of the forest.

"In time the barbarian force swept down from the north like a great tempest, ravaging the edges of the Heartwood as they journeyed around it toward the city. Many brave clans fought and fell to keep the invaders from the forest, and many clans who had fought fiercely one against the other now stood back to back as if born of the same womb, binding together their gifts and their swords striking as one against the enemy. Still the invaders won deeper into the forest, ravaging its very heart so that it seemed that the forest must fall.

"Inside the human city, those who had gone to shelter fought bravely as well, but in a great strike the barbarians slew Chyrie's mate. So it was that Chyrie, heavy with child and dark with grief, flung her spirit into the very heart of the Mother Forest and raised the forest itself against the invaders, raising vine and tree and every beast of the forest against the barbarians. And a great shaking came from the earth, and the barbarians fled northward once more, leaving the forest gutted and half-dead behind them.

"And in these great trials the alliance of the elvan clans was no more, for many clans had died and many others had lost their lands, and there was little game. But Chyrie in her time bore twin children of elvan and human blood mixed together, and she gave her daughter Ria to the human lord Sharl and her son Valann to Rowan as the Mother Forest willed, as a symbol of hope that humans and elves might once more thrive and dwell as peaceful neighbors. And Chyrie returned to the forest, where she who was most greatly tried and most greatly blessed by the Mother Forest dwells and stands as guardian of the peace and prosperity of our lands.

"And so it is that the Mother Forest has decreed that a great destiny awaits the children of Chyrie, that one day all the peoples of the forest will once again stand together in friendship, and that peace will be made between the forest and the humans as well.

"And so it was that Rowan set about rebuilding the village of Inner Heart, where many had perished and the lands had suffered and the game had fled . . ."

RIA

"Come back here, you savage little beast!"

Ria darted around the corner and ducked through a doorway, knocking furniture aside as she leaped for the window. Almost she didn't make it; this was the council chamber, and the small windows were set high in the wall for security reasons. Her tiny fingers and bare toes, however, found purchase between the stone blocks, and Ria scrambled merrily through the opening, shrieking delightedly as Lady Sivia raged impotently behind her. Ria jumped down from the window ledge and glanced frantically around her for a hiding place; the keep's grounds, however, were level and bare of trees and bushes.

Without hesitation, Ria ran for her one sure sanctuary: the stables. Lady Sivia was as terrified of horses as Ria was fond of them, and Ria had fled to the stable loft to escape her governess so many times that the horses no longer startled when the tiny barefoot figure charged into the stables and scrambled recklessly up the ladder to the loft. She burrowed into the hay and curled up in her hasty den, giggling to herself even as the dust of last autumn's hay made her sneeze. In a few minutes, if events followed their usual pattern, one or two of the guards or servants would appear on Lady Sivia's behalf, hunting for the governess's errant charge. They'd look around the stable, and search even in the loft, but thanks to what Ria thought of as her "don't-see-me," they'd leave baffled and tell Lady Sivia that Ria must have somehow sneaked back into the hall and hidden there. Where else could the child have gone, after all?

Where else, indeed? This was only a small country holding belonging to her foster father Sharl's brother Emaril, with but a few outbuildings—and those were now so tightly packed with supplies that even tiny Ria could not have wriggled into a hiding place there. It was early in the year and, although the kitchen gardens had begun to grow their crops of vegetables and herbs, there wasn't enough foliage there to hide a good-sized cat. And there was nothing else within the keep's wall except the keep itself.

Outside the wall, the land was similarly featureless. The few stands of trees that had once grown near the holding had been burned sixteen years earlier, the year of Ria's birth, when the great barbarian army had swept down from the frozen lands beyond the great northern mountains. The main thrust of the army, Ria had been told, had passed west of this small holding, but the surrounding lands had been looted and burned by small raiding parties looking for food, and ravaged again later when the defeated barbarian force had retreated northward. The lands around the holding had been replanted in crops to feed the citizens of Cielman through the postwar famine, and even after the famine was over, the lush flower gardens and topiary mazes Lord Sharl had often described had never reclaimed their rightful places from the usurping wheat fields.

And a topiary maze would have made a wonderful hiding place just now, too. The thick, green late-spring grain was almost tall enough now to hide Ria's slight form, but anyone standing on the wall of the keep and looking down could easily spot her. No, there was nowhere to hide but here in the stables, and unfortunately everybody knew it.

Footsteps outside the stable—to Ria's sensitive ears, the tread of the slipper-shod feet seemed as loud as the clopping of horses' hooves. Ria smiled to herself and burrowed deeper into the hay, although the scratchy blades insinuated themselves down the neck and sleeves of her tunic and itched almost intolerably. She quieted her breathing and imagined herself small and insignificant, silent as shadows, an invisible part of the hay around her. The stable door creaked open and feet scuffed in the scattered hay on the stable floor. The horses stirred in their stalls and snorted at this less familiar intruder.

"Ria?"

Ria almost jumped in surprise at the sound of the voice. If her foster brother Cyril, son of Lord Sharl and Lady Rivkah, had been sent after her instead of one of the servants or the guards, either Lady Sivia was far cleverer than Ria would have believed the stout matron to be, or she'd been so angry that she'd stomped straight off to Lord Sharl and Lady Rivkah to complain, and that boded disaster. Ria and Cyril had been the best of friends since they could do little more than toddle, but for the last few years Cyril had seemed more annoyed by her presence than otherwise, uninterested in what had always been their favorite games and pastimes, and he rarely sought out her company anymore of his own volition. If he'd come looking for her, he'd been sent.

"Ria?" She could hear Cyril climbing the loft ladder now. "I know you're here. No use hiding from me."

We'll see, Ria thought smugly. She almost gave herself away by giggling as Cyril stomped through the hay, once nearly stepping on her, prodding suspicious piles with his scabbard. Cyril knew better than to trust his eyes where Ria was concerned. Mice scattered through the hay, one running heedlessly over Ria's leg. The tiny paws tickled unmercifully. Ria shook with stifled laughter, a burning ache starting in her chest from holding it in.

"Ria!" Cyril's voice held a note of impatience now. His

boots stopped right in front of the tiny peephole Ria had left in the hay. "Will you stop playing and come out? I need to talk to you."

Ria waited until Cyril took the weight off one foot, preparing to step away. Suddenly she reached out and seized his ankle, pulling it out from under him, and Cyril roared indignantly as he tumbled into the hay. Ria leaped from her hiding place and jumped on top of Cyril, tickling him and stuffing hay down the front of his tunic until Cyril, laughing helplessly even as his face reddened with anger, finally flung her aside and scrambled back to his feet. The cracks between the rough-hewn wooden slabs of the barn walls were to Ria's small fingers and toes as good as any ladder, and she fled up one wall, unmindful of spiders and splinters, and scrambled out onto one of the rafters where she perched, grinning down triumphantly at her foster brother.

"Will you be still and listen for one moment!" Cyril snapped, scowling upward furiously as he brushed hay and dust out of his golden hair. "If you don't, I'll tell Mother and Father about the lizard you stuck down the back of Lady Sivia's gown."

That sobered Ria. She'd be punished for her trick, no matter how the stout and pompous matron had invited it with her overdignified stuffiness and courtly posturing. Lady Rivkah might even confine Ria to her rooms until the departure for Allanmere, and then Ria would lack even the poor diversion of watching the supplies being readied and the wagons loaded—let alone her favored pastime of pestering the guards and servants with tricks and endless questions. Life in Emaril's keep was boring enough that any entertainment at all was precious, and the very thought of being penned up behind walls, unable to escape, made Ria shudder.

Ria sighed and settled herself resignedly on the rafter on her belly, hands under her chin, ankles crossed and knees hanging down on either side of the heavy wooden beam like one of the holding's cats. Anything, even a lecture from her foster brother, was preferable to confinement.

"All right," she said, sighing again.

Cyril plunked himself down on a bale of hay, scowling up at her.

"I don't suppose you'd come down here to talk?"

Ria shook her head firmly. She was fair game for revenge on Cyril's part, and he might be trying to trick her down from her safe perch. On high ground she had the advantage.

"You know we're leaving for Allanmere in only a couple of days," Cyril began. "As soon as all the preparations are finished."

Ria nodded impatiently. Talk around the keep had been about nothing but the impending journey. Emaril's servants and guards would likely be glad enough to be rid of Lord Sharl and Lady Rivkah and their son and mischievous foster daughter and the extra work they occasioned, although Ria liked to believe she had endeared herself to a fair percentage of the staff. Ria herself was desperately eager for the journey and an end to the placid and uninteresting life at the keep, broken only by a very few journeys to Cielman for Lord Sharl to visit with his brother. Sometimes she felt so restless, so caged, that it seemed she'd burst if she wasn't set free. Often she ached until she nearly wept for something she could not name; sometimes she ran around and around and around the keep's walls until her sides ached and her stomach heaved, and still it was not enough. This place, this life, was not enough.

Ria knew her discontentment was wicked and ungrateful; High Lord Emaril had been more than kind to give Lord Sharl and his family the use of the keep after the near destruction of Allanmere, when Lord Sharl had returned to Cielman all but penniless. High Lord Emaril had been supportive, too, of Lord Sharl's efforts to raise money and settlers to rebuild the city, although Ria had heard Lord Sharl confide to Lady Rivkah that High Lord Emaril thought it a foolish venture.

Ria didn't care how foolish Lord Sharl's plan was. If it got her out of this stifling place and back to her true homeland, the home of *her people,* that was good enough for

Ria. Seeing the glum look on Cyril's face, however, Ria realized that he, perhaps, saw the journey a little differently.

"Won't it be fun?" Ria said, her deep blue-green eyes sparkling excitedly. "New places to see, a whole city all for us, and a forest and a river and a real journey. It might take *weeks* to get there."

"It's not going to be much fun for a while," Cyril told her glumly. "The stonemasons will have finished rebuilding part of the castle at least, but there won't be many servants. It won't be very comfortable, either, traveling by wagon, and it may be dangerous."

"Dangerous? Really?" Ria almost trembled with eagerness. Until now, "dangerous" was distracting Yvarden, her foster parents' mage, while she was casting leakproofing spells on the barrels. "Dangerous" was running too fast down the stairs while they were still wet and slick with soapsuds after being scoured. And "dangerous," of course, was slipping a lizard down the back of Lady Sivia's gown when the plump matron's bulk was between Ria and the door. "Dangerous how?"

"Brigands," Cyril said grimly. "Floods. Tornadoes. Earthquakes. And the elves near Allanmere, of course."

"The elves?" *That* made Ria's pointed ears prick up eagerly. "Why are they—we—dangerous?"

"They were dangerous before," Cyril pointed out. "Read the histories. They used to shoot arrows at any human who got too close to the forest."

"That was before the alliance between the elvan clans, remember," Ria said practically. "Before the barbarians came. The elves allied with the city during the war. Why should they be dangerous now?"

Cyril shrugged.

"It's been sixteen years," he said. "They may have decided that now that there's no threat to them, they don't have any need for an alliance. According to the messages Father and Mother have gotten back, there's been no friendly contact from the elves. Father's sent envoys to the edge of the forest, but the elves there shot arrows at anyone who came too close. Father said some of the border clans were always hostile to the humans, and he thinks those clans have claimed most of the border lands, so the envoys can't get through to meet with clans who might be more friendly. If you'd ever sit still long enough to listen to what Father and Mother talk about at supper, you'd know that."

Ria fell silent. Somewhere in that forest she had a mother, a brother of her own blood—a brother she'd never seen, a mother who had handed her over to the humans like a piece of shoddy trade goods. Her brother had run free in the forest for sixteen years, not caged behind stone walls, not raised by strangers. Had her brother Valann or her mother Chyrie thought about her in all those years? Had they wondered how she fared? Had Valann ever longed to know her? Had Chyrie ever, even for a moment, regretted flinging her daughter aside like a piece of refuse? Or had they both put her out of their minds and gone their own way? Until now, Ria could only wonder. But soon she'd be near them, perhaps even meet them. Eagerness and resentment—well mixed with less definable emotions —warred in her mind.

"But I didn't come to talk about that," Cyril said, breaking Ria's train of thought.

"What is it, then?" Ria said warily. Likely a lecture, then, after all. That, or he was simply acting as an agent of his parents to tell her how much trouble she was in—if not for the incident with Lady Sivia, then for something else.

"Lord Emaril is arriving tonight," Cyril told her. "He's going to be talking to Father about the money Father wants to borrow, and the ships to bring supplies down the Brightwater."

"Ships?" Ria asked in surprise. "I thought we were going in wagons." Traveling down the river by ship might be *much* more interesting. Why, Ria had never so much as seen a real river before, much less a ship.

"We are," Cyril said, dashing Ria's hopes. "But more supplies will be shipped down the Brightwater later. It'll take so long to build the farming community back up, Father's hoping to establish Allanmere as a river trade stopping point. It's in a good spot for trade ships to stop between the northern cities and the south coast, and to pick up trade goods brought in by caravan from the east. Father's going to try to persuade Lord Emaril to send a few supply ships down to try it. If Allanmere can get the river trade, the city's more likely to attract the merchants and artisans it needs to succeed.

"So these negotiations with Lord Emaril are very important," Cyril continued hesitantly. "Mother and Father need you to behave politely for a change, while Lord Emaril's here. He and Father have never gotten along well anyway, and Father has to ask him for a lot of help. So you mustn't do anything that might make Lord Emaril angry while he's here. Mother and Father wanted me to ask you that."

Ria scowled. She never quite understood what everyone wanted from her. "Behave politely" and "be good" were ambiguous and confusing concepts. It seemed impossible to predict whether her behavior would meet with approval or not. Sometimes seemingly everything that was any fun whatsoever was "wrong," and only boring things like sitting still and reading tedious scribblings, or uncomfortable things like sitting still and wearing too much itchy clothing, were "right." And sometimes even *that* wasn't enough; "right" meant remembering when to curtsey and what to say and when to say it, too.

Seeing Ria's hesitation, Cyril added, "Without Lord Emaril's help, we won't even be going to Allanmere."

That did it.

"All right," Ria said grudgingly. "I won't make any trouble while he's here. I promise." She'd just have to puzzle out how to get along without "making trouble."

"All right." Cyril looked vaguely relieved at Ria's promise, but he did not get up and leave as Ria had expected. He sat there in the straw, staring at her broodingly until Ria squirmed.

"What?" Ria said uncomfortably. "I promised, didn't I? What else do you want?"

"Ria, do you remember that ceremony when we were

younger?" Cyril said at last. "Where we said those
pledges?"

Ria remembered it dimly. It had been more than a decade before. There'd been a priest wearing ornate robes
who chanted and told her what words to repeat, she remembered that much; more clearly she recalled the discomfort of her formal gown and the huge feast afterward.

"I remember the feast," Ria giggled. "You bumped my
arm and I spilled the gravy all over you."

"And you kicked off your shoes under the table," Cyril
chuckled, smiling, "and the dogs ran off with one of them."

"You made a face at me," Ria remembered, "and I
threw a roll, and you ducked and it hit the Duke's daughter
sitting next to you. But when Father was going to punish
me, you said it was your fault."

"Well, it was," Cyril admitted. "Sort of. And we still both
got punished."

"They locked me in my room for two days," Ria said,
shuddering. "But what about that ceremony?"

"It—well—" Unaccountably, Cyril blushed, then
abruptly got to his feet. "Never mind. It's not important, I
suppose."

Ria shrugged and watched him leave. Her foster brother
was almost impossible to understand, too, and she'd mostly
stopped trying. Only a few years ago they'd been the closest of friends, playing together constantly, getting into
trouble together to fight the deadly boredom of the day-to-
day routine at the keep. Suddenly his voice had started
sounding funny and he'd started growing hair in strange
places. His scent had changed, too, growing stronger and
somehow harsher. At first Ria had thought Cyril was sick
and that Lady Rivkah, even with her great healing ability,
had overlooked it; sometimes it seemed that everyone
around her was half-blind and deaf and could smell practically nothing. She'd expressed her worry to Lady Rivkah,
who had only laughed and told her that Cyril was merely
growing up.

And as if it wasn't enough that he no longer looked or
smelled or sounded like the Cyril she knew, almost over-

night he'd begun to act like a stranger, too. He wouldn't wrestle in the loft with her anymore, he no longer enjoyed sneaking off to the stream to swim—well, truth be told, he didn't want to do much of anything interesting anymore. And more and more he gave her funny looks, too, the same sort of look the horses gave the stable boy when he was late with their grain.

It wasn't only a boy thing, either. The young ladies at court, many of them younger than Ria, were stuffy and boring, prancing around in the stiff and heavy finery Ria so hated, prattling on tediously about the most idiotic subjects. If that was "growing up," Cyril could have it and welcome. He seemed in a ridiculous hurry to do it, to Ria's way of thinking.

As soon as she was sure Cyril was gone, Ria climbed down from her perch. Lady Sivia would still be looking for her, and Ria would quickly be found if she returned to her rooms, but it was nearing suppertime and Ria had no intention of missing a meal. She could always count on the scullery maids for a hot meal in the kitchens, and even a hiding place under a table or, if necessary, Cook's voluminous apron if Lady Sivia made an uncharacteristic foray below stairs. Fortunately, as no new horses had been brought to the stable, it was obvious that Lord Emaril had not yet arrived, so there would be no repercussions from Lord Sharl and Lady Rivkah if Ria supped alone.

Ria sneaked into the kitchen by way of the kitchen garden entrance. By this time word of Ria's latest exploit had already reached the kitchen, and the scullery maids knew Lady Sivia was looking for her charge, so there was a good deal of giggling as the girls picked choice tidbits from the pots to fill a heaping platter for Ria. She repaid the maids by telling the story of Lady Sivia's gown and the lizard, mimicking the governess's dance and expression as she'd tried to shake the reptile out the back of her gown, until every maid in the kitchen howled with laughter. That brought the serving maids and stewards, and Ria told the story three times before she finally finished her supper.

The merry party in the kitchen was interrupted by the

news that Lord Emaril and his retinue had been sighted by the wall guards, and the scullery maids quickly returned to their cooking pots to have a private supper sent up. That meant that Lady Sivia would be helping Lord Emaril's governess mind Lord Emaril's four youngest children, so Ria judged it safe to creep back up to her rooms. To her dismay, however, she found her foster mother Rivkah there, laying out one of the gowns Ria hated so much.

"There you are," Lady Rivkah said relievedly, scowling at Ria's grubby state. "Have a quick scrub at the washbasin and get dressed. How ever did you manage to get all that hay in your hair? Lord Emaril's here, and you and Cyril must be at the meeting."

"Whatever for?" Ria said, dismayed. Other than the occasional obligatory appearance at feasts and so forth, she'd always escaped formal occasions with visiting nobility.

"Ria, don't argue," Rivkah said firmly. "We'll talk later. You promised you'd behave; Cyril told me so. Now please get dressed."

Ria knew her foster mother better than to argue with that tone; it meant that Lady Rivkah was worried and distracted and not likely to give any quarter. Ria disgustedly wriggled into the finery, hating the thick, binding layers of cloth that itched and stifled and weighted her down miserably. Even more disgusting were the stiff, uncomfortable shoes that cramped her toes and made her teeter precariously when she walked. And whatever was the use of the wretched things? Nobody could see her feet under her skirts anyway.

Lady Rivkah inspected Ria's hands and face critically and sent her back to the basin to scrub the dirt from under her fingernails and comb the last of the hay from her tumbled black curls. The comb caught in a tangle, and Ria growled an oath she'd once heard the stable boy use.

"Ria!" Lady Rivkah's voice was heavy with disapproval. "Young women don't use such language."

"I wish I could cut it," Ria complained, giving the comb another tug and wincing. She wanted to retort that she'd heard Lady Rivkah mutter similar invectives, or worse, on occasion, but that would only provoke an argument.

"Young women don't cut their hair either," her foster mother said impatiently. "And neither do your mother's people, as I recollect. Now come along quickly."

Lady Rivkah hurried Ria down the corridor to the small meeting chamber, where the maids were hastily laying out a late supper. Lord Sharl was there in his formal surcoat, and Cyril, wearing his finest tunic and trousers, looked so dignified that Ria longed to tickle him. The temptation faded, however, when High Lord Emaril and High Lady Vesana entered, flanked by their personal guards.

Ria stared interestedly at the High Lord and Lady of Cielman. When Lord Emaril and his family had visited on previous occasions, or when Lord Sharl and Lady Rivkah had taken Ria and Cyril to Cielman, Ria had taken good care to avoid the adults, lest she be obliged to attend some of the formal suppers and meetings such a visit always brought. Now she was surprised to see that High Lord Emaril didn't really seem all that much older than Lord Sharl, even though Emaril was the oldest of five brothers and Sharl the youngest. In fact, they looked a good deal alike, with the same steel-gray eyes and strong features, although High Lord Emaril's hair was a slightly lighter blond than Lord Sharl's, and High Lord Emaril had grown a short beard over his rather square jaw, while Lord Sharl remained clean-shaven. But Lord Sharl, like High Lord Emaril, had a few gray hairs scattered through his blond locks, and both men had the same frown lines between their eyes.

The two lords, however, had chosen very different ladies. High Lady Vesana was a tiny wisp of a woman, hardly taller than Ria, pale and fragile, with great dark eyes and soft brown hair. She dressed exquisitely and spoke very little; when she did speak, her voice was soft and musical. Lord Emaril tenderly helped her to a chair, and servants scurried to bring cushions for her feet; Ria remembered hearing somewhere that High Lady Vesana had almost died after the birth of her last child a year ago and was nearly an invalid now. The frail little doll of a woman could not have been more unlike Lady Rivkah, long-legged and golden-haired and full of life, a competent partner to Lord Sharl and a powerful mage as well.

The lords and ladies exchanged greetings, and, to Ria's surprise, Lord Sharl introduced Cyril and Ria. In deference to High Lady Vesana's comfort, Lord Sharl quickly had the large table moved aside and smaller tables placed beside each chair.

Already full from her earlier meal in the kitchen and wretchedly uncomfortable in her finery, Ria could only sit and squirm in her chair—her feet dangled far above the floor—while the adults discussed supply shipments and trade routes. To her amazement, Cyril seemed to know what they were talking about and made comments at several points, to which—even more amazing—the adults listened thoughtfully.

Lord Sharl had a map, nailed to a board and propped against the wall, that Ria found marginally more interesting. He showed Lord Emaril how the Brightwater River flowed past Allanmere to the south coast, emptying into the sea much closer to the southern trade cities than the Dezarin River leagues to the east of Cielman. Moreover, ships reaching the southern coast could then take advantage of the east-flowing current that skirted the south coast. The only disadvantage was that the Brightwater had never been completely charted or run by large ships, although rafts had taken measurements, and there was no positive assurance that the river was deep enough all the way down to the coast to support a heavy shipping trade.

"But this is the chance to find out," Lord Sharl said. "If a river trade route can be established this far west, it'll open up huge quantities of land for settlement. The trade roads already pass less than a day's ride east of Allanmere; using the city as a midpoint where the ships and the overland caravans can exchange goods, the distribution of those goods can reach almost any part of the settled country in far less time and at a greatly reduced cost."

"I can arrange two ships," Lord Emaril said after a mo-

.

ment's thought. "I won't risk valuable cargo and ships on an uncharted river, but the thought's worth testing. The ships will stop at Allanmere to deliver supplies; that'll lighten the load for the southern leg of the journey, where the depth may be shallower than we know. If the route can be navigated successfully, we'll discuss including Allanmere in a permanent river route—as soon as Allanmere can show that it has something to trade, that is, or that it can bring in the overland merchants to do their business in the city. That's all I can offer."

From the disappointment on Lord Sharl's and Lady Rivkah's faces, Ria could tell that it was far less than they wanted. Lord Sharl nodded, however.

"It's a start," he said. "At the present I don't know that we'll even have sufficient buildings repaired to house the settlers, much less establish shops and businesses. I think, though, that once news of the river route begins to reach the merchants, they'll come on their own. The prospect of greater profits and a wider distribution will bring them."

"For both our sakes," Lord Emaril said grimly, "I hope it's as you say. I've put a great deal of money—Cielman's and my own—into this venture of yours. And you haven't even managed to make your peace with your elvan neighbors."

"Ria and Cyril are the key to that peace," Lord Sharl said. "We'll have the ceremony as soon as we reach Allanmere. It'll give the settlers time to gradually accept the idea of the alliance and pave the way for negotiations with the elves as well. If I can establish a trade between the city and the elves, the city will be able to trade in goods available nowhere else in the settled country, and open up a new market for our own goods, too."

"You have a grand dream, little brother," Lord Emaril said, smiling a little. "But so far that's all it's been. And you can't feed your people on dreams. I'd have thought you'd learned that lesson already."

"No one could have expected a barbarian invasion," Lord Sharl said with a sigh.

"And nobody expects fires, floods, droughts, crop blight,

hail, plague, dragons, and blizzards," Lord Emaril said wryly. "Yet they come anyway. And a newborn city's a fragile thing."

"If there's another disaster the likes of the invasion," Lady Rivkah said quietly, "any city in the world might fall, newborn or not. Cielman itself was spared only because the main force of the army passed too far to the west."

Lord Emaril had to agree with that. Bored, Ria nibbled at a sweet cake while High Lord Emaril, Lord Sharl, and Lady Rivkah talked about the proposed journey. Their endless discussions of quantities of seed grain, building materials, trade routes, and expansion rates continued until, despite her discomfort, Ria found herself nodding in her chair. She propped herself up and let a few curls fall into her face to cover her closed eyes and dozed, letting the conversation slide by her.

She'd never seen a forest, not a real one, but she dreamed of trees all around her, of cool green shadows and the smell of fresh warm earth and growing things. Trees would tower over her as tall grain towered over her when she lay down among it, but the trees would be much taller—taller even than the wall of the keep, as Lady Rivkah had said. She dreamed of innumerable sounds around her, birdsong that she recognized, other rustlings and swishings and cheepings she could not define. This was the world that should have been hers, her brother's world. For a moment she could almost see him as Lady Rivkah had described the baby she'd seen only briefly, more human than elf, ears round as a human's, black hair straight, but with their mother's tawny gold eyes. He'd be tall now like a human, maybe starting to show muscles like Cyril and with hair growing all over him now, too. Unlike Cyril, though, surely he'd understand her, be her friend. He could understand how trapped she felt in these walls, how she longed to run and run without stopping, to strip off her clothes and feel the wind and the sun caress her skin as she ran. He'd lived with the elves, like wild animals free in the forest, and he'd understand how his sister felt caged within the keep.

For a moment she could feel him near her, see him solidly before her, his eyes wide and glad to see her, and she thought if she reached out, she could touch him, clasp that callused brown hand that would be so large beside her own—

Ria jolted awake just in time to see everyone rising to make their goodnights. Ria quickly slid from her chair and bobbed as Lady Rivkah had taught her, her tongue stumbling over the formal pleasantries she'd tried to memorize. At last she was able to slip away to her room, wriggle out of her finery, and crawl into bed.

Despite her weariness at the meeting with High Lord Emaril—or perhaps because of the surreptitious nap she'd had there—Ria was awake as usual when the sun was no more than a thin white sliver barely peeping over the grain fields. Ria bounced out of bed, splashed her face with water from the basin, and dressed hastily, but she took the time to hang up her finery. Lady Rivkah would be furious if she knew Ria had left the gown crumpled on the floor the night before.

Stopping at the kitchen for a piece of bread and honey, Ria learned to her amazement that High Lord Emaril and High Lady Vesana's carriage had left to return to Cielman only a few moments before Ria had come downstairs. Still, it wasn't so surprising, as most of the household would be busy loading the wagons for tomorrow's departure, and the bustle and confusion around the keep would be exhausting to Lady Vesana. Ria was sorry she'd missed seeing High Lady Vesana's newest baby, but at least their departure would save her further boring meals and hours in itchy gowns and *shoes*.

The servants quickly chased Ria away from the loading operations; her tiny form was all too easy to trip over. Disappointed, Ria found a perfect vantage point on the stable roof to watch the process. Some of the supplies had been stored in the small outbuildings; others had to be brought up from the keep's cool cellar. There were so many sacks, barrels, and crates that Ria wondered how all the goods would ever be packed into the small train of

wagons. Maybe, Ria thought hopefully, there'd be no room
for sitting in the wagons and they'd all have to ride horses
all the way to Allanmere and sleep on the ground at night.
Maybe there'd be no room to take such luxuries as fine
gowns and shoes!

By midday, however, the entertainment of watching the
wagon loading had palled somewhat, and Ria was preparing to climb down from her perch and see about some
dinner when Cyril unexpectedly emerged from the back
kitchen entrance, carrying a large covered basket. He
waved to Ria from the ground.

"I've brought dinner," he said. "Want to come down?"

"Uh-uh," Ria said firmly. "You come up." She mis-
trusted Cyril's sudden desire for her company; he could
well be seeking revenge for yesterday's ambush or her falling asleep last night at the meeting, if he'd noticed. He
wouldn't chance a scuffle, though, on the high stable roof;
Cyril had never been very good with high places.

Cyril sighed.

"All right," he said. "How do I get up?"

"You remember," Ria said impatiently. "From the loft,
just climb the wall beams to the trapdoor."

"I can do that," Cyril said with a shrug, "but not with
this basket."

"Then send it up on the rope." Ria jumped to her feet
and ran to the front of the barn, where the ridgepole of the
roof projected several feet outward. At the end of the
ridgepole was a pulley used to lift bales of hay to the loft.
Cyril placed the handle of the basket over the iron hook
and pulled on the pulley rope until the basket reached the
ridgepole.

Ria sat down on the ridgepole and scooted out to the
pulley. She wasn't such a fool as to walk out and then bend
over to pick up the basket, although sometimes she and
Cyril had jumped off the ridgepole when there was a great
pile of hay beneath. The basket was heavy, and Ria's keen
nose quickly told her the contents—roast fowl, cheese, hot
rolls stuffed with chopped dried apples and honey, and

pies made from last winter's potted meat and new spring greens.

By the time Ria had taken the basket back to the relative safety of the rooftop and inventoried the contents, Cyril had climbed through the roof trapdoor and crawled rather less confidently up to join her. He looked down and shivered.

"Why in the world do you want to sit up here?" he asked. "It's hot, and the wood's hard and splintery, and the flies from the stable are everywhere." He swatted one of the offending insects as he spoke.

"I've been watching them load the wagons," Ria said, scowling. What else would she be doing, and where else could she go to do it properly? "I can't read the markings on the sacks and boxes and barrels from here, so I try to guess what they are."

"You could've saved yourself the trouble," Cyril shrugged. "Mother's got the whole list of every morsel we're taking on a scroll in the kitchen, and they're crossing it off as the stuff is loaded."

Ria stifled a retort. What else was there for her to do, after all, with everyone else in the keep so busy and snappish? At least sitting atop the stables, she *knew* she wasn't doing anything likely to get her foster parents angry with her.

Cyril was silent for a long time, staring down at the wagons.

"What did you think," he said at last, "about what Father and Mother and Lord Emaril said last night?"

"It was boring," Ria said, shrugging. "I slept through most of it."

"What about the part about the ceremony?" Cyril asked hesitantly. "Did you sleep through that?"

"Lady Rivkah said we'd have a ceremony as soon as we reach Allanmere," Ria said, fishing in the basket for a roll. "Do you think we'll have a feast, too?"

"Well, probably." Cyril gave her an odd look. "What do you think of it?"

"A feast would be nice." Ria bit into her roll. "At least if

Cook's coming with us. Then we can see all the people who have come to Allanmere. What kind of ceremony will it be, do you think, a planting ritual, or maybe a blessing on the new buildings?"

"Ria—" Cyril unaccountably flushed. "They were talking about our wedding. Yours and mine."

For a moment Ria's mind refused to understand, and she sat just as she was, mouth full of unchewed bread, roll and hand poised. Then she flung the roll over the side of the barn, spit out her mouthful, and exploded to her feet.

"Wedding?" she protested. "I'm not marrying you."

"Of course you are," Cyril said, looking away. "We've been betrothed since we were little. You remembered the pledge ceremony."

"We were just little children then!" Ria said hotly. "The priest had to tell me how to say half the words. Nobody ever asked me if I'd marry you!"

"Nobody ever asked me either." Cyril still wouldn't meet her eyes. "Mostly the children of nobles aren't asked; they're told."

"Well, I'll tell *you* something," Ria said furiously. "I'm not marrying you, and I don't care what anybody says about it!"

Before Cyril could reply, Ria ran to the end of the ridgepole. Too angry for caution, she swung under the beam, grasped both ropes under the pulley, and fitted her small foot into the curve of the hay hook. Letting the pull rope slide through her hand, she lowered herself to the ground at a speed just less than falling, ignoring Cyril as he called after her.

Now there really *was* no place to hide; Cyril was in the stable, and all the outbuildings were swarming with servants moving things. Ria stormed back to her room and, for lack of any better hiding place, crawled under her bed, which had been raised high for the sake of coolness in the warm spring weather, and curled up on the cold stone of the floor.

She expected Cyril to come after her, but it was Lady Rivkah who eventually rapped on the door, then pushed it

open. Furious as she was, Ria managed to think herself
small and insignificant and invisible. There was nothing her
foster mother could say that Ria wanted to hear, not now.

Lady Rivkah didn't waste time searching vainly. Her fingertips traced a symbol in the air, and she murmured a
short incantation; immediately she turned toward the bed.

"Come out from under there, Ria," Lady Rivkah said
flatly. "I'm sure you can't expect to hide under the bed like
a mouse forever, not unless you want to be left behind
when the wagons leave. And I've never known you to miss
a meal yet."

Ria sighed and crawled out. Sometimes it wasn't altogether handy to have a powerful mage for a foster mother.
She climbed onto the bed and folded her arms, eyes stubbornly averted, too angry even to speak.

Lady Rivkah sat down beside her.

"Cyril told me what you said to him," she said. "Don't
you think it's a little late for you to balk and act outraged
now? You've been betrothed to Cyril for more than a decade."

"Mostly what I remember from that ceremony was being
kept in my room because of the roll I threw," Ria scowled.
"Nobody ever told me what it meant, not in words I could
understand."

"But I've talked to you about your duties and responsibilities when you're married," Lady Rivkah said patiently.
"We've talked about it dozens of times."

"Well, 'when you're married' means married *someday*
when I *want* to be married to *somebody*," Ria protested
hotly. "It doesn't mean married when I'm *sixteen* to *Cyril*,
whether I want to or not!"

"Ria." Lady Rivkah reached over and patted her shoulder. "Your betrothal to Cyril has never been a secret. It
never occurred to me that I'd need to sit down and say,
'Ria, you're expected to marry Cyril.' You've read the histories I wrote of our time in Allanmere, or you should
have, at least, to understand that the two of you were always intended to marry. If you've remained ignorant all
these years, it's because you've wanted to."

Ria scowled silently. It *couldn't* be true. She *had* read the histories—well, some of them, anyway, mainly the exciting parts about the battles and Lady Rivkah's accounts of what they'd seen in the elvan village. She'd sort of skipped the rest. How could anybody be expected to read every single word of such boring stuff? She'd done much the same with Lady Rivkah's instructions on her future and her duties; she hadn't precisely *ignored* what Lady Rivkah had to say, but usually her mind had been filled with more interesting things and somehow a good bit of those talks had—well, just drifted by somehow without too much of it lingering in Ria's mind.

Ria glanced again at Lady Rivkah and then away again, grinding her teeth. Somebody *should* have talked to her, plain and straight, in words a child could understand. But even so, would it have made any difference? Ria thought not.

When it became plain that Ria would not answer, Lady Rivkah sighed and shook her head.

"Ria, you've met many of the noble families in Cielman. You know how the marriages of their daughters are arranged, usually almost from birth. Most of those daughters are married far younger than you. Emaril was only fourteen when he married Vesana, and she was only twelve. By your age Vesana had already borne her first child."

"But he wasn't her foster brother," Ria said sullenly. "And nobody made you and Lord Sharl marry somebody you didn't want before you were ready."

Lady Rivkah laid her hand on Ria's shoulder, and her voice was kind.

"So far as I know, no humans have ever been given an elvan child to foster," she said gently. "The eastern elves in their cities are a remote and aloof people who've never given us a chance to learn much about them. But Sharl promised your mother that you'd be married to our first-born son. Besides that promise, a marriage between our House and one of the elves is the best way to make an alliance between the city and the forest. The elvan clans may not want to deal with the humans of the city, but they may consent to negotiate with an elvan High Lady and the daughter of an elf who helped save the forest. I believe, and Sharl does too, that that's why your mother chose to give you to us."

"Then let Cyril marry some other elf," Ria said sourly. "One who wants him."

"If the elves won't talk to humans, I think it's fair to expect none of them are going to come walking out of the forest asking to marry one," Lady Rivkah told her wryly. "Ria, living in a noble family means that you always have good food and warm clothing and a solid roof over your head, healers when you need them, a warm fire in the winter. It means you don't have to work in the fields or exhaust yourself at a trade or sell your body as a whore. It means you can sit on the stable roof and watch the wagons being loaded instead of loading them yourself. But it also means that you're responsible in many ways for the well-being of a lot of other people, and that means that sometimes what's necessary for your people is more important than what you want for yourself. You're no different from the rest of us in that regard."

Ria was stubbornly silent. She wasn't a noble to be obligated, nor a peasant to be ordered, either; she was an elf, and if she could just find her way back to her mother's people, she'd show Lady Rivkah and all the others just how different that *did* make her.

"There's no use sulking," Lady Rivkah said patiently. "And you've picked a bad time if you're making this fuss to get attention. We've all got too much work to do to cater to you while you feel sorry for yourself. Even Cyril's seeing to the packing of his own things; I'd have you do the same, but I know if I did, the only clothing that would be brought would be those patched old breeches and tunic. At least you should be pleased that Lady Sivia won't be coming with us."

That was a surprise. Ria's pointed ears pricked up with interest despite her effort to look stubbornly indifferent.

"She won't?" Ria asked warily.

"No. Married ladies don't have governesses, and in any

event, Lady Sivia wouldn't want to accompany us to Allanmere where the conditions will be so rough." Lady Rivkah glanced sternly at Ria. "I've had trouble enough getting her to stay this long after the trouble you've given her. If you and Cyril want teachers after you're wed and have assumed the throne of Allanmere, you'll have to find and hire them yourselves, and good fortune to you finding ones who can put up with your tricks."

Lady Rivkah stood, patting Ria's shoulder.

"Now if you want to go off and sulk, go ahead. If you want somebody to be angry at, though, come to Sharl or me, not Cyril. We're the ones to blame, if you like."

Lady Rivkah's exit from the room was quickly followed by the entrance of a bevy of serving maids bringing a box for Ria's clothes. Ria fled to the kitchen, where she found to her disgust that a similar state of chaos reigned. Even the cellars, which Ria had always disliked because of their dark, close atmosphere, were too crowded and bustling to give her sanctuary. At last there was nowhere to go but back to the stable, where thankfully the horses were not inclined to irritate her further.

Ria picked up one of the stable boy's brushes and began grooming one of the horses, comforted by the huge, gentle presence of the animal. Lord Sharl and Lady Rivkah had told Ria that her mother could hear animals' thoughts, speak to them in the same way, even see through their eyes. Ria had tried and tried and tried, but although she could befriend the most ill-tempered dog in the keep and coax the most feral of the barn cats to eat tidbits from her hand, that appeared to be the extent of it. Ria had been inconsolable when she'd realized that, like magery, such a gift didn't seem to be a matter of trying; one either had it or one didn't, and it appeared that Ria simply didn't. She'd have given—well, just about anything in the world to fly with a bird the way her mother had.

She'd been so looking forward to the trip to Allanmere, the prospect of escaping the monotony of Lord Emaril's country keep. Now it seemed, however, as if Ria was walking into a cage even smaller and far less escapable—marriage.

Oh, to be a bird, to fly high above the cage walls that closed more tightly around her every moment.

Ria froze where she was.

Yes, a bird could soar over cage walls.

But a mouse, small and insignificant and nearly invisible, might very well slip through the bars.

II

Valann

Valann could only cough weakly now, his eyes burning, the thick smoke choking him so that he wavered in and out of consciousness. Sweat ran down his body in rivulets, but he was too weak to raise his hands to wipe it away. In a moment he would surely die, his aching lungs no longer able to draw even a little air to sustain him from the roiling smoke. He almost reached for the cord fastening the tent flap; then he let his hand drop back. He *would* die, and gladly, before he'd fail his passage trials.

The fire was dying as the smoke choked it, too. Val's body was weakened by the burning herbs and powders, but not his gift; he inched his hand toward the brazier. Almost before he focused on the dying flames, they flared anew. Val had just enough consciousness left to be dimly surprised at how effortlessly he prodded the flames to burn higher. Just as Dusk had said, the fasting and the rigors of his passage trials strengthened the spirit.

It seemed forever, but likely it was only a short time

before the tent flap opened, admitting a wonderful rush of cool, clear air. Dusk leaned in.

"Are you ready to come out?" he asked gently.

Valann tried to answer but could only cough weakly, wheezing helplessly.

"Yes. I think you are." Dusk slid his hands under Val's shoulders and pulled him carefully from the tent, then leaned back in to pour a dipperful of water over the smoking brazier. Dusk gently wiped Val's face with a moist cloth, nodding sympathetically while Val coughed and retched. When Val was finally able to breathe quietly again, Dusk gave him water, heavily laced with medicinal herbs, a tiny sip at a time.

"You are almost ready," Dusk said gently. "Perhaps I put too much dreamweed on the brazier, a poor thing for a Gifted One to do. Did you dream in the smoke? Some say the dreams of passage trials are visions of the future."

"No." Val shook his head. His voice was a hoarse rasp. "No dreams."

"I dreamt." Dusk's eyes had that pale, faraway look that meant that his mind had drifted away to that distant place it sometimes went. Sometimes his mind brought back visions, too, from that place.

"What?" Val wanted to question Dusk as he'd seen his heart-mother Rowan do, gently leading the Gifted One through the mists of his thoughts to bring the vision into the light, but he had no breath, no voice to do it. Each word was a scratching torment on his throat, and he couldn't seem to concentrate.

"I felt your sister walking unseen in the wood," Dusk said, his eyes fixed on some point just beyond Val's face. "I saw a legion of humans clad in furs, carrying fire and steel, their hands red with blood, their feet trampling the forest. They came behind your sister, far behind, like a great dark storm cloud rising over the forest, a storm bound to rend the trees from the earth, and she was a small light against that darkness, bright and pure, her brilliance piercing the great cloud like a single golden ray of sunlight. And you walked to meet her, holding out a precious gift in your hands, a gift of freedom."

Rowan had always said that Dusk's visions were important, but Val only half understood what Dusk was saying, his head spun so dizzily from the potent herb smoke and the potion Dusk had given him. He was weak, too, from hunger; he'd fasted for four days while cleansing potions and ritual baths purged his body of all impurities, while ritual chants and meditation exercises cleansed his spirit. He forced himself up to a sitting position, shaking his head to clear it.

"What?" he asked groggily.

Dusk's eyes cleared suddenly, and he smiled sympathetically at Val.

"Too much dreamweed on the brazier," Dusk said again. "You have a little time to rest before the sun sets, but remember that you must not sleep yet. Come, you can lie down and Lahti will stay with you. When I left Rowan after mixing the potion, the other elders were still arguing."

Val was miserably glad to crawl to the furs Dusk had spread on the ground and lie down, closing his eyes so he would not have to watch the dizzy spin of the world around him. Oh, for only one hour's peaceful sleep. But he was forbidden sleep until his dreaming time came at sunset. Val grimly forced his eyes open again.

Lahti appeared at his side as if by magic, her long brown braid tickling his face until she flipped it back over her shoulder. Her warm brown eyes, usually sparkling with mischief, were now wide with worry.

"I've brought you some cold minted water," she said, easing her forearm under Val's shoulders. "Dusk said it would ease your stomach." She lifted him with some difficulty; although she was tall for her age and her clan, like most of the elves in Inner Heart she was small compared to Valann. Val helped as best he could, and Lahti was able to support him in a half-sitting position and hold the wooden cup to his lips.

His senses almost painfully heightened, Val breathed in Lahti's scent, a mixture of the leather of her clothing, the

pungent odor of the herbs she'd bathed in to purify herself
so she could assist Dusk and be with Val during the rituals,
her own slightly musky scent—but over it all, the sharp
tang of her fear. She was terribly afraid for him, as he knew
Dusk and Rowan were despite their seeming calm—no elf,
to anyone's knowledge, had ever taken the trials of passage
into adulthood so young. And there had never been, to
anyone's knowledge, a youth of only part elvan blood to
face the trials at all.

"Dusk said the elders were still arguing," Val rasped
painfully.

"Still." Lahti smiled a little. "Don't make that fierce
scowl, my friend. The elders are only concerned for you, so
young and your blood not pure. What if the potion
poisoned you, like the mushrooms you ate three years ago
that almost killed you? Even Dusk can't be certain, and
he's tended you all your life. And what if your spirit isn't
old and strong enough to make the journey to the Mother
Forest and back? Some have failed on their first journey;
some have even died, or been spirit-lost and worse than
dead. I have two decades and five years, and I've trained
with Dusk for years, and my spirit still hasn't called for the
journey. How can your spirit be ready almost a decade
sooner?"

As always, Lahti's touch, her scent, were almost as much
a torment as they were soothing. He fumbled for her hand,
held it over his heart where the springy black curls had
grown, so that she felt the quickened beat of his blood.

"My spirit is ready," he whispered.

"I know." Lahti glanced around her, then smiled mischievously and ran her fingers up the inside of his thigh,
making Val gasp involuntarily. Then she took pity on him
and stopped. "I feel your body calling. I wish mine could
answer. I wish I could be the one to come to your hut after
you return from the Mother Forest."

"I wish that, too." Val shivered as a new wave of nausea
washed through him, banishing his arousal as abruptly as it
had come. "But for now I only want this all to be done. It

seems like forever since I last had a mouthful of meat, since I last slept."

"It can't be rushed. Without the trials to strengthen your spirit, you might not return safely from your journey." Lahti lowered Val back to the furs and glanced around again. This time she laid one small, callused palm on Val's forehead, the other over his heart, and Val felt her healing power flow into him as smoothly as the sunlight flowed down through the leafy canopy. Immediately his stomach eased and his reeling head settled in a wave of cool well-being. Val caught at Lahti's hands, pulled them away from his body.

"You shouldn't do that," he whispered.

"No tradition says you must be left to suffer," Lahti whispered back. "Rest now until Dusk returns."

Val sighed and relaxed, his head cradled on Lahti's lap, for the moment as at peace from his desire as he was from his dizziness and nausea. So skilled already, her gift, although—or perhaps because—she still ran with the child-pack. There were always plenty of bruises, scrapes, and even broken bones for her to practice on, plus the occasional more seriously wounded animal. Her gift of healing had shown itself so early that Dusk had perforce been training her in its use for years. Now he was teaching her the use of herbs and other materials to supplement her natural gift.

Healing—the most welcome of all the old gifts. Nobody saw in Lahti's gift, in her very flesh, an unpleasant reminder of the devastation of their world. But even the children had run, at first, from Val's gift of fire.

And some of his own people—or as much his own people as they could ever be—argued even now to deny him his most fundamental right, his passage into adulthood. Would he be more acceptable, more harmless to them if he could somehow be frozen in childhood? But there was no holding back the change of seasons of his body; the Mother Forest had come months ago in a dream of Lahti to waken his flesh, as She came to all children in their time. Only the doubts of some of the elders in Inner Heart—

surely it could not be his true waking dream, not when he was hardly more than a decade and a half old!—had prevented his passage ritual from being conducted immediately. But his body knew beyond any doubt that he was done with childhood.

And just as he'd always felt the need to run twice as fast, climb twice as high, shoot twice as far as any of the rest of the child-pack, he'd been doubly painstaking in his observance of the preparations for his passage. Most young hunters made the bowl for their passage potion from the skull of a deer killed in an ordinary hunt; Val had set out alone with only spear and dagger to kill one of the fierce boars that roamed the Heartwood, and he'd succeeded. He'd prepared the bowl with his own hands, and the meat was likely even now roasting over fires in Inner Heart. He'd traded dearly for the finest, sweetest oil for his purification and had bathed with sweet-smelling herbs twice each day during his passage instead of the required once. Despite her station as the Eldest of the clan, his heart-mother Rowan had chosen the finest, softest hides and taken the time to tan, dye, and bead his ceremonial jerkin and trousers herself, and Val had brought his finest bow and one of the boar's great curled tusks to leave as his offering to the Mother Forest. Val had fasted for four days instead of the required three, foregoing even the permitted herbal teas. None of the clan elders could fault his preparation, at least. What more could they possibly ask of him? How could they dream of denying him? The sudden surge of anger at that thought surprised Val with its intensity.

Perhaps a frown furrowed his brow. Lahti smoothed her hand gently over his forehead, and Val opened his eyes to her smile.

"Dusk is returning," she said. "He must have spoken successfully on your behalf. I can smell your dreaming potion in the bowl he carries."

Val sat up, too fast; his head swam again and he sank back to the furs. Mysteriously Lahti had vanished; this time it was Dusk whose arm supported him. The Gifted One's face was drawn with concern.

"Come," he said. "Can you walk? We should hurry. The sun is setting."

"What?" The world swam around Val again. Dusk's smooth shoulders were strong under his arm, the scent of the potion strange and heady. Then the scattered stone slabs of the Forest Altars were around them, and Val could feel the sun-warmed hardness of stone under the fur on which he lay like an offering.

Suddenly, despite the Forest Altars around him, despite the certainty of the Mother Forest's protection in this sacred place where the elves came to worship, he felt frightened, alien, and alone. What if the elders who protested his passage were right? What if the Mother Forest rejected him because of his human blood? What if his spirit *was* unready for passage into adulthood?

"No doubts," Dusk said kindly, as if reading his thoughts. "You fear death, and you must in truth die a kind of death. Valann the boy must return to the Mother Forest, and Valann the man will come back to us changed greatly by his journey. But the man is strong enough in spirit to return. I prepared you myself for this journey, and it is a trail I know well. I've walked it many times."

He held the bone bowl to Val's lips, and Val swallowed thick, bittersweet liquid. Fire poured down his throat and into his vitals, and for a moment Val remembered Lahti's words and knew terror that this potion might poison him as he had nearly been killed by eating the common white-capped tree mushrooms that every elf ate from childhood. Then the burning passed, left him feeling cold and weak and empty. Could the Mother Forest fill that emptiness when he was not truly a part of it? Alone. So alone.

"We all walk alone in this world," Dusk seemed to say, or perhaps Val only imagined it. "But in the Mother Forest we never walk alone, and you least of all."

Val was tired, so very tired. Without opening his eyes, he knew somehow that Dusk had gone. Had the sun set? Despite the warm air he was cold, then hot, then cold again. There were warm furs over him, but somehow they did not fight the chill—was it fear?—that came from somewhere within him.

It seemed that he was sinking slowly into the earth, as softly and comfortably as he might sink into a thick pile of furs to sleep on a cold winter's night. He slid down along the roots of the trees, digging deep into moist, rich soil fairly bursting with life. But below the roots, he could feel himself approaching an unknown realm where there were no stars to point his way, no trails he knew. What waited there was powerful and hungry and alive, alive, wild and fierce and old and strange—

Your gift is fire, Dusk had told him during the days of fasting, of purification rituals. *But fire's not a part of the Mother Forest. Fire is a tool, but a tool of death, not allied with the green growing things. It cannot guide you to the heart of life. You must find another guide. Turn toward the earth and ask for help.*

But what help might there be? He had friends, many friends among the child-pack, but they had begun to draw away from him when his body had rushed unexpectedly toward adulthood, when hair began to sprout bizarrely from his arms and legs, his chest, even his chin and upper lip. Already he was almost as tall as most of the adults in the clan, his shoulders broader, his muscles large, ungainly lumps on his body. The children drew away not only because of his strangeness, but because he was no longer one of them; they knew, if the elders did not, that Val had charged headlong into the adult world.

The adults of the clan had always loved him and cared for him as impartially as they had any other child, but some of them, too, had lately begun to draw away. Their distance was less open, tinged with concern, perhaps even pity, but also with a touch of fear—fear perhaps not *of* him and his human blood, but because he and his human blood became every day more a part of the clan. And he would be an adult soon, old enough to couple and perhaps to mate, old enough to sit around the fire with the other adults when there were decisions to be made. Most important, he would be old enough to sow his seed in High Circles when women ripened, and that seed, if it took root in a woman's womb, would carry to the child Val's half-human blood. *Tainted blood.* No one had ever said the words, but they had hovered unspoken, a tangible presence. *Tainted seed in the wombs of our women.* Val was certain that that thought, more than any other, was the topic of the arguments likely continuing even now at the hide tent Dusk and Rowan and the elders who had accompanied them to the Forest Altars had set up.

Yet what more could he have done, ever, to prove himself one of them, a valuable member of his clan? He was stronger than any elf he knew; he could sling a good-sized deer over his shoulder and carry it alone, and he'd done it, too, on many occasions. Three summers ago a bear had charged their hunting party; Val alone had stood firm while the others escaped. He'd killed the bear alone, with only his spears and his dagger, although he'd spent the next moon cycle under Dusk's care, recovering from his wounds. He'd driven himself relentlessly to master every skill any adult in the clan would teach him, bitterly resenting his own clumsy bulk, hating it that he had to struggle hard at some lessons, such as tracking by scent, where his friends in the child-pack succeeded so effortlessly. He could fling a spear farther than any hunter he knew and pull a bow heavier than any other in the clan, but that hardly lessened his humiliation when he realized the clumsiness of his own steps beside the easy grace of his kinfolk in the dance.

Sometimes it seemed that all he could do would never be enough. How could anything he did ever be enough, when it was what he *was* that was wrong?

For a few moments the dreaming potion had given Val's thoughts a remarkable clarity, as sharp and cold as the icicles that formed at waterfalls in winter; then another wave of confusion came. What was he doing here, his thoughts running in helpless circles like hopeless prey driven mist-witted by fear? If his own clan feared him and set him apart, what hope that the Mother Forest would welcome him? Maybe the elders who doubted him were right. At the moment he felt very much still a child, albeit a child misplaced in a man's body, lost and alone in a frightening place.

Help me, he thought desperately. *I am so alone, so afraid.* If he could weep in his thoughts, he might have been weeping. But who would there be to help him?

Abruptly another wave of clarity lit his mind, and he remembered Dusk's vision. *I felt your sister walking unseen in the woods. And you walked to meet her, holding out a precious gift in your hands.*

His sister. His twin, cradled in the same womb, curled against him as they dreamed together to the beat of their mother's heart, sent to horrible exile among the humans, yet bearing the birthright of visible elvan blood Val himself lacked. She'd be small and slender and graceful like other elves of the clan, not oversized and lumpy, her skin smooth and soft, not overfurred like some shaggy beast. How he wanted to resent that, to envy his sister for merely *being* everything he was not. But more, he wanted—no, *needed*—to know her. Was she the part of his life, perhaps the part of his very self, that was missing? Would she resent and envy him, too, because she'd been torn away from her home, her people, and he'd remained? Might she even hate him, or would she understand his plight and help him if she could? Did she, too, feel herself a stranger in her world, alone and longing for another's understanding? How had she fared in the years since their birth? Was she, perhaps, even at this moment, thinking of him?

He could almost picture her in his mind. Rowan had often described the tiny baby with her delicate features, her curling black hair and nut-brown skin, her eyes blue and green together as if spring leaves and clear sky had blended together there. She would be slender and unformed yet, small and agile, her blue-green eyes twinkling with the carefree joy of elvan childhood, her black curls always tumbled, her face always smudged, her knees and elbows always scraped and bruised, her tiny fingers nimble and quick and always moving. If he spoke to her, she would turn quickly like a startled doe and her large, sparkling eyes would grow wide and surprised—

For a moment she was there before him, just as he'd pictured her, and some communication passed between them, a flash of understanding as fleeting as a finger of lightning reaching for the earth. He could almost touch her, almost clasp her tiny fingers, and he reached desperately for her, but already she was fading, drawing away as so many others had drawn away from him. Her image dwindled and was gone, and he was alone again in the darkness as he sank deeper into confusion. There was so much life boiling and seething around him that somehow it made him seem infinitely small and insignificant, unworthy, less than nothing. Oh, he could drown in this no less than in a spring-flooded stream, roaring, sweeping him away—

Warm fingers, strong and comfortingly solid, seemed to close about his own. That small point of contact anchored him, made him somehow real again, gave him *somewhere* to be. He clung desperately to the small digits and let them draw him through the confusion, through sights and sounds and scents that meant nothing to him even as they bombarded his senses, and the warm hand clasping his drew him inexorably deeper into the seething confusion—

—into sudden silence.

At the center of chaos, as at the center of an autumn whirlwind, peace and stillness as unbroken as the surface of a forest pool in the moonlight. And reflected in that pool was himself, and beside him a small figure clothed only in the sparkling green leaves of vines that twined around her slender limbs, with tumbled gold-brown curls and tawny gold eyes, one brown hand clasping his. Her eyes were wild, like a beast's, but somewhere in those eyes was something warm and familiar, something very like love.

Startled, Val turned and looked all around him. There was no one; he stood in darkness at the edge of a pool. That was all. Yet when he turned back to the placid water, the small figure still stood beside him, firmly clasping his hand.

Val's lips barely moved.

"Mother?"

There was no answer, at least none that Val could see or hear. Yet somehow he felt in her touch that she understood him, acknowledged him, accepted him. In the reflection she stood on tiptoe and reached up with her free hand to touch the contours of his face, and Val could see now a hint of her own features mirrored there. Her fingers were rough and hard, her arms contoured with wiry muscle. She smiled, and Val could see a little sadness in that smile. Then she released his hand and turned, facing Val directly out of the pool, and extended both hands toward him.

Hesitantly Val reached toward her, expecting to touch warm flesh or, possibly, the cool surface of the water. Instead his hands plunged into fire and he was pulled forward into an inferno. Fire swirled around him and through him, consuming him body and spirit, and for a moment it seemed as if the flesh would be seared from his bones. Then the fire passed, leaving him untouched in its path, leaving a glowing trail of embers as it moved on. Val followed the trail of fire, his feet unburned by the embers as he walked, then ran, reaching for the flames that had for one moment been a part of him. Closer he came to the dancing flames, and closer, until he reached out and grasped them, and—

Val yawned and stretched, groaning as stiff muscles protested the movement after hours of immobility. The furs were soft and cozy over and under him, even the stone was warmed by the sun and his body, and Val luxuriated in the comfort a moment longer before he grudgingly opened his eyes.

Sunlight flowed like warm honey over the skin of his face, promising a hot day despite the early hour, and a soft breeze ruffled his hair. He could smell Dusk somewhere nearby, and the tempting aroma of roast meat and hot baked tubers made his mouth water. Val sat up and stretched again, reaching up to trace the contours of his face and smiling to himself. Despite a slight light-headedness from the days of fasting and the rigorous rituals of preparation and purification, Val felt wonderfully rested and refreshed, more contented and at peace than he would have thought possible. And why not? If his mother Chyrie, who lived closer to the Mother Forest than any elf in the Heartwood, thought that he was elf enough, then he was elf enough. Had he somehow touched the spirit of his mother in truth, or had the Mother Forest sent a vision of her as She had sent a vision of Lahti to wake his body to adulthood? Did it truly matter? He had made the journey to the Mother Forest and returned, and he was well content with what he had found there.

Val picked up the furs and followed his nose to Dusk's camp just outside the borders of the Altars. Lahti was sitting outside tending a haunch of venison as it roasted, and her dark-shadowed eyes—had she waited up all night?—lit with delight and relief at Val's approach.

"Fair morn," she said. "You look well. And ready to break your fast, I imagine." She cut off a thick slab of meat, impaled it on her dagger, and held it out.

"Yes, and yes," Val said emphatically, accepting the dagger and sighing contentedly as he sank his teeth into the juicy meat. It was tough, barely warm, and still bloody—easily the most wonderful meat he'd ever tasted in his life. He swallowed several bites before he paused long enough to speak again. "But where are Dusk and Rowan?"

Lahti's smile wavered a little, and she gestured to the tent. Glancing to the south, Val could see that the other two hide tents, in which the other elders who had accompanied them had been sleeping, were gone. Val turned back to Lahti, raising his eyebrows in surprise.

"Dusk slipped out of the camp with the potion for you yesterday before the other elders had decided whether or not to give him permission," Lahti said, shrugging apologetically, "and they were furious when he returned and told them. There was more argument, and Dusk was so upset that he became unwell. Rowan and I tended him all night, and the elders started back for Inner Heart. Dusk and Rowan are sleeping now."

"He had a vision yesterday," Val said, but now he was

not so sure. He could barely remember what Dusk had said —something about Ria and a storm cloud, wasn't it?—and sometimes it was difficult to tell whether the healer's babblings were visions or delusions. "He spoke of my sister."

Lahti nodded sympathetically, understanding Val's doubt.

"He seems well enough now," she reassured him. "His illness and the elders' doubts shouldn't mar your passage. He'll be glad to know all was well with you." There was a hint of regret in her voice; however much she might wonder about his passage ritual, and however much Val might have liked to hear what she thought of his passage dream, it would have been inexcusable for Val to discuss his journey to the Mother Forest with her, as she had not yet passed into adulthood herself.

Apparently Rowan had heard their voices, for she emerged from the hide tent, smiling although fatigue ringed her eyes as darkly as Lahti's.

"Fair morn, Valann, Lahti," she said. She touched Lahti's cheek affectionately, but smiled again as she embraced Val. "I shall miss my boy, but I greet the man with pride. Valann, share our food and fire, and be made welcome among us."

Val flushed with a mixture of pride and embarrassment at Rowan's recognition of his new status as an adult. With all the argument and anxiety surrounding his passage, he'd hardly spared a thought about what would happen afterward. Of course, he was no longer an infant to share his mother's hut and fire, nor a child to run wild in the forest with the child-pack and sleep and eat in whatever temporary shelter he chose. He was an adult now, and a hut of his own would have been prepared while he was gone from the village.

"I am honored to share your food and fire," Val said, a little awkwardly. "May joy and friendship be my contribution." He appreciated Rowan's recognition of his adulthood, but it seemed a little foolish to mouth the formalities as he stood there with a half-eaten piece of meat already in his hand and Lahti trying to keep from chuckling at his discomfort.

Rowan chuckled a little too, and Val felt a bit less awkward as he sat down again, eager to stuff more venison into his achingly empty stomach.

"I hear Dusk was unwell last night," he said between bites.

Rowan sighed and nodded, but said nothing. There was little enough to be said. Beast-speaking was the oldest and best developed of Dusk's gifts despite his skill as a healer. The Gifted One had been flying in the mind of a hawk during the barbarian invasion sixteen years earlier when a human spear had struck his body, prematurely severing the link between man and bird. Dusk's body had been long in mending, and his spirit had never fully recovered. Sometimes he took strange fits in which his body jerked and twitched; more often his spirit wandered to strange places, sometimes bringing back powerful visions but more often only leaving Dusk mist-witted for a time. There was nothing to be done for the Gifted One but to honor and care for him and pray to the Mother Forest that his spirit would continue to return from its strange journeys. Still, Val had never known Dusk any other way, and Dusk's visions had often spared the clan great hardship.

"He's sleeping easily now," Rowan assured him. "I sent the other elders back still infuriated that Dusk had gone ahead without their consent. All the quarreling served no purpose but to upset him further. And you have returned from your spirit journey safe and strong as Dusk said you would. When we return I'll call the elders to my speaking hut and you can tell us your passage dream, and then there will be an end to all this wondering and arguing." She patted Val's shoulder and her eyes twinkled over her smile. "And an end to your waiting. Lahti has acted as elder sister for you. Come, we'll tidy the camp and ready the packs before we wake Dusk."

To Val's relief, Dusk was clear-headed and cheerful when they woke him. The four of them had to carry the packs a good distance on their backs, but once they had left the smell of roast venison behind them, Dusk was able to summon graceful spiral-horned deer to bear them back to Inner Heart.

For Val, the ride was something of a triumphal procession; he had ridden out of the village a boy and was returning a man. While he was gone, the elves of Inner Heart would have prepared a symbolic feast of memory, as if for a death, to acknowledge Val's return to the Mother Forest. Many elves, Val knew, feared (he prayed to the Mother Forest that none had actually *hoped*) that because of Val's youth and his human blood the feast would be more than merely symbolic. His friends in Inner Heart, he knew, had been praying and offering to the Mother Forest for his safe return and would be deeply relieved that he lived; some, however, would find his very return a new source of worry.

And one of the clan's women would be preparing, too, to come to Val in his new hut and teach him the ways of man and woman. Ordinarily it would fall to a man's oldest sister to choose his teacher, or, if he had no older sister, his mother. It was very like Rowan that she would not usurp the role of Chyrie, Val's true mother, but it was not unfitting that Lahti, his dearest friend, would, as Rowan had joked, act as his older sister. And yet there was a little bitterness to the joke, for he would have chosen Lahti above any woman in the village, but until she passed from childhood, like a real sister she was forbidden to him.

Riding the deer until they were near the village, it took only part of the day to reach Inner Heart, something which faintly surprised Val. He felt he'd journeyed far from home, perhaps not in distance, but in spirit, so that it seemed strange to return so quickly. Strange, too, that Inner Heart would appear no different from when he'd left it, the huts and firepits exactly where they'd been before, the elves going about their everyday tasks as always. Well, that wasn't exactly true; somewhere in the village there'd be his new hut. But Inner Heart could never have changed as much as he felt *he* had in the last few days.

The lookouts raised glad cries when they saw Rowan, Dusk, Val, and Lahti, and they were met at the edge of the village by a crowd of laughing elves waiting to embrace Val and hang garlands of leaves and flowers around his neck, to sweep him off his feet and carry him, laughing helplessly, to the speaking hut.

It took a little time for the elders to assemble. There always seemed to be so many of them, enough to make Rowan's large speaking hut—in Val's lifetime they'd made the hut larger twice—seem crowded. Rowan said it wasn't that there were so many elders; it was that there were fewer young adults since the invasion. The oldest elves, together with the sick, fertile or pregnant women, and children, had been sent to the human city to shelter and had survived the invasion, while so many of the younger warriors had fought and died in the forest, that sometimes it seemed that half the clan were elders.

The fire was lit in the speaking hut and food was brought —cold food from the memory feast last night while Val had made his strange journey, although Val knew that even now they'd be preparing a new feast to celebrate his return —and Val spoke quietly of his passage dream. He felt a brief pang as he spoke of his mother. He had never seen her with his own eyes; no elf, to his knowledge, had seen Chyrie since she had brought him to Inner Heart and abandoned him there. Some thought that Chyrie had returned to the Mother Forest in body as well as spirit. Valann didn't really want to speak of her; he wanted to keep her his secret, his very own vision, if a vision was all she'd been. But if that was the vision the Mother Forest had sent him, the elders had a right to know it.

One by one, the elders nodded as he spoke. When he finished, Janan, a Redoak almost as old as Rowan, spoke at last.

"Your mother's spirit guided you to the Mother Forest," she said slowly, "and the fire guided you away. What can it mean? Is it that your elvan blood will bring you to us, and your human blood lead you away?"

"We can hardly interpret a passage dream in such a way," Rowan protested. "Each of us must find our way to the Mother Forest at passage, and each of us must find our way back again. You might as easily suggest that his elvan blood leads him into death and his human blood back toward life. What is plain is that he made the journey and returned as he must."

Janan was silent for a moment, and Val understood the glances that several of the elders exchanged. They were thinking of fire and human blood and High Circles. Then Janan stood and walked to Valann, tall like most Redoaks so that she met his eyes squarely.

"When my clan joined with Inner Heart," she said, "there had been no children born to Redoak for two decades. We feared there would never be more. The Inner Hearts and Moon Lakes and Owl Clans were strange to our eyes, very different than us, but we danced in their High Circles and some of our women were filled again with life, and my daughters have children with the black hair of Inner Heart and children with the pale eyes of Owl Clan." She embraced Valann a little stiffly. "If the Mother Forest acknowledges you one of us, I can do no less."

One by one, other elders rose to give him their embrace. Val knew there were some who left silently without the proper acknowledgment, but he could not manage to care. More than anything, he simply wanted this awkward moment to end so he could have a little time alone.

When the other elders had left, it was Rowan, as Eldest of the clan, who led Val to the edge of the village and showed him the new hut that had been built on the ground for him, Moon Lake fashion, as Val had never favored the hanging bowers preferred by most of the Inner Hearts. Val's belongings, the carvings he had made and the hides he had prepared, his weapons and clothing, had been moved into the hut, and by tradition a fire had been laid but not lit. A skin of wine and a single small cake had been placed by the firepit so that Val could, as an adult, offer food and fire to the Eldest of the clan. When Val would have drawn out the rock he used to strike sparks from his dagger, however, Rowan laid her hand over his.

"Every member of this clan," she said gently, "has the duty—and the right—to use his Gifts in the service of his clan." She smiled. "And you were never very deft with stone and steel in any wise."

A great tension vanished somewhere in Val, and he laughed with his adopted mother, focusing carefully on the tinder until it burst into flame. How they had all cried out and fled from the hut, Val no less frightened than the rest, the first time when his untrained Gift had caused a cold fire to blaze up so furiously that it had burnt off most of the thatched roof! How wonderful, too, that now he could laugh at the memory.

Rowan stayed only long enough to share the small cake and a sip of wine, as tradition required; then she left Val to himself to gather his thoughts, lowering the tent flap behind her as she left. By custom, other clan members would leave gifts outside the door during the night, small tokens to make his new hut more comfortable—warm furs, carved wood bowls, pottery vessels, and the like—but they wouldn't disturb him unless he raised the tent flap, signifying that visitors would be welcome, or called out to invite them into his hut.

Val lay down by the fire, his mind too full of the day's events to let his weary body relax, and listened to the shuffle of feet and the soft murmur of voices as objects were laid on the ground outside his tent. Nothing forbade him from admitting visitors, although custom excluded children from his first night as an adult, but Val left the door flap closed and remained silent. Feeling unaccountably shy and awkward in his new status after all the ritual and formality, Val was glad enough to sit quietly in his hut, though he would have welcomed Lahti's merry company to distract him.

Through the smoke hole Val saw the sky darken as the sun set. He could smell the odors of the feast his entire clan was sharing, and his stomach rumbled. Yes, there was the smell of roasting boar among the other appetizing aromas. If he'd only cross the short distance of clearing to the firepit, someone would have saved him the boar's heart and other choice portions, as tradition demanded. He stayed where he was.

The moon was rising. Soon a woman would come to his tent to give him the greatest gift of adulthood, his initiation into the delights of coupling. But who had Lahti chosen? Mira, the young tracker who so often accompanied Val and Lahti on their hunts, less than a year out of childhood herself? Ilea, who had initiated more young men than any woman in the clan, and who loved to boast of it? Might Lahti, thinking of the arguments among the elders, have made an uncharacteristically circumspect choice and selected a woman known to be barren, or past her childbearing time?

Light footsteps approached, then hesitated outside, and a slender hand lifted the edge of his door flap. Val's heart pounded, and he was amazed to feel his hands trembling as he recognized Doeanna, Lahti's mother's mate's younger sister. The Owl Clan woman was as tall as Lahti, but reed-slender and pale where Lahti was wiry-muscled and dark. Doeanna's long pale braid was beaded and coiled on her head, as befitted her age and stature, but her large, dark eyes with their perpetual wondering expression gave her a sort of childlike air. She carried a large platter of food, which she placed quietly by the fire before she turned to speak to him.

"Lahti asked me to come to you," she said, her voice as always a soft murmur. "I was honored to accept. Does her choice please you?"

"Very much," Val admitted, ashamed of the quiver in his own voice. Of all the women in the village who might have come to his tent on this night, he would never have expected Doeanna. She was a dancer of exquisite skill and had borne two children; at least six men had asked her to be their mate, but Doeanna was a solitary creature and content to live alone. Despite her love of solitude, however, rumors of Doeanna's skill in the furs were such that Val had no doubt that Doeanna never lacked companionship when she wished it.

"Here is roast fowl, venison stewed with fresh herbs, some of the boar you killed, acorn meal cakes and honey, and the season's first berries, and Sun Flower Nectar in celebration," Doeanna murmured. "Surely you are hungry after your fast and the other rigors of your passage."

"Uh—" Val swallowed hard. Only moments before, his stomach had been grumbling its hunger; now he was sure he couldn't swallow a bite of the finest food the Heartwood could offer.

"Ah, you hunger indeed, but not for food," Doeanna said softly, smiling. Her large, dark eyes shone softly in the firelight. "So impatient, as the young always are, so ready to bolt down their wine before they can truly savor the full richness of its flavor. Well enough, sweet Valann. There will be many hours tonight to teach you patience."

She tied the side cords of the door flap to the door frame so the flap could not be lifted, then turned back to him, drawing her tunic over her head. Warm firelight flickered over her willow-slender, moon-pale body as she knelt beside him on the furs.

Val thought fleetingly of Lahti, smiled nervously, and reached for the lacing of his tunic.

III

RIA

• Lush green plains rolled by the wagons. For a few days Ria had seen fields thick with green-gold grain or planted in rows of vegetables as they passed through Cielman's outlying farmland. Often there were peasants working in the fields. Gradually, as they moved farther south and west, the farms became fewer and the fields gave way to these endless grassy plains.

Ria, however, was not bored despite the seeming monotony of the scenery around them. No matter how similar the view each day from her place on the wagon seat, it was a different view from the one she'd seen every day of her life from the walls of Emaril's keep. When the jolting of the wagon tired her, Ria ran beside it or climbed up behind one of the guards on their horses, or rode the patient draft horses pulling the wagons. Sometimes as she ran through the grass, she'd stop to chase butterflies or watch small snakes and become so engrossed that one of the guards would have to ride back to reclaim her. Lady Rivkah, however, did not chide her; Ria wondered whether her foster mother found it less trouble to let her do as she pleased than to try to keep her in the wagon, or whether her new-found liberty was merely because she was supposedly the bride-to-be of the future High Lord of Allanmere. Whatever the reason, Ria was fully prepared to enjoy it.

Ria found the plains endlessly fascinating. Small animals she'd never seen lived in the tall grass, and colorful butterflies and rainbow-hued flowers dappled the green-gold plains. Every night when they stopped to camp, Ria had new prizes to show her foster parents and the utterly disinterested Cyril. She pestered the guards, cook, and mages to show her which of the roots, berries, mushrooms, and young green plants of the plains were good to eat, and every night she'd present sacks full to the cook, together with a dozen other plants and two dozen questions. Lord Sharl joked that she'd see them all poisoned, but Ria could tell he was proud of her cleverness.

She and Cyril, however, found some common ground in a new pastime—hunting. Both had been taught the bow, but there had been little game in the settled lands near Emaril's keep, and they were not allowed to join the occasional hunting parties that ranged far from the keep. Now, however, there was an endless variety of game of all sizes available, and Ria and Cyril were permitted to ride with the guards to hunt the evening's meat.

Ria found her first hunt an unforgettable experience. She'd never killed so much as a mouse in her life and wondered whether she'd be able to do it at all; the first time the guards surprised a small herd of plains deer, however, a sort of hungry joy filled her, and her arrow flew to its mark before she knew she'd shot it. She'd felt a brief pang of regret when she'd seen her kill lying before her—it was such a beautiful creature, so graceful and harmless in life—but the smell of its blood woke that strange hungry joy again. When she cut her arrow free, she'd been unable to resist the impulse to raise a small strip of the bloody raw flesh to her lips, and the taste had made her tremble. She'd quickly cleaned her knife and her arrow and turned away when Cyril arrived, knowing he'd never understand the fierce excitement Ria was certain must show on her face. Somehow she knew that whatever pleasure Cyril got out of hunting, it wasn't the same.

Hunting, however, quickly became a competitive game. Ria could not match the range of Cyril's longer bow, but Cyril admitted that he could not best Ria's deadly accuracy, nor her keen vision, which could spot the plains deer almost invisible in a thicket. Lady Rivkah abashedly admitted that she'd never mastered the bow, but she and Lord Sharl sometimes joined the hunt simply for the joy of riding and relief from the jolting wagon seats.

Ria did not mind the roughness of their night camps. It was exciting to sleep in the open, a treat to wake to wind and birdsong instead of the clatter of pots from the kitchen. It tickled her pride to know that when they sat down to eat in the evening, she'd been the one to supply some of the meat and fresh vegetables they ate. When it rained, Lady Rivkah or one of the other mages cast a spell to keep water off them, and Ria was almost disappointed at how comfortable their camps were. It was delightful, too, to have no tiresome lessons, although Cyril had taken to hunkering over maps and scrolls with Lord Sharl and Lady Rivkah in the evenings, talking about crops and shipping and other equally dull subjects. Ria, meanwhile, was happy to spend her evenings avoiding her foster parents and Cyril altogether, sitting unobtrusively in the shadows near the servants and guards' fires and listening to the gossip, learning all the bawdy and "unsuitable" songs that Lady Rivkah had always tried to keep her from hearing.

The trade road itself was a source of occasional interest. This far south of Cielman it was hardly even a road, by Ria's observation, just a dusty and well-rutted dirt track, but Cyril told her it was one of the most heavily traveled trade routes between the north and the southern cities this far west. It ran near to Allanmere, very near, which was how Lord Sharl had taken the idea to build a trade city in that particular spot.

Sometimes they passed riders on the trade roads, messengers carrying their tidings north or pilgrims journeying

to northern temples. Once they met a merchant caravan—
it would stop in Cielman, in fact, as part of its trade route
—and although it was only late afternoon, the merchants
and Lord Sharl agreed to make camp for the night. That
was a jolly night; Lord Sharl and Lady Rivkah and Cyril sat
up most of the night talking with the merchants, discussing
trade routes and the possibility of including Allanmere as a
new stop between north and south, but Ria befriended
some of the children in the merchant caravan and spent
the night listening to the stories of their travels and nib-
bling sweets they'd brought from faraway cities. By morning, Ria had traded her silk scarf with the gold embroidery,
plus the matching slippers, for a chirrit pup from the litter
of one of the children's pets. As soon as she'd seen the
fuzzy, tumbling pups, as curious and full of energy as Ria
herself, Ria had known she had to have one; Lady Rivkah
had told her that Chyrie, Ria's mother, had had a chirrit,
so of course Ria should have one, too.

Lady Rivkah, however, was less delighted with Ria's new
acquisition the next morning.

"Oh, Ria, don't you think we're going to have enough
trouble in the new city without pets to watch out for?" she
asked, dismayed when she saw the strange little creature
peering out of Ria's pocket.

"He won't be any trouble," Ria said defensively. "They
told me how to take care of him. I'll feed him and keep
him out of the way."

Surprisingly, it was Lord Sharl who came to Ria's rescue,
picking the little animal out of her pocket and stroking its
large, tufted ears gently, chuckling as the chirrit clasped his
finger in its tiny, handlike paws and chirp-whirred with
contentment at the attention.

"I suppose a little thing like this can't eat all that much,
and he could hardly be more bother than you are by yourself, Ria," he said with a smile. "What did you trade for
him?"

"Well—" Ria squirmed. "My red scarf."

Lord Sharl gazed at her sternly, but his eyes twinkled
suspiciously.

"And?"

"And the slippers," Ria admitted.

Lady Rivkah groaned, and Lord Sharl snorted with laughter.

"That scarf and those slippers must've been worth a good twenty-five Suns, maybe more," he said, shaking his head, "and that chirrit pup wasn't worth more than six or seven, even to a mage needing a familiar. You'll have to learn better bargaining than that as the High Lady of a large trade city. Well, it was your first lesson, and a poor bargain's no crime. Let the child be, Rivkah. She's been lonely enough these years, and she'll be lonelier still as the High Lady of a half-empty city still being rebuilt."

"Well, you were lucky," Cyril commented in an undertone, settling down beside Ria in the wagon.

"I know," Ria said happily. Poor bargain or no, she couldn't have been more pleased. Now she'd never have to wear the irritating scarf or slippers again. "He's beautiful, isn't he?"

"I mean you're lucky Father's talks with the merchants went so well last night," Cyril chuckled. "If he hadn't been in such a good mood this morning, you'd probably have gotten punished instead. At least you could've traded for something useful instead of an animal only a mage might need. They had some hunting hound pups that looked to be a good bloodline."

"Then you should have traded for one, instead of spending your evening sitting by the fire," Ria retorted without rancor. Cyril was only jealous, she was sure, that Ria had managed to acquire such a marvelous little creature.

The chirrit pup was so young that Ria carried it in the front of her tunic despite Cyril's joke that it was long past time she had *something* there. He was an odd-looking little creature with round, wondering eyes, large tufted ears, and remarkably handlike paws. His fluffy squirrellike tail was amazingly dextrous and strong, able to wind firmly around Ria's upper arm or, unfortunately, her throat to keep himself steady on her shoulder. He seemed to eat just about anything Ria would—meat, fruit, tubers, bread, cheese, sweets—and even Lady Rivkah was amused by the way he ate, clasping morsels of food securely in his little paws as he sat and nibbled, his bright, intelligent-looking eyes darting around as if to ascertain whether anyone nearby might have something more appetizing to offer. Soon even the roughest guard was saving choice tidbits for Ria's pet.

The plains rolled on until Ria lost count of the days. Occasionally there were small fords to cross—branches of the Brightwater River, Lord Sharl said, signs that they were getting closer to Allanmere. Ria was disappointed that the caravan rarely stopped at these fords; she'd never seen a body of water larger than small streams, and she was fairly aching to tear off her clothes and jump into the cool water.

One night, however, to Ria's delight they camped by one of these small branches. Ria lay in her bedroll listening to the water chuckle over the rocks until she could bear it no more; then she slipped quietly out of the tent. The guards walked slowly around the camp; it was a surprisingly simple matter to stand quietly against one of the wagons, think herself small and unnoticeable, and then dart off into the tall grass when the guard was safely past. When she had worked her way downstream out of earshot, however, she was surprised to see that someone had arrived at the idea of a midnight swim before she had; she was even more surprised to recognize the shadowy figure pulling the tunic up over its head as none other than Lady Rivkah.

Ria thought she'd moved silently, but she must have made some sound, for Lady Rivkah turned and peered up into the darkness.

"Ria? Is that you?" The High Lady kept her voice very soft. She beckoned almost furtively.

"Uh-huh." Ria sighed and scrambled down to join her foster mother. "I'm sorry I sneaked away. I just—"

To Ria's amazement, Lady Rivkah smiled and dropped the tunic over a bush.

"I know," she said. "I felt the same way. Hang your clothes up and come on."

The water was almost too cold for swimming, but Ria

and Lady Rivkah waded in the shallows and scrubbed their skin with the soap Lady Rivkah had brought, splashing each other in the moonlight and giggling as quietly as they could. When they grew too chilly, they shiveringly pulled on their clothes and sat on one of the boulders edging the stream.

"You know," Lady Rivkah said quietly, "you're not the only one who sometimes feels trapped and dreams about just breaking loose in some way."

Ria glanced sideways at her foster mother. Lady Rivkah seemed the very image of a perfect High Lady—disciplined, self-contained, competent. But she could remember from childhood a different image—Lady Rivkah in old patched leathers, staging mock swordfights with Ria and Cyril using sticks for swords, having snowball fights in the winter, building mud castles in the soft plowed earth after a rain. Where had that woman gone over the years?

"Once when Sharl and I were riding through the forest with your mother," Lady Rivkah said, "it was raining hard. Very hard. Chyrie and her mate Valann wouldn't let me cast a rainproofing spell for them to ride under, and I worried about her becoming chilled and sick—she was pregnant with you then. But before I knew what was happening she'd jumped down to the ground, pulled her clothes off, and was pelting off down the trail as fast as she could go." Lady Rivkah chuckled. "When Sharl and I caught up with her—on our horses, mind—she'd run herself out and was on her knees in the mud *howling,* I do believe. At first I was horrified, and embarrassed, but for a moment—just a moment, mind—I saw that look in her eyes and I wanted to be there howling with her in the rain. Her mate said it was the wild blood in her. The same wild blood that runs through your veins, Ria."

Lady Rivkah shook her head.

"But don't ever believe, Ria, that only you—or only elves—ever feel that wild blood. No matter what you think, we all want to run in the rain and howl sometimes. Now let's get back to camp."

Ria thought about Lady Rivkah's words in the next few

days. She could certainly sympathize if Lady Rivkah felt caged and trapped as Ria herself did; however, that didn't change the fact that Lady Rivkah had chosen her cage and Ria had not. Moreover, why should Lady Rivkah, if she understood Ria's need for freedom, be so eager to cage Ria ever more tightly? No, Ria thought with some pity that Lady Rivkah had left her howling days behind her with the snowballs and mud castles. With any luck, however, Ria hoped, hers were only beginning.

Ria could scarcely believe her eyes when abruptly the forest loomed before them, cool and green and huge. There had been no forests near Emaril's keep or near Cielman, and Ria could never have imagined the immensity, the ancient grandeur of it, even in her wistful dreams. Nor could she have anticipated her sudden certainty that this was something more than a simple stand of foliage— this was in its own way a living being of sorts, an entire little world. Even more startling was the sense of home- coming as soon as Ria saw it, the sudden yearning to rush headlong into its leafy arms and drown herself in its shad- owy depths. Her breath came short and she trembled, clenching her fists in anger as much as longing. So close and yet so unreachable. The guards would stop her before she got more than a few steps away.

"I know," Lady Rivkah said softly, her hand on Ria's shoulder. "The first time I saw it, I was amazed, too. It's like another world, isn't it?"

Another world indeed. Ria shivered. Her mother's world, her brother's world, her people's world. Her world, if she hadn't been exiled from it. No, whatever her foster mother might be feeling, it wasn't this.

The road curved to avoid the forest by a good margin. Around midday Lord Sharl halted the wagons, and he and Lady Rivkah saddled their horses and rode off toward the forest alone, much to the dismay of the guards and of Ria, who had begged hard to go with them. Lord Sharl and Lady Rivkah rode back and forth along the forest's edge for almost an hour, occasionally calling out in Olvenic without result, and then returned discouraged to the wagons.

"Nothing," Lord Sharl said disgustedly. "Not even arrows. We'd have been throwing our lives down the privy to ride in there, though, no doubt."

"There'll be other chances," Lady Rivkah said comfortingly. "Remember, so much of this part of the forest burned. A good deal of that's new growth, and that means the trees won't be large enough for their hanging huts and so on. Likely the outermost clans moved deeper into the forest with the game. There may simply be nobody living here now."

"No sentries, no wide patrols to watch the edge of the forest?" Lord Sharl said skeptically. "The elves must have grown a good deal calmer and more trusting, then, than they used to be."

It took days to ride around the northeastern side of the forest, and Ria continued to marvel at the size of it. At the southeast edge of the forest, a smaller track branched off from the trade road, and Lord Sharl said this was the road to Allanmere.

"The south side's much narrower," he told her, pulling out a map to show her the wedgelike shape of the forest. "It'll only be a short ride around the southern tip, alongside the river, and then we'll be almost at the city."

On the south side of the forest, the road passed through a narrow strip of open ground separating the forest to the north from the broad expanse of the Brightwater River to the south. It was Ria's first glimpse of the river on which her foster father was laying so many of his hopes, and Ria was rather disappointed. It was big and deep-looking, yes, but it was placid and muddy and not much different otherwise from the streams Ria had seen.

At the southern edge of the forest they stopped again. Lady Rivkah told Ria that this part of the forest had once been the territory of a friendly elvan clan called the Brightwaters, who had allied with Rowan and the city during the barbarian invasion, and Lord Sharl had hopes of contacting them. Once again, Ria and Cyril were not permitted to approach the forest, and they amused themselves along the riverbank, even Cyril eager to stretch his legs after the long wagon ride. Poking in the rushes at the river's edge, Ria saw a length of what looked like rope tied to a stake driven into the bank and trailing into the water. She nudged Cyril.

"What's that?" she asked, pointing.

Cyril pulled on the rope, eventually drawing to light a sort of woven basket of willow switches.

"It's a fish trap," he said. "The elves must have set it. It's too far from the city."

"Then there *are* elves here," Ria said, delighted. "We've come around most of the forest edge. I thought they'd all gone away or something."

Cyril gave a short chuckle of derision.

"Where would they go?" he said. "A whole forest full of elves? They're not like the elves in the eastern cities. They wouldn't fit in anywhere else, and they don't know anything outside their own forest. There's nowhere else they *could* go, even if they wanted to." He glanced toward the forest, then gasped, pointing. "Look!"

Lord Sharl and Lady Rivkah were riding away from the forest as fast as the terrified horses could run. Ria could see what looked like flies buzzing out of the forest after them; then Ria realized that what she saw must be arrows. Guards rode out to meet them, but Lord Sharl and Lady Rivkah were fortunately already out of range of the deadly missiles. One of the guards, more heavily armored, risked the lethal rain to ride in closer and retrieve one of the arrows.

Lord Sharl examined the feathered fletching and the painted band on the arrow shaft and shook his head grimly.

"This isn't a Brightwater arrow," he said. "It looks like Blue-eyes to me. Gods know I'll never forget the arrows we pulled out of ourselves and our horses and—" He glanced at Ria and did not finish whatever it was he would have said. "That's bad news. It means that the Blue-eyes must have claimed a good part of the border lands, as I'd feared.

The Brightwaters might have dealt with us peaceably. The Blue-eyes will never let us close enough to be heard, no matter what gestures of friendliness we make, and getting past those lands to even try to reach Rowan is going to be difficult."

Ria could see that her foster parents were sorely disappointed by this turn of events, but there was nothing to be done. They quietly returned to the wagons and continued along the river.

Once they rounded the southern edge of the forest and turned back to the northwest, Ria caught her first sight of the city of Allanmere. Again, she was disappointed. The size of the wall indicated a large city indeed—larger even than Cielman, it appeared—but the wall was crumbled and ruined in many places, the great stone gates fallen into disrepair. Ria could not see much over the wall, but the few structures she could see through the crumbled gaps were fallen in and roofless. Ria remembered from the histories how the city had been bombarded with boulders and fireballs by the barbarian army before the wall had finally collapsed in places to admit the invaders. She shivered. Had they come this far only to live in a ruin?

"It's not as bad as it looks," Lord Sharl said kindly, riding beside Ria. "A good part of the inner keep has been rebuilt. Most of what you're seeing now were barracks and guild halls. The west and north sides of the city are in much better shape, and the wall's almost entirely intact along the river and the swamp. The south and east sides of the city were the worst hit, and those buildings will be the last repaired, too. Most of the people moving into the city want houses nearer the market at the center."

"How many people are in the city now?" Ria asked dubiously. Could anyone live in a city as tumbledown as this one appeared? There was certainly nobody to be seen—no, surely those tiny moving dots atop solid sections of the wall were guards, or possibly stonemasons.

"In the city itself, somewhere between a thousand and half again as much," Lord Sharl told her. "Probably another hundred or two farming the surrounding lands. The farmers will be the slowest returning, I'm afraid. Most of those who left have settled elsewhere. When we first founded the city, good farmland was hard to find in the settled lands and there were plenty of families looking for land of their own. Since the invasion, there's more good farmland available near the larger, well-established cities than there are farmers to work it. Farmers aren't quite so ready to pack up their families and take a chance anymore."

Ria looked back at the forest, so tantalizingly close to the city. How many elves lived in the cool shade of the mighty trees? Surely they'd scorn crumbling stone walls and half-deserted cities.

Riders approached from the city—guards, but none Ria recognized. These were guards Lord Sharl had been hiring for the past two years, sending them south to oversee the reconstruction of the city. They were recognizable as guards only by their chain armor and military bearing; under the padding, they wore rough homespun like any peasant.

The guards cheered Lord Sharl's arrival, and Ria was surprised at their casual familiarity. Despite their "milords," they greeted the High Lord of their city much as they might one of their own number, clapping him on the shoulder or clasping wrists with him. Lady Rivkah they treated with rather more deference, but Ria wondered whether that was not because she was a mage or a woman, rather than their High Lady. High Lord Emaril had apparently demanded much more formality from his guardsmen, if the behavior of the guards at his keep was any indicator.

Instead of entering at the south gate of the city, the guards led them around the wall to the east gate, what they called the Sun Gate, telling Lord Sharl apologetically that the south side of the city was still in very poor shape and some of the buildings fronting the street were of dubious stability. Ria didn't doubt it; riding past the wall, she could see huge gaps, many ringed with scorching even sixteen years' worth of rain had not washed away. The Sun Gate had been repaired to some extent, but obviously it had

been the target of a more sustained attack, and to Ria's
untrained eye it seemed ready to collapse. As Ria rode
through the cracked street, tumbled buildings choked with
debris on either side of her, she wondered how any of the
city could possibly be any worse than what she saw. In one
spot they had to detour through alleys to skirt a huge crack
in the earth, the edges of which had crumbled alarmingly.

To Ria's amazement, Lord Sharl rode perilously close to
the crack, chuckling as he peered down into it.

"Rivkah, I think between you and your teacher, you did
more damage to the city than the invading army," he
grinned.

"You did *that*?" Ria asked her foster mother, greatly
impressed.

"Of course she did," Cyril said irritably. "It was in the
histories."

"Well, we meant to cause an earthquake," Lady Rivkah
said, flushing slightly. "We just didn't mean to cause quite
that *much* of one. You know," she added defensively,
"we'd hardly more than experimented in pooling our magical energy and working together. It's not as though we had
much time to perfect a multiimage lattice, with barbarians
pouring through the walls and half the city on fire. It was
no small trick to manage the earthquake and such a large
illusion at the same time, either."

Ria grinned in appreciation, both at the feat of magic
and at the size of the crack it had left. Lord Sharl had
commissioned a tapestry depicting the event, and now that
Ria associated the crack with the event, she could truly
appreciate the skill of the weavers—she could never have
otherwise imagined the huge fiery figure climbing up out of
the flaming crack. It had been a clever idea, to create the
illusion that the fire-god enemy of the barbarians' ice god
was crawling forth to defend the city. Ria had been proud
when Lady Rivkah told her that her mother Chyrie had
been the one to suggest it. That idea had likely won the
war, even if the city had been all but ruined afterward,
even if most of Lord Sharl's hard-won settlers had abandoned the place.

As they rode farther into the city, however, Ria saw that
the city was not, in fact, deserted. Nearer the center of
town, several buildings had been nicely restored into shops
or houses, complete to weathertight shutters and baked-
clay tile roofs. There were peasants, too, in the streets,
bent on various errands of their own. Some were clearing
rubble out of buildings or setting stone blocks in place,
apparently refurbishing houses or shops for their own use;
others were repairing the roads for more general use.

Children running in the streets stopped to watch the
wagons curiously, many of them pointing to Ria and whispering excitedly. Most of the adults stopped to look, too,
and Ria fancied that their expressions when they looked at
her seemed to show rather more hostility than simple curiosity. Ria shivered and drew herself up. Hadn't they been
told that High Lord Sharl's foster daughter (and their
soon-to-be High Lady) was an elf, or were they simply that
unhappy about it?

There were other signs of life in the city, too. At the
center of the city where the road turned north was the
market, and there were stalls there although it wasn't even
midweek, peasants selling early vegetables and other wares
from trays or carts, and even a few small merchants offering their wares directly from their wagons. Ria had never
been allowed to prowl the market in Cielman, and she
pleaded to have a chance to look around, but Lady Rivkah
shook her head sternly.

"When there's time, I'll take you to the market," Lady
Rivkah said gently. "It isn't safe for you to go alone just
yet. Sharl has had to take who he can get for settlers here,
and some of them are rough people. And after so many
have been shot at just for getting too close to the forest,
I'm afraid you wouldn't be very well received in the city
until the citizens come to know who you are."

A smaller wall separated the keep from the rest of the
city, and this wall was largely intact. There were more
guards here, mostly working on the wall at the moment,
and what might be servants going about their business in
preparation for the High Lord's arrival. Many of these folk

stopped what they were doing, too, to rush to greet Lord Sharl and his family as they rode along the outside of the keep's wall toward the gate.

As Lord Sharl had said, the northern and western portions of the city, largely protected from attack by the natural barriers of the Brightwater River to the west and the swamp to the north, had remained relatively undamaged. A few buildings had fallen, but Ria speculated that that might have happened during the earthquake Lady Rivkah had spoken of, as she saw little of the fire damage she'd seen farther to the east. As Cyril had speculated, however, the keep itself, incomplete when the battle had begun and struck by massive attacks, had suffered tremendous damage. One of the keep's two large towers had collapsed completely, and the jumbled blocks, shattered and scorched, still lay where they'd fallen at the corner of the keep. Ria stared at the ruined tower and shivered. Her mother's mate had died on that tower, and Lady Rivkah's teacher, too. Might the ruined tower, or even the whole keep now, be haunted?

The chirrit pup scrambled out of Ria's tunic to sit on her shoulder, nuzzling her ear, and Ria was unaccountably comforted. This shabby stone city might not be where she truly belonged, but it was better than Lord Emaril's country keep. Who knew what manner of adventures a curious young elf could have here? Certainly something more interesting than baiting her governess and hiding in the stable loft. And the forest *was* closer, much closer than it had ever been in her life. Yes, this place might suit her very well, indeed.

A few unfamiliar servants hurried to the yard to unload the wagons. Ria did not wait for a guide, but ran into the castle, the chirrit chattering nervously at the bumpy ride and half-throttling Ria with his tail. At least the halls were clean, although Ria wondered whoever had designed the place—the halls wound like the tunnels in an anthill, rather than following any logical pattern she could see. To Ria's amazement, she realized she was very nearly lost in the place, and she had to find a window and look out to get her bearings. Turning back, she met Lady Rivkah in the halls.

"I thought you might like the room where your mother stayed," Lady Rivkah said tentatively. "Chyrie and Valann were only here a short time, but still—come and see it, at least."

The room was nothing special; Ria's room at Lord Emaril's keep had, in fact, been larger and had more furniture and tapestries. But the windows looked out over the ruined tower and toward the forest.

Lady Rivkah followed Ria's glance to the tower.

"Chyrie and Valann loved that tower," Lady Rivkah said rather wistfully. "They'd spend almost every evening up there. Sometimes they'd even sleep at the top of the tower. I don't think they much cared for being indoors."

Ria looked at the tower again.

"Do—do I look much like her?" she asked impulsively. "My mother."

"Very much like." Lady Rivkah smiled affectionately. "Her hair was curly like yours, but it was a kind of golden brown, not black, and her eyes were a sort of gold color, not blue-green. But the set of your face is just like Chyrie's, and you're small like her. I always wondered how such a tiny thing could have so much fire inside her. She'd not give ground before the brawniest elf-hating fellow in the city, and give back as good as she got, too, even when she was heavily pregnant."

"*She* wouldn't have let someone marry her off to a man she didn't want," Ria said pointedly.

"She didn't want to come to Allanmere," Lady Rivkah replied quietly. "She didn't want the elves to ally with the city, and I doubt she wanted to give up her children, either. But your mother was wise enough to put aside what she wanted for the welfare of others. It's not only nobles who sometimes must make sacrifices for the good of their people."

Ria was stubbornly silent, although she wanted to protest that she heartily wished her mother *hadn't* given up her children, no matter what noble reasoning had gone into that decision. She wondered if Chyrie had considered that the "sacrifice" she was making condemned her daughter, too, to life as an oddity, a stranger among people who would use her only as a political tool. Suddenly she was furious, as angry at the mother she'd never known as she was at her foster parents. Why had they done this to her, all of them?

"You've taken good care of him," Lady Rivkah said suddenly, breaking Ria's train of thought, and it took Ria a moment before she realized that Lady Rivkah was speaking of the chirrit on her shoulder. "Have you given him a name yet?"

Ria shook her head, still too angry to speak.

"You'll need to name him soon," Lady Rivkah said. "Chirrits are very intelligent; that's why mages like them for familiars. No intelligent creature likes to live without a name."

When Ria still said nothing, Lady Rivkah sighed and shrugged.

"I'll leave you to settle yourself in," she said. "If you want another room, choose for yourself, but you'll have to wait until the maids have time to clean it. After supper I'll show you where the baths are. By that time the clothes should be brought in."

Ria ignored Lady Rivkah's exit, but a moment later the High Lady's statement finally sank in. *Where the baths are?* Why in the world didn't the servants bring up the tub and water as usual? Maybe there were so few servants that a bathing room of sorts had been set up near the kitchen so the water wouldn't have to be carried so far. Wait—Lord Sharl had spoken of springs of hot water being found far below Allanmere that the mages had tapped and brought to the surface in various places in the city and in the castle, too. That must be what her foster mother had meant. Well, that would be interesting, at least.

Ria glanced around the room. It could have been anyone's room, rather small and a little barren. There was no sign that anyone extraordinary had ever stayed there. Inelegant quarters for the future High Lady of Allanmere. But then, likely after her marriage she'd have other quarters, with Cyril.

That thought made her grimace. Marriage—and to Cyril, yet! Doubtless he'd want to do the man-woman thing, too, that the High Lord and Lady did in their rooms and that the servants sometimes came out to the stables to do secretly, unaware of Ria in the hayloft. The whole thing looked clumsy and uncomfortable to her, maybe even painful, although from what she'd seen, the servants certainly seemed to like it. Ria was curious enough to give it a try—someday.

Still, marriage to Cyril! She didn't want to wear scratchy gowns and shoes and attend stuffy formal suppers and sit in audiences. She didn't want to arbitrate boring land disputes or figure tedious crop inventories, and most of all she didn't want to spend her days and nights inside stone walls instead of outside in the fresh air.

In a rush of daring, Ria dashed to the window and climbed up on the ledge. She could work her way along the wall of the castle and climb down the tumbled blocks of the tower easily enough, and from there the debris might hide her until she reached the inner wall. And then—

Ria stopped, shaking her head.

And then the peasants working on the grounds, clearing debris and mending the walls, would surely see her and stop her, and if they didn't, the guards on the inner wall would. She'd never even tried making her don't-see-me work while she was moving. *Then* she'd have to get through the northern part of the city to the outer wall. At the very least she'd be sighted crossing the broad expanse of bare land between the wall and the forest. The only possibility would be to make the journey on a night when the open land wouldn't be lit by moonlight; Ria had learned, to her surprise, that everyone but she seemed pitifully unable to see in the dark.

And what if she reached the forest? Ria was no fool; she knew the elves of the border clans—likely Blue-eyes, as Lord Sharl had said—might welcome her onto their lands no more than they did her foster parents. But she thought it likely they wouldn't shoot an elf appearing to flee from the human city, at least until they questioned her. Lady Rivkah had made sure that Ria and Cyril learned Olvenic, both the kind spoken in the eastern elvan cities and the kind spoken by the elves near Allanmere, and even Lord Sharl had insisted on regular practice; one day, after all, they'd be negotiating with those elves in the Heartwood. The Blue-eyes just might listen to Chyrie's daughter, might let her continue into the forest. Might even know where her brother could be found.

Maybe they'd even—

"There you are." Lord Sharl leaned against the door frame. He was wearing his patched traveling leathers, liberally besprinkled with dust. "Rivkah said you probably wouldn't stick your nose out of your room for some time. Come and see this anyway."

Ria sighed irritably, but she followed her foster father through the halls of the castle to the west side, then across the grounds to the wall. The wall here was largely intact, as was the western tower when Lord Sharl led Ria up through it. The guard at the top of the wall bowed, eyes wide, when Lord Sharl emerged from the doorway.

"Look at that," Lord Sharl said, turning Ria gently to face westward and indicating the view with a sweep of his hand.

Ria looked. Almost directly beneath them was the broad expanse of the Brightwater River. Southward lay a number of sturdy wooden docks built out into the stream of the river, piles of stone buttressing each support against the strength of the water. Ria could see stacks of debris where likely one or more of the old docks, probably fallen into disrepair, had been torn apart and rebuilt. The docks now were fresh and new; even now Ria could see Yvarden standing there, doubtless casting the antirot and worm-repelling spells to keep the wooden beams sturdy.

Across the river to the west lay fields. Those fields were green-gold with ripening grain now, or green with the tops of vegetables. Here and there Ria could see a break in the fields, winding lines of streams branching out from the Brightwater, or darker blots of farms.

"What are you seeing out there?" Lord Sharl asked after a moment.

Ria shrugged. "The river. The docks. Farms." What else was there?

"Hope," Lord Sharl corrected. "Hopes and dreams. More than a thousand people who have tied their lives and the lives of their children to this city. I brought them from all parts of the known world—folk whose homes and lands were destroyed or rendered unusable by the invasion, folk from uninvaded countries where all the good land was already taken, folk from large families who had no more land to parcel out, folk who weren't born to land and who didn't have the money to better themselves. They came because I made them a promise. Sixteen years ago I made the same promise and I broke it. This time I'm going to keep it."

Lord Sharl gestured down at the muddy river.

"That's why I'll keep my promise this time. I've spoken to merchants in the north—dozens, maybe hundreds of them. As settlement moves west, the Dezarin becomes more and more impractical. This was the only site convenient to both the river and the trade road; that's why I chose it. The Brightwater River will become the new supply line between north and south, and we'll be the only trade city *on* the Brightwater. Emaril frets about the depth, but I've had depth readings taken all along the length of the Brightwater from rafts. Sixteen years ago we had supply ships carrying down full loads of *coal*, by the gods, in high summer when there hadn't been rain for weeks. That river can carry anything we load it with, and it'll carry it right to our door."

Ria eyed the river dubiously. It didn't look all that special to her.

"There's only one thing as important to the success of this city as the river," Lord Sharl continued. He turned Ria around to look in the opposite direction at the forest. "The elves. Their goodwill might not save this city, but I can assure you that their continued hostility will destroy it. If the border clans made a determined effort, they could make it so dangerous to pass around the southern tip of the forest that nobody could get to the city from the trade road. It wouldn't take much to dissuade merchants from diverting their caravans to Allanmere—just a few arrows now and then, or even one or two very decisive bloody raids, and then the river trade I'm counting on will be just another empty dream.

"We need timber from the forest for building. Even if we build every house and shop out of stone, we'll still need beams for the roofs, for floor supports, and wood to burn until we can bring in shipments of coal. As the plains around the city are dug up for fields, we'll need to hunt in the forest for food and furs, too, until enough livestock can be bred to feed the city. Even healing herbs—most of them grow in woodlands, not on the open plains. Those are commodities the elves could trade in, if they'd trade."

Ria remained silent. She could see where this trail ended.

"But we can't negotiate with the elves if we can't talk to them," Lord Sharl said after a moment's silence. "Sixteen years ago some of them would have talked to me—perhaps most of them, thanks to Rowan's alliance. Even the squabbling between the clans over territories might have worked to our advantage, made our trade goods seem more desirable. That alliance had fallen apart when last I talked with Rowan, though, and that was right after the war, just before Rivkah and I returned to Cielman. Since the invasion I imagine there's a good deal more free land than there are elves to claim it. Any shortage of game should have long since replenished itself. They have everything they need, and they've had sixteen years to enjoy it and let their hatred of the humans grow, with a poacher picking at the edge of the forest now and then to keep their anger and their arrows ready. A good many of the clans that might have negotiated with us sixteen years ago won't do it now, even if we can reach the inner clans at all. I'm not sure they'll even talk to you. But we have to try."

Ria clenched her jaw stubbornly, stroking the chirrit pup.

Lord Sharl patted her shoulder gently.

"I understand your feelings," he said. "I and each one of my brothers grew up knowing our father might arrange a marriage for us with one of the neighboring families to bring whatever advantage they could—land, mercantile affiliations, whatever. Even when I met Rivkah, for years we didn't marry because of the possibility that I'd need to make an alliance marriage later. I could gain great advantages by marrying Cyril to landed nobility, possibly obligating several merchant families to us and vastly facilitating later trade. But he'll marry you because of a promise I made before he was even born, that you'd be wed to my firstborn son. And wed you'll be, not only because of that promise or because I need that link with the forest—although both of those are factors—but because it's the best I can do for either of you."

"I don't want to marry him," Ria protested hotly. "And *I* don't think it's best for me. But nobody ever bothered to ask me what *I* thought."

Lord Sharl turned and smiled a little pityingly at her.

"And what's the matter with Cyril? He's intelligent and strong, a fair fighter and training to be a mage. You've known him all your life. You used to be such great friends. Don't you like him now?"

Ria squirmed.

"I like him well enough," she said reluctantly. "But not *that* way. I like him like a brother and a friend. When he has time for me," she added quickly. "Mostly he doesn't want to be bothered with me these days."

"All boys pass through a stage where they don't want to be bothered with girls," Lord Sharl chuckled. "But I think Cyril's past that time and quite ready for marriage. I don't believe he doesn't want to be bothered with you; I think he's simply outgrown the games you used to play, and you haven't." He glanced sideways at Ria. "Do you know, your mother was over eighty years old when she bore you, and she *still* looked like a child to me. And her mate was centuries old."

"Well, there," Ria said eagerly. "You see, I can't possibly marry Cyril. He'd be old and dead in a few decades, and I'd still be young."

Lord Sharl was silent for a long moment, and Ria was surprised to see the weary sadness on his face.

"Rivkah and I spoke of that many times," he said. "I've discussed it with Cyril, too. It's a possibility, yes, that you'll live far longer than my son, and if he died, I can't imagine you ruling the city without him. But that may not be the case. Despite the way you look, you have some human blood. It may be you'll grow old with Cyril. If not, I hope you'll be wise enough to abdicate to your heirs when Cyril is gone." He shook his head. "But that's a future that you and Cyril will have to decide. And I think he'll be glad enough to marry you, elvan foster sister or not. Would you rather I'd done as other noble fathers do and married you to some fellow you didn't even know, someone you might not like at all?"

"No!" Ria said quickly. The thought sent a spear of alarm through her. "No. I don't want to marry anybody."

"Ah. So you'd rather live on Cyril's estate as a hanger-on," Lord Sharl said, nodding sagely. "You came to us with nothing of your own, so you'd be happiest leeching Cyril's wealth instead, letting him keep you in comfort while you give nothing in return."

"I don't want Cyril's wealth," Ria said hotly. "If that's what I wanted, I *would* just marry him. You know, I didn't exactly ask to be fostered with you at all, much less in order to steal his money!"

"Not that there's much to steal, as almost everything we own has been invested in this city," Lord Sharl agreed. "All right, so you don't want Cyril's wealth. How do you plan to live, then? You don't know any trade well enough to support yourself. What exactly is it you *do* want to do, Ria?"

"I could—I could go back to the elves," Ria said defiantly. There it was, her poor, timeworn hope made plain.

She'd hardly ever dared put that wish into words even in her own mind all these years. Her people, her home, had always seemed so distant, so unreachable. But her brother was somewhere in that forest. Even if her mother hadn't wanted her, surely her brother, her twin, would welcome her. Surely he would. Wouldn't he?

"Ah, I see." Lord Sharl nodded again. "And knowing that they live rough in the wilderness, doubtless you've picked up thousands of skills useful to them during your sixteen sheltered years in my brother's keep. Or were you expecting that they'd pamper and keep you as we've done, while you yourself contributed nothing?"

"Well, it's hardly my fault I wasn't raised among them," Ria mumbled. "Anyway, I'd learn. I can hunt already, and I've learned plants that can be eaten, too."

"Yes, doubtless you'd learn," Lord Sharl agreed. "You're clever and quick to master a skill when you actually apply yourself. There'd be a great deal for you to learn, a tremendous change in your life. But it's been my experience that the elves are inclined to be patient with their own kind. Still, your mother gave you to us to raise for a reason. Have you thought about what that reason might be?"

"I suppose she was just like you, wanting an alliance between the elves and the humans," Ria grumbled. Actually it was a question she didn't much like to think about. She was far too afraid of the answer.

"Would it surprise you to know that she hated me," Lord Sharl chuckled, "and disagreed with almost everything I believed in, and for a long time would have liked nothing better than to see me dead, if not kill me herself?"

"It certainly *would* surprise me," Ria said sourly. *That* hadn't been in the histories! A part of her, however, cringed inside. How could her mother have hated her so much as to give Ria to her enemy?

"Well, she did, and she didn't want the alliance, either," he said. "But she knew we needed it—both the humans and the elves. Because the alternative is another war someday, a war between the city and the forest, and this war we'll both lose, because in a war between neighbors who should have been friends and allies, there are no winners, only losers."

"The alliance with the elves didn't save the city before," Ria pointed out.

"No," Lord Sharl admitted. "We didn't have enough time to prepare, we didn't have enough troops, and Rowan didn't have complete support among the elves. If we'd had more time to learn to work together, just a few more months maybe—well, we didn't. We won, but in winning we lost the city. The elves lost, too, a good part of their lands and game and several whole clans of elves, your mother's clan among them. Nevertheless, every life we saved—human or elf—was a victory of sorts. I think your mother gave you to us to raise in the hope that such a thing would never have to happen again. And whether you agree with the idea of an alliance or not, I think you can at least agree with that."

Ria scowled. She hated it when her foster parents used that reasonable, patient tone that was so hard to argue with; it was even more infuriating than when they snapped at her or ignored her as if she was an idiot.

"You're sixteen years old, not a child anymore, however much you look it," Lord Sharl said a bit more sternly. "It's time you started assuming some of your responsibilities as my foster daughter and an adult of noble family. As I'm sure Rivkah told you, most young women your age would be long married by now and likely with a child or two at their skirts. Because we were waiting for the city to be ready to live in again, we postponed the wedding—kinder to you and Cyril, we thought, to let you have time to get used to each other, and good for the people's morale to have the wedding in the city. That may have been a mistake on our part. At any rate, we'll announce the wedding as soon as we're settled in—say a week. I suggest you put that time to use working out your differences with Cyril and learning to be of some use to this city as High Lady instead of sulking in your room."

He left Ria there on the wall in a state of utter panic. A week! Then say another week between announcement and event; Lord Sharl and Lady Rivkah likely wouldn't bother with too much preparation and ceremony in this half-populated, half-ruined city with so few people living here yet. No more than two weeks and she'd be shackled like a prisoner in this keep even more securely than she'd been at Emaril's keep. And breaking free of this prison would be much more difficult than simply slipping a lizard down a governess's gown!

Ria turned and stared down into the city itself. The sun had all but set, and only a small portion of the buildings showed the glow of firelight or lamplight. So many uninhabited buildings might offer limitless hiding places for a nimble-footed elvan girl—if the tumbledown structures didn't fall in on her and crush her, that is. And under cover of darkness, that elvan girl might be able to slip through one of the openings in the outer city wall, less heavily guarded than the inner wall. The only problem remained crossing the distance between the city and the forest unseen. The moon was waning, but there'd be no moonless nights for some time yet, and with only two weeks before the wedding, Ria didn't dare to wait. Maybe with practice she could manage to make people ignore her while she was moving as well as when she was still, but that practice might take time she could ill afford, and how could she test her skill? How frustrating that she couldn't manage a simple feat that any apprentice mage could!

Then Ria paused.

Apprentice mage—

Ria hurried back to the castle, then ground her teeth in frustration as she realized that she had no idea where Cyril's room might be. It took quite some effort even to find a chambermaid, and then the flustered girl, as newly arrived as they, was no more certain of the interior of the keep than Ria herself. Eventually Ria gave up and began searching on her own, theorizing that Cyril's room would be in the same wing as her own since so much of the castle had not yet been repaired. When she eventually found a room where she recognized some of Cyril's belongings, she found to her disgust that Cyril was not in it; the idiot was no doubt poring over plans or figures with Lord Sharl, or busy with some other equally boring task.

Ria rummaged through Cyril's chests until she found his books and scrolls, and there she found pen and ink and a scrap of hide. She penned a quick note asking Cyril to meet her in her room as quickly as possible, and as soon as the ink dried, she rolled the note and laid it on Cyril's pillow.

On the way back to her room, Ria chanced across one of the baths of which Lady Rivkah had spoken. It was an impressive bit of magic to tap into the hot springs far below the surface, much less to pipe the hot water to the upper floors of the castle. Ria was less impressed, however, with the end result; the bathing pool itself needed cleaning and repair and the hot water, though appealingly bubbly and clear, smelled like bad eggs. Ria paused long enough to dabble one hand in the delightfully warm water, but when she realized the egg-stink clung to her fingers, Ria wrinkled her nose and continued back to her room.

Her few daily necessities were still in their pack, not yet unloaded. With the bustle of servants in the kitchens and around the wagons, there'd be no chance to sneak a few supplies, but she could hunt, and she'd learned a good many plants she could forage if need be, although most likely she'd have no use for either skill. Surely the elves would give her food, too, while they helped her find her mother and brother. So the only problem remained reaching the forest and contacting the elves once she got there, and Cyril was an apprentice mage who could likely cast a simple invisibility spell—if he could be persuaded to help her.

Now she was glad for the repeated practice conversations in Olvenic her foster parents had pressed on her. Ria had picked up the language far more easily and instinctively than Cyril, although they'd both received their basic grounding in the language magically at the same time. With any luck she'd be speaking nothing but the musical elvan language for the rest of her life.

Lady Rivkah had told her endless stories of the elves'

customs, the proper thing to say when greeting them and the kinds of gifts they seemed to like. Ria had learned those lessons easily, too; somehow it was much easier to remember what she was told than what she read off scrolls. Ria had practiced the greeting till she could say it backward if she liked, and she'd accumulated, over the years, a small packet of exquisite gem-bead necklaces and bracelets and two small but marvelously forged daggers. The gifts had cost her most of her pocket money, but it would be worth it if the proper gestures of respect to the Eldest of her brother's clan could possibly win her a place among her own people.

For the first time in her life, freedom.

"Jenji," Ria murmured. It wasn't an exact translation; in Olvenic it meant something like *the freedom of fast running against the wind.*

The forgotten chirrit pup on her shoulder chirp-whirred in her ear, and Ria reached up to caress the little round head.

"That's the name for you, little one," Ria murmured. "I think I'll call you Jenji."

There was a tentative rap at the door: Cyril. Ria smiled and thought of tall trees and cool green shadows.

IV

V ALANN

• "Try again," Rowan said encouragingly. "Once more."

"I have come to speak of peace—" Val sighed explosively in frustration as his throat rebelled against the ugly grating sounds. "How can anyone speak this wretched human tongue without choking?"

Lahti giggled, and Dusk had to chuckle, too.

"Your mother once made that same face when she first spoke their words," he said. "But it's not so difficult. A little time and practice and you will speak well."

"You speak it far more skillfully than I," Valann grumbled. "So does Rowan. I don't speak for Inner Heart; I'm not even an elder. One of you should be the one to speak to them."

"How are we to approach them without being killed?" Rowan said practically. "We can't be certain that the humans we once dealt with are even among those living in the city now. Surely they will kill any elf who comes out of the forest to approach their city. But you they won't kill, because you are somewhat like them in appearance, and we must learn if the human Sharl or his kin rule the humans who have come again to the city." Rowan shook her head grimly. "If not, I don't know what hope we have to avoid conflict, even battle."

"The same hope as always," Val said crossly. "They can keep to their city and their open lands or face arrows and spears when they near the forest."

"And the metal coverings humans wear into battle will repel those arrows and spears. And when they tire of spears and arrows and bring their swords and crossbows into the forest, they will face less than a hundred ferocious Blue-eyes," Dusk said. "And when they have killed the Blue-eyes, they will kill the eighty or so Black Rocks, and then go on to the next clan, and the next, until there are no more spears or arrows to stop them. Once, just before the great war, when other clans were willing to listen to us and possibly even lend support, we might have faced and defeated a city filled with hundreds upon hundreds of humans with huge swords and metal over their skins to protect them from our spears and arrows. And then again, we might have fought and died and left our forest all but empty for the humans to plunder as they would. Now as a few handfuls of scattered small clans as ready to cast their spears at one another as at the humans, we have no chance at all. We must make peace with the humans if we can."

"And what do you hope to gain even if they'll speak with me?" Val asked bitterly. "Only a tiny handful of clans will even accept your envoys now. Even fewer will trade with Inner Heart. We have no alliance amongst ourselves to offer the humans."

"I know." Rowan sighed. "It will take many years to build ties between the clans again, if it can be done at all. I can only hope that the human Sharl, who dreams far beyond his own short lifetime, will agree to leave the forest in peace long enough to build that alliance, or perhaps offer his aid. The humans know the way of uniting many peoples into one; we know that from what we heard of their own city. Perhaps they can help us find the way."

"They'll likely help us find our way to destruction, and

gladly, so that they can freely hunt our game and cut away
our trees for their own use," Valann said, scowling. "And
then I would be the one who helped them do it. Hasn't it
been enough through my years that half my clan has
doubted me and sometimes even feared me, thinking me
more human than elf? I was almost denied my adulthood
because of those suspicions. Must I now be seen as the
traitor who consorts with the humans as well?"

Lahti patted his shoulder comfortingly but said nothing.

"You are no traitor while doing the bidding of your
clan's Eldest," Rowan said gently. "Listen to me. For sixteen years I have thought to wait until the human lord
Sharl came to us as he said he would. When Dusk's birds
showed humans returning to the city, I thought surely he
would come to the forest. But he has not come. Dusk's
vision spoke of your sister, and it spoke of an invasion of
the forest following far behind her. That vision will allow
us to wait no longer. We *must* know whether the humans in
the city mean us no harm or whether we can expect to be
crushed between two enemies like a nut between the teeth.
If your sister is in the city, we must speak to her and to the
human Sharl and learn whether they still desire our friendship. You are Chyrie's son and Ria's brother. You *must* be
the one. Sharl will greet you in friendship, or at least without hostility. If he and your sister have not arrived in the
city, we must know whether the humans there are loyal to
him or to his enemies, and if the latter, we must find a way
to stop Sharl and your sister before they reach the city. It's
for your sister's sake as much as ours that you must go."

"I saw you walking to meet her," Dusk agreed. "Therefore you must be the one."

"Then I have no choice?" Valann asked slowly.

"Always there is a choice," Rowan said, shrugging. "I
can't force you to obey my bidding, nor would I, any more
than Dusk's vision forces you. You must follow the voice of
your own spirit. But an adult of this clan who sits at my fire
must also remember that each decision he makes affects
not only him, but each member of our clan—and perhaps
other clans as well."

"And who is to accompany me on this pleasant journey, if I go as you bid?" Valann asked bitterly. A hard, sullen ache had settled around his heart. The Mother Forest might have accepted him, but apparently he was not yet finished proving himself to his clan.

"I can send others with you, if you wish, as far as the edge of the forest," Rowan said, ignoring his sarcasm. "But the more of you traveling together, the greater the chance you will be seen passing through other clans' territories. The Blue-eyes at least would certainly attack you and take you prisoner, if not kill you. Only you must approach the city itself because you are"—she hesitated, but continued unflinchingly—"apparently human, and any elves you take with you would have to wait in danger in a territory not our own until you returned. It would be wise to take as few others as possible."

"I'll go with him," Lahti said suddenly, and everyone jumped. She had sat so quietly in the shadows behind Valann that they had all but forgotten her presence.

Dusk raised one eyebrow thoughtfully, but Rowan shook her head.

"You are still awaiting your adulthood, little one," she said kindly. "I cannot send a child who may one day become a ripe woman into such danger."

"I may be a child, but I'm a healer," Lahti argued. "You have no other healer to send with him. I can track better than Valann and run almost as fast and twice as silently."

"Not you," Valann said quickly. "I'll go alone."

Lahti gave him one of her sidewise glances, her dark eyes half-closed slyly.

"I will go with you," she said silkily, "or I will follow after."

"And if I order you to stay?" Rowan said sternly.

Lahti said nothing, but her dark eyes never left Valann's. Rowan groaned.

"And I thought Valann had given me all the trouble a youngling could give," she said with a sigh.

"You can't think of allowing her to leave our lands!" Valann said hotly. The thought of Lahti injured, perhaps killed, by hostile clans or, worse, by humans, was intolerable.

"And what do you propose?" Dusk said, chuckling. "That Rowan tie her to a tree or cage her in a hut? She too must follow the voice of her spirit."

Valann glared at Lahti, who only smiled. He shook his head furiously. Now that Lahti had shamed him with her eagerness to run off into danger with him, he could scarcely refuse Rowan's request. Oh, he'd go—if for no other reason than to meet at last the sister he'd seen in his dreams—but now he'd have to creep away in the nighttime to get away without Lahti. He'd have to be careful, too, to cover his tracks; Lahti was every bit as good a tracker as she claimed. Bad enough to have to dodge all the hostile clans between Inner Heart and the edge of the forest; now he would have to cover his back trail, too. And all for the dubious privilege of walking alone up to the gates of the human city to demand entrance.

"I'll consider it," he said at last. With any luck, he could gather his supplies and creep away at night before Lahti even knew he'd decided to go.

"Tonight I will dream and ask the Mother Forest for a vision to guide you," Dusk said, ignoring Rowan's sharp glance of disapproval.

"And I will see that Valann eats supper and doesn't spend all evening brooding," Lahti said merrily. "By the time I pour three or four skins of moondrop wine down his throat, he'll be ready to agree to anything you want."

For probably the first time in his life, the very last thing Valann wanted was Lahti's company; he wanted solitude to think and plan, and he certainly didn't want Lahti to see any preparations he might be making to leave the village without her. But perhaps this was for the best after all; if he could convince Lahti that he would never agree to the journey, it might be all the easier to slip away without her.

"Now, this looks more like a proper home," Lahti said approvingly, glancing around the inside of Valann's hut. Valann had strewn the hard-packed earth floor with furs he'd taken and prepared, and likewise he had decorated the walls with other furs, hides, and antlers from successful hunts, together with the gifts he'd received after his passage. Valann had hung his new adult's sling bed—by elvan custom, wide enough to hold two comfortably—and decorated nooks in the walls with carvings, strings of beads and teeth, and arrangements of feathers and colorful stones. It was still a barren hut by elvan standards, but that was to be expected of a young man only just passed into adulthood.

In preparation for his passage, a few months before Valann had begun joining the clan's hunting parties instead of hunting smaller game alone or with a few others of the child-pack, or perhaps a deer with some adult mentor. Tonight he had two plump brush fowl that he had cleaned, stuffed with berries and tubers, wrapped with herbs, and coated with mud to cook slowly in the embers in his firepit. Lahti poked the lumps out of the embers and used one of the firepit stones to crack open the hard mud, filling the hut with the rich aroma of herb-flavored fowl.

"Just because Rowan has been as mother to you, you often forget to show her the respect due our Eldest," Lahti chided as she picked mud from the leaf-wrapped fowl. "She speaks with the wisdom of many centuries. And Dusk's visions have eased our trail for many years. Are you not even a little curious to meet your sister, to see these folk whose blood is partly yours?"

"They are none of my blood," Valann growled. "My father was a stinking northern barbarian who took my mother by force. My human blood is a shame that I can't seem to escape. I've spent my life trying to prove I'm elf enough for my own clan, and now I find that even Rowan thinks me more human than elf, human enough to fool a whole city of them, with my life most likely the price if I fail."

"All our lives might be the price," Lahti said soberly. "There are bare places in the forest still, burned to the roots so that almost nothing grows there. I've heard it said that the surviving elves of the forest were months finding and returning all of the dead to the Mother Forest. Whole clans were slaughtered down to the merest infant. But even that victory, if we can call it a victory, was with the aid of the human city and the strength of many elvan clans united together. If Dusk's vision truly showed a second such invasion, how will the forest fare with so few of us all scattered throughout it and wasting our arrows on each other, and the humans our enemies instead of our allies? And this time our children, our sick and helpless, our pregnant women, will die as well, for we'll have no stone city to shelter them."

Valann sighed. His bad luck that Lahti was wise as well as gifted beyond her years—if only her body was equally precocious!

"Perhaps Dusk will have a new vision that will set a different course," Valann said hopefully. It was, in fact, his greatest hope—that perhaps Dusk's vision would show at least that now was not the time, that his sister's arrival and any possible disasters to follow were far distant in the future. Or perhaps a vision might show that Rowan and Dusk were to accompany him to the human city—or better yet, two or three dozen elves armed with the stoutest spears and sharpest arrows.

"Rowan hates it when Dusk takes potions to bring his visions," Lahti said soberly. "She fears his spirit will go out to the Mother Forest and never wholly return again, like—" She stopped abruptly.

"Like my mother," Valann said grimly. "I know the stories. But I think—" He remembered Chyrie's eyes, the warmth of her rough fingertips against his face. "I think the stories are only guesses. I think no one quite knows the entirety of what has become of my mother's spirit—or what my mother's spirit has become. And after my passage journey, I think—"

"Oh, Valann, you mustn't speak of—" Lahti began disapprovingly.

Valann smiled and touched Lahti's lips to silence her.

"I think that Dusk's spirit is in no danger, unless it's the danger of his own desire," he finished. "Just as a beast-speaker faces the danger of becoming too much a part of the beast he touches, Dusk's spirit dares a seductive flight when he seeks his visions. But he's made that journey and returned many times. Dusk's love for Rowan and for his people roots him well in our world. We all return to the Mother Forest in the end, in any event, and while that journey may be a joyous one, with great wonders at the end"—Valann smiled—"the great oak, rooted deep in the earth, doesn't fall before its time, and Dusk knows that even better than we."

"Nor does the tree bear fruit before its time," Lahti sighed. She tore off a leg of the brush fowl and nibbled at the rich meat. "When we have eaten, shall I ask Doeanna if she will come to you?"

Valann chuckled.

"Doeanna devoted four of her nights to my instruction," he said. "I think that was as much of her solitude as she was willing to sacrifice to any one man."

Lahti nodded.

"It's always wise for a young man new to adulthood to avoid fastening his affections unhealthily on a single female," she agreed soberly, although her eyes twinkled slyly. "Perhaps I should ask Badea or Kynda instead. And Ilea's been waiting for you to ask her. Her pride will suffer a terrible blow if *she* has to ask *you.*"

"Ah, pardon me, 'elder sister,'" Valann said with mock sternness. "I'm no longer new from my passage and am quite capable of choosing my own partners, thank you. And tonight I choose to choose no one, but to eat my baked brush fowl in peace and sleep—quite alone, thank you. Perhaps the Mother Forest will send *me* a vision tonight." He smiled at Lahti. "Unless you'd like to stay with me. You always slept with me in the child-pack, and now I miss your presence."

Lahti smiled back, but there was a little sadness in her eyes, too.

"I miss your warmth in the night, and the feel of your heart beating, and even the annoying sound your breath makes through your nose while you sleep," she acknowledged. "But it would be cruel to lie here, you a man and me a child. Better we both find someone else to warm us in the night." She smiled again, mischievously. "And if you've learned a great deal from Doeanna, perhaps on the night after my passage journey, you'll be the one to come to me in the night and teach me the dance that men and women dance together in the furs. But tonight I've promised Tava that I'll play my pipes at her High Circle." She ducked her head almost apologetically as she spoke.

Valann understood the gesture, as he understood why Lahti did not ask whether Valann would be dancing the dance with Tava. He had not been asked to join Tava's High Circle, as he had not been asked to join Senie's four days ago, or Ranata and Dawn's last week. At one of the clan firepits, Dawn, the green ribbon of fertility proudly tied around her upper arm, had started to approach Valann, but Ranata beside her had shook her head warningly. Dawn had turned away, giving Valann one last look with the same apology in her eyes that he now saw in Lahti's. Dawn had come to his hut two nights later, bringing moondrop wine and caresses even more intoxicating than the potent liquor, but her touch couldn't heal the wound in his heart, and her cries of pleasure could not eradicate from Valann's memory the silence in the clearing as others near the fire had looked away, too.

Lahti was right; he should go to the clan firepits and find a lover to warm his furs tonight. There were many women who would gladly and without reservation share pleasure with him; Doeanna had even told him that first night that some were jealous that she'd been the one chosen. Dawn had confessed that she'd been curious to know how his hairy skin would feel against hers. There were probably some women of the clan, too, Valann had to admit, who would joyfully take him to their furs even when they ripened, as ready to accept a child of his seed as of any other man of the clan. There were others, too, even more puzzling, who sought him out because he was the son of Chyrie, himself touched by the Mother Forest and destined for great things. It was unreasonable to expect to be chosen for every High Circle danced in the clan; few men were. But the exclusion still stung, and Valann knew that many women in the village would even rather remain childless than to bear children tainted with Valann's part-human blood.

Valann drifted restlessly around the inside of his hut, touching the decorations, comforted by their familiarity. Each fur hanging on the wall or strewn on the floor, each carving, each cluster of feathers carried a story, some humorous, some sad, some embarrassing. Even the gifts he'd been given after his passage held special meaning, small reminders of the love of his kinfolk. Being surrounded by these talismans of his childhood, each imbued, so Dusk told him, with a small portion of Valann's spirit, gave Val a sense of himself, a sense of being *here* and *now,* a sense of belonging in this place and time. Yes, like any adult of the clan, he was growing roots, roots that bound him to this world, this place, that drew nourishment from deep in the forest and fed him life. Just as he fed, in his own way, every life that touched his own, as leaves from the tree fell to rot on the soil and fed other trees, as its limbs gave shelter to squirrels and birds, as its branches brushed and twined with those around it. And if perhaps he was not as fully a part of this place as some of the others around him, still he was enough a part of the forest to put down his roots here and grow with these people—*his* people. And the years to come would only bind him to them, and them to him, ever more firmly.

And did that not make him their tool in a sense, as they were all tools of the Mother Forest in a sense also, just as his hand or his eyes were a part of him and therefore his tools? And was not that very kinship his obligation, and the reverse, too? And had not Chyrie, even the very act of his birth, placed upon him certain obligations, too? But if he was obligated, was it not to the Mother Forest, rather than to the interpretations of what Rowan thought best for them all? And if he disagreed with Rowan, how was he to know, then, what to do? *You must follow the voice of your own spirit,* Rowan had said.

Dusk's vision—that Valann would meet his sister. That much Valann could agree with wholeheartedly. Once he'd had the chance to see how a lifetime among humans had molded his sister, he could better assess in his own mind what association with these humans might do to his people —and perhaps, a small voice within him said, learn something of the human blood that ran in his own veins.

And more, too: He'd never admit it, even to Lahti, but a great curiosity burned in him to see this human city and the wonders there. Imagine a whole city of dwellings built from stone! Imagine stones piled upon stones far higher than his head to form a great wall surrounding the city! He'd heard the stories told by the women who'd sheltered in the city during the battle, and he could scarcely believe what they'd told him—cakes of bread as light and soft as feathers; pools of hot water that bubbled without boiling, drawn up by magic from deep within the earth; clothing made not from leather, but spun from threads like a spider's silk; and best of all, metal so common that everyone could have a new knife whenever they liked, arrows were metal-tipped, and even cooking pots were made of it!

All right, then. Best done before he began to doubt again. Valann quickly packed the few belongings he would need for the trail—his best bow, his sword and dagger, flints, fishhooks and leather cord, light sleeping skins, and a few supplies. He had just tied a waxed skin around the pack when he heard a scratching on his door flap. Hurriedly he pushed the pack into the shadows in case the visitor was Lahti; to Valann's surprise, however, it was Fox, Dusk's cousin and sometimes assistant, who leaned his head in but did not enter.

"Rowan sent me for you," he said quickly. "She asks if you would come to her hut."

Surprised, Valann hurried after Fox, who, to Valann's amazement, did not enter that hut either, only indicating to Valann to go in.

Rowan's hut was almost dark, lit only by a single scented fat lamp. Dusk was sitting before the lamp, staring raptly into its flame, with Rowan anxiously beside him. Rowan glanced up at Valann and hurriedly beckoned him over.

"Come and listen," she said. "He speaks of your sister."

Dusk turned toward Valann, but Val could see that the Gifted One's eyes looked upon some point beyond him.

"She is near," he said. "She stands on a narrow line between one world and another. You will meet her on that line. She is the light burning against the darkness of the great storm to come, but you are the spark that will light the lamp. She is our hope for today, and you will be the one to give her the hope for tomorrow. Strong walls are but half the answer; strong roots must be their anchor."

"Tell us where she walks," Rowan said quietly but insistently. "Tell us where Val must meet her and how he will reach her safely."

"They came from the north, but they have passed the eastern edge already," Dusk said. Then his brow furrowed and he shook his head, as if losing the vision.

"Has she passed the south?" Rowan asked gently. "Where does she walk, Dusk?"

"She walks—she walks—" To Val's alarm, Dusk began to shake. Great droplets of sweat broke out on his skin and rolled down his face. "She—sh-sh-sh—" Dusk's voice trailed off in a stuttering gurgle, and he tumbled stiffly backward to the furs.

Immediately Rowan seized the Gifted One's hands, swiftly binding them with a strip of leather. Val was already carefully prying apart Dusk's clenched jaws to force a piece of wood between his teeth. Dusk had bitten his tongue and the inside of his mouth severely on occasion when he'd been similarly afflicted, and Rowan and Val had long since learned how to deal with his strange ailment. It took both of them to capture and bind Dusk's jerking legs, but when that was done, there was nothing to do but leave the Gifted One on soft furs, far from the lamp, until he was well again.

Ordinarily Rowan would have given Dusk a sleeping powder that the Gifted One kept prepared for such occasions, but now Rowan hesitated. Val knew why; dreaming potions had such a profound effect on Dusk that to give him another mixture of any kind would be dangerous. Rowan and Val exchanged worried glances, Val praying silently but fervently that the Mother Forest would once more return his father-by-love's spirit.

At last Dusk's jerking motions stopped and he slumped quietly to the furs. Rowan moistened a soft skin to wipe the sweat and drool from his face, removing the wood from his mouth; more slowly, Val unwound the bindings from Dusk's wrists and ankles, leaving the strips ready to hand. It wasn't unknown for the Gifted One to suffer a second attack of his shaking illness immediately after the first.

It was some moments before Dusk wearily opened his eyes, but Val thanked the Mother Forest to see that the Gifted One's eyes were clear and knowing again. Dusk turned his head to face Val.

"I saw your sister," he murmured, still panting for breath.

"I heard you," Val said quickly. "Rest yourself."

Dusk shook his head.

"I remember," he said. "She was in danger. Great danger."

"Did you see where she was?" Rowan probed gently.

Dusk frowned, then sighed and shook his head again in frustration.

"I don't know," he said tiredly. "My thoughts turned south, and I saw violence and danger, but I did not see her. I think you should wait, Valann. She will come to you, I think."

"From the south? Past the Blue-eyes who would kill any who set toe-tip on their lands, elf or human alike?" Val retorted. "She would need to walk unseen, indeed! No. I won't wait." He turned to Dusk. "Lahti must not come after me. Not into Blue-eyes' lands. When you've rested and recovered, will you tell her I've gone east?"

Dusk smiled, his tired eyes twinkling a little.

"I'll speak to her now," he said. "Hurry and go. A deer will be waiting at the southern edge of the village."

"You mustn't exert yourself further," Rowan protested, but Dusk waved a hand weakly, dismissing her concern.

"We've asked Valann to take a terrible risk," he said,

struggling up to a sitting position. "I'd be ashamed to deny him that small assistance. Go, Valann."

Valann hurried, skirting the edge of the village to return to his hut so that Lahti would not see him. He quickly poured water over his hut fire, making sure that the last embers were dead before he shouldered his pack. No time for further preparations; what he'd packed already would have to suffice. Then there was the short, careful journey back around the edge of the village again to make his way south where, true to Dusk's word, a large stag grazed peacefully, unalarmed by Val's approach. The stag was a bit more skittish as Val carefully strapped his pack to its back—Val did, after all, smell of fire and cooked meat— but it allowed Val to mount and headed rapidly south with no urging from its rider. Val settled himself as best he could far back on the stag's back to avoid the hard ridge of its spine and resigned himself to a long and uncomfortable night. He'd have to get as far as he could on the stag; when he stopped to camp it would undoubtedly wander off, and he had no way to summon another.

As long as he was riding, he moved swiftly enough to risk using one of the common roads that led from different sections of the Heartwood toward the Forest Altars. He could easily be seen by patrols as he passed through their territories on the common road, but it was doubtful that they would offer him harm as long as he stayed on the road. Many clans, while not openly allied with Inner Heart, knew that Val was Rowan's son-by-love and would likely permit him to pass through their lands with no hostility despite his human appearance. Even hostile clans would probably not bother with a lone elf—even an odd-looking one—on the common road, passing swiftly through their territories and offering no obvious threat. It was when he left the road that he'd be in danger.

Valann rode until the sky was beginning to lighten and he was so weary he thought he'd fall off the stag's back. Valann let the tired stag go its own way; he himself had barely enough energy to find a suitably hidden spot for his sleeping furs and make certain that his shelter was not visible from the outside. He crawled wearily between his furs and was quickly asleep. Like any hunter in a dangerous territory, he slept well but lightly, his ears straining for any sound of danger, half-rousing periodically to sniff the air for any strange scents.

When Val finally roused, it was well past midday and quite warm, and he was dripping with sweat between his sleeping furs. Val took a cold meal from his preserved supplies and stayed where he was in the thicket. If he was, as he suspected, in Golden Flower territory, he would be wisest to wait for the cover of darkness before he continued on. The Golden Flowers were no friends to Inner Heart, but fortunately they were one of the few elvan clans who lacked good night sight. Once he passed through Golden Flower lands, however, and reached Swiftfoot territory, he would be wiser to travel by day; the Swiftfoots were so nocturnal that few would be about during the daylight hours.

Val had finished his meal of dried meat and was rolling up his sleeping skins when an oh-so-faint rustling in the bushes made him freeze where he was, all senses alert. There was a faint scent, familiar and yet strange—there! Val's nose wrinkled at the unmistakable scent. What in the Mother Forest would a ripe female be doing wandering the woods alone? Surely no Golden Flower would be fool enough to—

"Valann?" The voice was familiar, and now Val realized why the scent had confused him so.

"Lahti!" Val groaned with dismay as two small hands parted the bushes and a familiar face peered through the leaves.

"There you are," Lahti said relievedly, scrambling through the brush to sit down beside him. "I almost lost your trail after you left the common road." She paused. "Well, you need not overwhelm me with your welcome, nor with congratulations on my skill at following your trail," she said sarcastically. "But you might at least offer me a sip of your wine, as I rode all night and a good part of the day catching up with you."

"How could you—" Val shook his head confusedly. Now that she was near, the scent of her ripeness was almost overwhelming. Then his eyes widened and he seized her shoulders, staring at the green band circling her arm. "Lahti! You ripened! But when—"

"Oh, no, no," Lahti said hurriedly, her cheeks flushing. "Dusk gave me the ribbon and made a scent for me so that I would be safe from harm while traveling through hostile territories."

Val groaned again. Betrayed by his own foster father. There would be no ridding himself of Lahti now. Still, it was a clever move on Dusk's part. No elf, no matter how angered, would ever harm a ripened female—nor her mate, most likely, especially under the excuse that Val and Lahti were traveling to the Forest Altars or returning to their own clan for the purpose of conceiving a child. No clan would ever dare interfere with conception; that was the one precept held universally throughout the forest, especially now that so many clans had only begun to repopulate their territories after the invasion. Travel to the Forest Altars, however, would not explain their presence this far south when Lahti was clearly a Moon Lake; Val would have to think of some other explanation if they were captured. It hardly mattered, though. No clan would believe that a man would have brought his ripe mate into hostile territory for any malicious purpose.

"All right," Val said reluctantly. "It was a canny thought on Dusk's part. And I'd be a fool to think you would return to Inner Heart now, nor would I send you alone. But I beg that you'll refrain from any needless risk. To take a child, and one who might one day become a ripe female in truth, into such danger is an offense against the Mother Forest Herself. Now, come; let's be away from here before some Golden Flower patrol hears our speech and finds us."

Lahti nodded, giving Valann a merry smile as she shouldered her own pack. She let Valann set the direction and the pace, and she stayed quiet except when Valann spoke. She stayed close, too, and Val found this a special kind of torment; the scent Dusk had made for Lahti perfectly simulated the musky aroma of a ripened female, only far stronger, and no male elf in the Heartwood could have failed to respond to it. Valann was hard-pressed to keep his attention on moving quietly through the forest.

Valann was glad for his day's inactivity, but he knew Lahti had had far less time for rest, and the effort of constant vigilance and stealth was exhausting. Valann stopped halfway through the night to rest briefly, and Lahti crouched panting beside him in the small thicket where Valann had taken shelter.

"Have we crossed into Swiftfoot territory yet?" Lahti murmured.

Valann shook his head.

"We could easily have missed the markers," he said. "But I think not. I think Golden Flower lands must be larger than what we've crossed. Can you continue?"

"Oh, yes," Lahti said, a little too hastily.

"We'll have to camp in a few hours, in any wise," Valann said. "We must rest before we start across Swiftfoot lands, and that must be during daylight when Swiftfoots sleep."

"Of course," Lahti agreed, but Val fancied he could hear a little dismay in her voice.

However tired Lahti might be, however, as the night continued Val had to acknowledge that Lahti's night sight was keener than his, her hearing slightly more acute, and it was not long before she was leading him rather than the reverse. Several times Lahti quickly pulled him into shelter behind bushes or trees, and it was often moments before Val heard the footsteps that had warned her of the approach of a patrol. Once they were forced to hide in the trees for nearly an hour as a wide patrol stopped to rest almost directly beneath them. The appearance of the patrol told Valann that they were still in Golden Flower territory, but as this was a wide patrol, equipped for days outside their village, they must be very near the border of Swiftfoot lands.

They proceeded a little farther, far enough to be certain that they were outside the circuit of the Golden Flower wide patrol, before setting up a camp. Val was delighted to learn that Lahti, who had left Inner Heart less precipitously than he, had brought more supplies; they couldn't risk hunting in hostile territories, let alone building the fire to cook their catch. They were too tired to savor the travel cakes of dried berries, dried meat, and acorn meal pounded together and bound with rich melted fat or the trail sweets of nuts and sap-sugar; they gulped down their hasty meal and crawled wearily into the sleeping furs to snatch a few precious hours of rest before sunrise when they'd continue on.

As exhausted as he was, however, Valann found that sleep eluded him. Lahti's warmth curled against him was comforting, sweetly familiar, and yet an exquisite torment. Her scent and the warm softness of her skin where it touched his were the keenest tortures. The nights that Valann had spent in the arms of Doeanna and other women of his clan might as well have never been; his body was as hungry as a youth straight from passage. Moving with infinite caution, Val stroked a lock of Lahti's straight black hair that had fallen over his tunic, then brought the soft strands to his lips. By the Mother Forest, her scent was more intoxicating than the finest moondrop wine, and what he'd give to quench that thirst!

Lahti murmured in her sleep and rolled over, pillowing her head on Val's shoulder, her warm body stretched against the length of his and her arm thrown over his chest. Val almost groaned in agony even as his arms reflexively folded around her. Oh, by the Mother Forest, this was asking more of him than he could bear!

Then Valann froze. Was there a new roundness in Lahti's slender hips beneath his forearm? And was—by the Mother Forest, yes, he could feel the slight swell of budding new breasts pressing against his side. At last Lahti was moving toward adulthood, however slowly. Surely it could not be more than a few weeks before she would be ready to undergo her own passage! Ah, and then there would be an end to waiting. Perhaps Lahti would agree to become his mate. Val had discussed it with her before, and Lahti had only laughed, protesting that they were both still children, and that even discounting that, they were far too young to think of such a thing. But once she passed into adulthood, she might be persuaded to change her mind, especially if she ripened and conceived. Val would have to speak to Dusk so that Lahti could be examined. If the Gifted One thought Lahti showed any signs of imminent ripening, why, they'd have to begin preparing for her passage immediately so as not to waste her time of fertility!

But the prospect of Lahti's adulthood perhaps weeks from now made it no easier to bear the torture of her warm flesh pressing against his here and now while she was still forbidden to him. Valann sighed again, grinding his teeth in frustration even as he buried his face in the softness of Lahti's hair.

Lahti rolled over and leaned on Val's chest, opening her eyes. She sighed, too, and smiled, reaching to run her fingertips through the thin growth of coarse, curling hair that covered Val's chin.

"You were right," she said. "Perhaps I shouldn't have come. I was thinking of you, but—but perhaps I was thinking too much of myself, too, of my loneliness while you were gone and my fear for your safety."

"I can't fault you for that," Val said, chuckling. "I think of you too much on occasion as well."

"Yes, you do." Lahti shook her head, not smiling now. "You have less than two decades, Valann. You're too young to have such strong feelings for me."

"And I was too young to pass into adulthood," Val reminded her. He breathed in the rich scent of her hair and groaned. "You smell so good. I wish Dusk had found another way to keep you safe."

"I wish I could be a woman for you in truth as well as seeming," Lahti said regretfully. She sat up. "It's almost dawn."

"I know." Val sat up, too, relieved and at the same time sorry to lose the contact between his body and Lahti's. "We should leave now. The Swiftfoots will be making their camps and returning to their village. With luck we can make it entirely through Swiftfoot territory and reach the edge of the forest today."

Lahti nodded and helped Val bundle up their sleeping skins. They could travel faster by day; even with their keen night vision, it was easier to see in the sunlight, and they were secure, too, in the knowledge that the Swiftfoots with their oversensitive eyes would not be about by day. The Swiftfoot territory was small—because of their relative helplessness by day, the neighboring Blue-eyes had captured most of the Swiftfoots' lands—and Val and Lahti were crossing the narrowest section of that territory. With a quick and steady pace, they saw the forest thinning ahead of them by early afternoon, and shortly thereafter, Val and Lahti were looking for the first time in their lives on truly clear and open land.

In the forest, elves thought of distance in terms of days' or hours' travel—a relative measurement at best, as travel varied with the weather, the amount of undergrowth, the directness of the route, the need for stealth and concealment, and whether the travelers were on foot or mounted on deer. Looking out across flat land where one could see what seemed an impossible distance to the dark, snaking line of what must be the Brightwater River, the world seemed unfathomably huge. The direct sunlight, unfiltered through the thick canopy of leaves, was unbearably bright, and Val and Lahti blinked tears from their eyes several times before they became accustomed to the light. To their dismay, however, despite the greater distance over which they could see, there were no signs of any humans or of Valann's sister.

"Perhaps they've not yet come this far," Lahti suggested hopefully.

"Dusk said they had already passed the eastern edge," Val said, troubled. "From here we can see across the whole southern edge of the forest, or nearly so. We would surely see them if they'd come around from the east."

"There's their road," Lahti said, pointing to a strip of earth worn bare of grass as a forest trail was worn bare of undergrowth, only far wider. "Dare we venture out to read the traces there? We could so easily be seen."

"But we could see farther as well," Val speculated. He shrugged at last, although the very thought made him tremble. "We'll try it. From this distance, if the Blue-eyes see us, they'll think us Swiftfoots."

"In the full daylight, and out there where nothing will obstruct their view?" Lahti said doubtfully. "And even so, might they not shoot at us anyway?"

Val shook his head.

"We're too far from the border of their lands for their arrows and spears," he said. "A short foray to study the trail, no more than a few moments, should be safe enough. And if they are close enough to see us, the Blue-eyes will be close enough to see the band on your arm."

There was no disputing that, and Lahti made no further argument. After scanning the outer limits of the forest once more as best they could, Val and Lahti stepped at last into the open, trying to look in every direction at once as they made their way to the road. Val fought against sudden panic, the inexplicable certainty that the obscenely great sky was going to fall down on them where they stood, forcing his feet forward one at a time, smelling Lahti's fear-rank sweat. It seemed an impossibly great distance, but once in the open there was nothing to be gained by turning back, so they continued onward, keeping as low to the ground as they could. They stopped at the edge of the hard-packed soil, eyeing the ruts and tracks curiously.

"So many scents," Lahti marveled, shivering nervously even as she sniffed at the crescent-shaped horse tracks. "I smell beasts and humans and wood and many other things. They passed this way not long ago. The tracks lead toward the city."

"But can we be certain this is the correct group of humans, my sister with them?" Val asked worriedly. "Perhaps it was other humans traveling to the city."

"If Dusk's vision is to be believed, and your sister has already passed the eastern edge of the forest, then these must be the traces of her travel," Lahti said. "She must have already passed around the southern edge, too. She may have reached the city already."

There was nothing to do but return to the relative safety and concealment of the edge of the forest. There they crouched in the bushes as their hearts gradually slowed and fear subsided, chewing on dried meat and disappointment.

"We should return to Inner Heart," Val said slowly. "Rowan and Dusk may have news for us, or new instruction."

"We've come so far," Lahti protested. "We've passed through hostile territories once. If we return to Inner Heart and then must come back again later, we're doubly at risk. If these clans see the traces of our passage through their land, they'll double their patrols and watch their boundaries closely."

"*We* would not be at risk," Val corrected pointedly. "To travel to the western edge of the forest I must pass through either Blue-eyes' lands or Hawk's Eye's. We know the Blue-eyes are hostile and the Hawk's Eyes likely so. I think Rowan and Dusk will reconsider allowing you to accompany me. And I'd ask you to reconsider, too," Val added softly, touching Lahti's shoulder. "Dusk's scent may keep you safe from harm, but that scent and your presence are a torment and a distraction I can't afford."

"Valann—" Lahti laid her hand over his, her dark eyes for once serious. "I think we should continue on to the western edge of the forest now. Dusk spoke of danger. I think we can't spare the days it would take to return to Inner Heart and then to come back, if the danger Dusk spoke of is to your sister."

Val groaned and rubbed his eyes, still dazzled by all that daylight. By the Mother Forest, what was he to do? Alone he would have risked continuing on to the western edge of the forest immediately. But there was Lahti to consider, and they were both so tired. There were not enough supplies for the two of them, either, even with what Lahti had brought, for the longer journey, not if they were to have food to eat on their return journey to Inner Heart. Hunting in hostile territories would be doubly dangerous. Alone, Val might have enough food, but there was no question of sending Lahti all the way back to Inner Heart on foot alone. Yet Lahti was right; if Dusk's vision was to be believed—and why were they here if not?—there was indeed no time to return to Inner Heart. Oh, for a beast-speaker to send a message to Dusk for confirmation!

"Very well," Val said reluctantly. "We'll continue on. But if I decide that you must stay out of Blue-eyes' and Hawk's Eye's territories, you must do it, and wait for me to return. Will you promise me that?"

Now it Lahti's turn to consider. At last she nodded.

"I dislike it, but if my safety makes you stronger, I'll agree," she said. "If you say I must, I'll remain in Jumping Mouse territory, east of Hawk's Eye's. Most of the Jumping Mouse lands are all but abandoned; I should have no difficulty there."

Val nodded grimly.

"Very well, then."

"I suppose that means we must start back across Swiftfoot lands immediately, while there's still some daylight left," Lahti said, sighing miserably.

"I fear so," Val said, sighing, too. The afternoon was well advanced already; they'd never be able to make it back to Golden Flower territory before dark. Then they'd still have Golden Flower territory to cross anglewise, heading west, during the night. Still, the alternative—to cross that strip of bare land and follow the Brightwater River, out of range of Blue-eyes' arrows, and hope to make their way back to the forest past the city to Hawk's Eye's lands—was unthinkable. They could possibly avoid the human sentries and patrols, even creep back into the forest safely, if they were careful, but the mere thought of all that naked land, with no cover or shelter to bolt to in case of danger—no, Val's whole spirit utterly rebelled. Once he'd thought of the bare lands as merely an overlarge clearing. He'd never realized —never imagined!

And I blithely agreed to cross all that open space alone and walk boldly up to that city of humans, he marveled to himself.

They moved as quickly as they could while still maintaining some caution and vigilance. Near sunset, however, Lahti pulled Valann to a halt.

"We must stop," she panted. "We're too tired. We're making sounds and leaving a trail."

Val shook his head, but not in disagreement. Lahti was right. They were still far from the Golden Flower border, and it was almost completely dark. Swift foot patrols would be out now, and Val and Lahti were too weary to outrun them; moreover, their tired, noisy stumbling was sure to bring pursuit. There was nothing to do but make a camp, hopefully one secure enough that they could stay for the remainder of the night and possibly through the day, too, and then start afresh.

"There," Lahti breathed, pointing. Val had to look twice before he saw what Lahti meant—a small cavelike space formed by the roots of a large tree, so cleverly concealed by undergrowth that it was barely visible.

Lahti sniffed around the entrance, then carefully parted the brush; the space had probably been used as some animal's den at one time, but it was so long empty that there was not even a scent left. Lahti and Val crawled inside and spread their sleeping furs over the bottom of the den, making sure the foliage was pulled back to conceal the opening.

"We should be safe enough here," Val said. "We'll take a rest and then start anew after daybreak."

"So long," Lahti said unhappily. "So much time wasted."

"A good deal more time will be wasted if we're killed by the Golden Flowers, or captured and must be ransomed," Val reminded her. "At any rate, best we're well rested in case we must continue far on foot before stopping again. Go ahead, eat and sleep, and I'll go outside and make certain we've left no trail and our shelter is well hidden."

Lahti was too tired to argue, and by the time Valann returned from concealing their tracks for some distance around their shelter, she was fast asleep, a half-eaten travel cake still clasped in her hand. Val gently put the travel cake away and curled up beside her, too tired to eat. This time, despite Lahti's warm presence and her scent, Val had no difficulty sleeping.

Val roused briefly twice: once jolting awake from a dream of his sister, and once when a Swiftfoot patrol passed a short distance away. The second time he awoke, it was full dark, but the moon had risen, as Val saw when he carefully peered out through the concealing foliage.

The Swiftfoot patrol paused not far from his shelter, and Val's anxiety was almost obliterated by pity. The Swiftfoots were thin and worn and harried-looking, jumping at the slightest noise. Likely the constant conflict with the Blue-eyes had chased most of the good game from their lands, forcing the Swiftfoots to relocate their village frequently within their territory. It had never before occurred to Valann that perhaps other clans were not prospering as comfortably as Inner Heart.

When he pulled his head back inside, Lahti was awake and watching him. She was as grimy as he, her hair matted with sweat and her clothes dirt-stained, but Val found himself marveling once again at how lovely she looked to him.

"Time to go?" she asked.

"If you're ready," he said gently. "A patrol only just passed by. I don't think there'll be another anytime soon. If we wait a short time, it should be safe to continue on to the borders. If it's as late as I believe, it should be near dawn when we reach the border of Golden Flower territory and leave Swiftfoot lands."

"And then what?" Lahti asked worriedly. "The Golden Flowers will be about by day."

"And the Swiftfoots still by night," Val agreed. "But we have no choice unless we lose another half a day or more. At least we're well rested. Have you eaten your fill?"

"We have plenty of travel cakes," Lahti assured him. "We can eat as we go. Come. I'll take the lead until the sun rises."

As Val had suspected, they passed through the remaining Swiftfoot territory without difficulty, as the wide patrol had just passed them by. Golden Flower territory was both easier and more difficult; they could see more clearly and move faster by daylight, but just as they could see more easily, so they could also be seen. Most of their extra speed was negated by the additional need to keep under cover of sheltering bushes, scurrying up trees or into hiding at the least noise, and zigzagging widely from their course to avoid patrol trails. By the time night fell, both were shaking with exhaustion. They camped only long enough to snatch a few hours of sleep, bolt their cold travel food, and stumble on. Without mounts, they'd be days working their way around to the western edge of the forest.

Then there would be no obstacles except the murderous Blue-eyes—and a city full of humans.

V

RIA

"This has got to be the most foolish thing you've ever talked me into," Cyril panted, swatting leaves out of his face. "More shame to me for letting you do it."

"Shhh," Ria scolded. "The wall guards will hear you."

"I hope they do," Cyril grumbled, lowering his voice nonetheless. "Then we'll both be comfortably locked in our rooms until the wedding, instead of out here risking our lives."

Ria ignored that last comment, especially the reference to the wedding, and pulled Cyril along the wall, waiting for the guard to pass. As soon as the footsteps faded into the distance, she turned back to Cyril.

"Hurry," she whispered. "We have to climb over."

"Over that?" Cyril asked incredulously, gazing up at the wall to the keep's grounds.

"That's nothing," Ria said impatiently, tucking the end of the rope she held into her belt. "We've climbed worse. Now come *on*." She scrambled nimbly up the stones.

"Not since we were children," Cyril growled, but he was

climbing behind her with rather more difficulty despite his greater height; his larger hands and feet did not fit as neatly into the cracks in the stone as Ria's, and his clumsy riding boots were less suited for climbing than Ria's soft leather footgear.

Ria reached the top of the wall, panting. She glanced around to make sure none of the guards had seen her, then braced her feet against the crenellations of the wall, giving Cyril a hand over the edge. They took the rope ends from their belts and pulled up the packs tied to the other ends of the ropes, then dropped them over the far side of the wall and half-scrambled, half-fell down after them. As Ria had planned, it was only a short run from their crossing point to the nearest tumbledown building, and they squatted, panting, as far inside the wrecked building as they dared.

A rat squeaked and scampered along one wall, and Ria shivered, but her disgust was almost drowned in excitement. This was a true adventure—nothing at all like raiding the pantry for sweets in the middle of the night, or pulling a good trick on Lady Sivia. Ria's heart pounded joyfully. She'd never felt this frightened—or this free—before. It was worth the risk of being caught and punished. It was worth *any* risk.

"Did they see us?" Cyril gasped.

"I don't think so. No." Ria watched the next guards cross the top of the wall right on schedule, peering vigilantly into the castle grounds and outside. "We'll wait here and rest until the next guard goes by, then start working our way east."

They waited, Cyril thankfully silent, until the next guard had passed. They scrambled from one ruined building to the next until they could see the outer wall, then stopped to rest again inside what looked to have been a bakery.

"At least we've made it this far," Ria said, sighing with relief. "You'd better cast your spell here."

"It isn't good for very long," Cyril said dubiously. "Especially when I'm trying to hold it while I'm walking around. I've only just mastered it."

"We don't need it for very long," Ria told him. "It's only

a few dozen steps to the wall. The spell's only got to hide us just long enough to get out of sight of the wall guards. It's dark enough that that won't be very far."

"You'll have to stay right with me, too," Cyril warned her. "I can't make it extend very far. I've never tried to cover anybody but myself before."

"I'll stay right beside you," Ria agreed impatiently. "Now will you do it, please?"

"All right, all right, don't rush me," Cyril said nervously. "I've only done this a few times. If you rush me, I'm sure to botch it up, and then it's right back to our rooms."

As Cyril began his spell, laying out herbs and powders and colored candles and reading a chant out of a book, Ria began to have her doubts. Lady Rivkah never needed such paraphernalia; most often she never even spoke a spell aloud, needing nothing but a gesture or a word or a brief pass with a rod to make the spell effective. She'd told Ria that an expert enough mage usually progressed beyond such trappings. Cyril must indeed be as rank a novice as he'd said. And what if he failed? Would they even know if the spell didn't work? Short of the guards raising a shout, that is!

Cyril continued his chant, weaving a complex pattern of gestures and tracing a design in the dust on the ground. Jenji chittered and poked his head out the neck of Ria's tunic, dancing from paw to paw, his little nose quivering excitedly against Ria's neck. Mage's familiar—was Jenji a magic-spotter, and did his excitement mean that Cyril's spell was taking effect? Ria fervently hoped so.

Well, nothing for it. As soon as Cyril finished his chant and stowed his book back in his pack, he turned and nodded to Ria, who nodded back. She felt no different, and she could certainly see Cyril, as well as herself if she looked; she'd just have to trust Cyril's paltry skill. From what he'd told her, his simple spell couldn't cover sound or scent, but hopefully they wouldn't be getting close enough to the guards to betray themselves in those ways. Cyril would have to concentrate on holding the spell, too, so Ria shouldered his pack as well as her own and led the way back out of the building, holding his hand. She'd just have to find a place in the wall gap where he wouldn't stumble and knock himself on the head while climbing through the debris, or the spell would surely drop.

Luck was with them. As rebuilding the defensive outer wall had been made a priority by High Lord Sharl, many of the fallen blocks had been cleared away, the broken stone reshaped and used in rebuilding the crumbling sections, or cut down to be used for other buildings in the city. Even the smaller debris had been cleared; Ria imagined it was probably being used to help fill in the great crack in the street before her foster mother and Yvarden tried to seal the top. There was a relatively negotiable path past what debris remained in the gap, and Ria took Cyril's arm, guiding him carefully through. They paused in the gap, waiting to be sure there were no guards close enough to hear them, before they continued onward.

Then there was the moat to cross, but it had fallen into neglect over the years and the water had mostly drained away, leaving nothing but a thin layer of scummy liquid over the foul-smelling mud at the bottom; the greatest difficulty in crossing was making certain that Cyril didn't slip in the sucking mud, or letting the wall guards see mysterious tracks appearing in the bare mud where it wasn't covered by water. Then they were on open ground, with nothing between them and the forest but grass and the occasional wildflower.

About halfway across the open space, Cyril sagged and sighed with weariness. Ria helped him down to the ground, sitting down beside him. Jenji, silent in Ria's tunic during their flight, clambered up to Ria's shoulder and sat there quietly, rubbing against her ear.

"That's it," Cyril said tiredly. "I can't hold it anymore."

Ria glanced back at the city. The figures of the wall guards seemed very visible to her.

"Can you see the guards?" she asked.

Cyril squinted back at the city.

"I can see the edge of the wall," he said. "I think. There's some light in the city, and I can see the outline against that. But no guards. Oh, wait—yes, there's something moving. I think," he added dubiously.

"Then they can't see us, not with the moon behind them," Ria said relievedly. "Rest for a bit and then we can go on easily."

"What about the elves, though?" Cyril asked, a frown wrinkling his brow. "How do we know where we should go? I mean, there's a *lot* of forest."

"You're the one who always tells me I should read the histories and look at the maps," Ria said impatiently. "Lord Sharl marked the road where he came out of the forest before. It goes right to the center of the forest where the Altars are; he said so. All we have to do is reach that road and follow it right on in. According to Lord Sharl's map, Rowan's village wasn't too far from the center. It's a pity your spell wasn't good enough to conceal horses. It'll take an awfully long time on foot. Days and days, at least."

"We couldn't have gotten them through all that debris or across the moat without being discovered, nor hidden them in those tumbledown buildings, anyway," Cyril said practically.

"You're right about that," Ria agreed reluctantly. "Maybe the elves can help us get to Inner Heart more quickly. Didn't Lady Rivkah say they rode on great deer? Maybe they'll give us deer to ride."

"They'll more likely shoot us," Cyril said sourly. "They shot at Mother and Father, remember?"

"Of course they won't shoot at us," Ria said impatiently, tucking the protesting Jenji back down into her tunic. "I'm an elf, aren't I? Your mother and father were humans, and your father said himself that the elves have always tried to keep humans out of the forest, but the common road is for all the elves to use, including me. Now come on, will you, before somebody realizes we're gone and raises an outcry. We're still close enough to the city that they could probably catch us before we reach the forest."

Cyril sighed, but he took his pack back from Ria and rose to his feet.

"You know, the only reason I agreed to this is so you

wouldn't run off and try it alone," Cyril said at last, as they walked. "And I wanted a chance to talk to you."

"If you just want to go on about how I owe it to all our people to marry you, don't bother," Ria said shortly. "I already got that lecture from Lady Rivkah and Lord Sharl, too."

"There's no need for you to be so angry at me about it," Cyril said mildly. "I didn't tell them to lecture you about it. For that matter, I didn't tell them to have us betrothed. I don't see why you're so upset, though. I know you haven't found someone else, and we used to be such friends, you know."

"Yes, we used to be good friends. I was good friends with Cook, too, and most of the horses and cats and dogs. Being friends with somebody doesn't necessarily mean I want to marry them," Ria retorted. "And you haven't been much of a friend to me these past few years, either. Every time we were together, you'd get impatient and shoo me off. I thought probably you didn't like me anymore."

"It's not exactly that." Cyril glanced at her sideways. "It's just I was tired of hiding in haylofts and playing seek-and-find about the keep. I wanted to get on with other things in life. You didn't seem to want to grow up. And then—"

Ria waited, but when Cyril didn't continue, she prompted, "Then what?"

"Then I started thinking about our betrothal," Cyril said a little hesitantly. "At first I resented it a little, too. I mean, I'd rather have chosen my bride myself; who wouldn't? But I guess I never got as angry as you did. I mean, I suppose I got used to the idea. And I liked you as well as anyone I'd known—better, really, than the few girls of noble family I'd met when we visited Cielman. They all seemed rather stuffy and boring and only interested in stupid, petty things. You've never been boring, even when you made me so angry I thought I'd kick your bottom from one side of the keep to the other. So I thought maybe it'd be all right, maybe we'd even learn to love each other in time like High

Lord Emaril and High Lady Vesana did. And as I got older, I started to think about you and me as—"

Again he stopped.

"As what?" Ria said impatiently. "As husband and wife? As High Lord and Lady of Allanmere, dressed in scratchy finery and stuck at stuffy formal suppers and council sessions?"

"As lovers," Cyril said at last, very softly.

Ria glanced over at him in amazement.

"You can't mean that you're really interested in *that* sort of thing," she said. "I mean, have you ever seen how strange it looks?"

Cyril gave her a funny look, and Ria could see the blood rush to his cheeks.

"Well—have you?" he said evasively.

"Oh, mostly animals," Ria said carelessly. "Sometimes some of the servants came to the stables to have a tumble in the hay when they didn't know I was hiding in the loft. And I peeped in through the keyhole at Lord Sharl and Lady Rivkah once or twice. What about you?"

"Well, never mind," Cyril said hastily. "But I thought it might not be such a bad thing. You and me, that is." He looked at her rather anxiously. "Don't you think?"

"Well, we can try it if you want," Ria said, shrugging negligently. "The servants and your mother and father wouldn't keep doing it if they didn't like it, I suppose. But I don't have to marry you for that, and I don't *want* to marry you. Or anybody else, either. And don't give me the what-else-will-you-do-to-live speech, either. I've already gotten that, too. I know I don't have any money or any goods or any useful skills to get by on my own in the city."

"So that's what we're doing," Cyril said, realization and anger beginning to tinge his voice. "After all that you went on about how wonderful it would be if we could make contact with the elves before Father did, how proud they'd be—that was all so much dung in the pile, wasn't it? You just wanted to run off to the elves, and you needed me to help you get away from the keep. That's it, isn't it? And what were you planning to do with me if they *did* take you

in? Leave me standing there at the edge of the forest looking like a fool?"

"Of course you wouldn't look like a fool," Ria said impatiently. "What could be better? There we'd be, talking
with the elves, and if I was *with* them, that'd make it all the
easier to get them to talk to Lord Sharl, too. What better
way to get them to negotiate than to bring me back to
them? They'd know you meant them no harm, and I could
tell them about what good allies the humans of the city
would be. Your parents *would* be proud then. And we
wouldn't have to leave you standing there," Ria added
hastily. "You could come along, too, if you wanted." She
grinned a little to herself; duty-stricken Cyril would *never*
leave the city and his parents for any great length of time,
so the offer cost nothing to make.

"Oh, thank you," Cyril said sarcastically. "After you lied
to me, I'm supposed to believe my father will be delighted
to find I've crept away with you in the night and helped the
city's High Lady-to-be run off to the elves? I should run
straight back to the city and tell Mother and Father what
you're up to."

"By the time you get back, I'll have already reached the
forest, and long since, so go ahead if you really want to,"
Ria said practically. "Or were you planning to throw me
over your shoulder and carry me back by force?"

"I should," Cyril said with a sigh.

"Then one of us is going to get hurt in the fight I'll put
up," Ria retorted. "I can match you wrestling most of the
time, and if I run off in the dark, you'll never catch me.
And even if you do, you'll *still* get in trouble for helping me
get this far, too. On the other hand, if we can meet with the
elves, at least you'll get credit for getting the elves to speak
with you." She shrugged. "Fight or walk?"

Cyril was silent for a moment; at last he sighed.

"Walk," he said resignedly.

They approached the forest a little more closely, then
stopped.

"Where's the road?" Ria asked puzzledly. "It should be
right ahead, according to the map."

"It *has* been sixteen years," Cyril reminded her. "A lot of this part of the forest was trampled and burned, too. They may have moved the road, or just let it grow up. Maybe they don't need a road anymore."

"There has to be a road," Ria insisted. "Remember what Lord Sharl said about the Forest Altars at the center? All the elvan clans visited them at least occasionally, and the road was how they got there. It's a holy place, like a temple. Maybe they've concealed this end of the road, but we know where it *should* be. We'll go a little ways into the forest there, and then start looking."

"If we get that far," Cyril said grimly.

"We will," Ria said confidently. "Look, we've gotten this close and nothing's happened." They were well within arrow range now, close enough to touch the leaves of the first thin growth of trees.

"I can't see a thing," Cyril complained, squinting into the growth. "Why couldn't you have picked a night when the moon was brighter, at least?"

"If you could see, we could easily enough *be* seen on that open plain between the city and the forest when your spell wore off," Ria said patiently, pulling Cyril into the cover of the trees. She towed him resolutely into the thicker growth as quickly as she could. "And if I'd waited much longer, there wouldn't have been much use in running off at all, would there? Anyway, I can see. Just follow me and we'll find—"

Ria's words were interrupted as something whistled by her cheek, leaving a stinging scratch behind. Jenji screeched a warning and clawed violently at Ria, trying to scramble out of her tunic. Stunned, Ria put up her hand, amazed to touch the shallow furrow that trickled blood down her face.

"Wha—" she began amazedly.

"Elvan arrows!" Cyril hissed, leaping to drag Ria with him to the ground even as another arrow whistled by. "Get back to the—"

"I can't!" Ria cried as another arrow thunked into the ground almost at her hand. "They're between us and the edge of the forest." Ria grabbed frantically for Jenji, but the chirrit wriggled free, darting into a thicket nearby and chittering imperiously at them.

"Here!" Cyril pulled Ria into the thicket after Jenji, sheltering her with his own body. Jenji crawled back into Ria's pocket, and she could feel him shivering there. "Can they see us in—uh!" He jolted forward, and Ria screamed as she saw the arrow protruding from his back. To her amazement, however, Cyril sat up again.

"I'm all right," he gasped. "Come on—let's find some way back out of the forest."

Ria's mind whirled. There were elves all around them— *my people,* her mind insisted—but they were shooting arrows at them, trying to kill them! Why? Why? She crawled blindly after Cyril, crying out again but not slowing as pain speared up her leg from her left calf. Looking back, she saw a wooden shaft thrust completely through her leg a handspan below the knee.

Suddenly Ria saw a flash of bright light somewhere to the north, then another, and a tremendous outcry was echoed from nearby. Fire! But where had it come from?

Light flared again, a flaming arrow sprouting like a blossom from a nearby tree, and suddenly Ria could see dark silhouettes against the light of the fire, scurrying to smother the dancing flames. Gratitude flared even brighter in Ria's heart, and with it a sudden inexplicable sense of a familiar presence nearby. Suddenly she was certain, utterly certain who her benefactor was.

"Valann!" she cried, even as Cyril dragged her out of the forest into clear land. Ria resisted feebly, but a sudden wave of sick weakness turned her limbs to water, and she could do nothing but slump limply against Cyril as he half-lifted her, pulling her away from the forest as fast as he could stagger in the darkness. She could hear arrows thunking into the ground behind them.

"We've got to go back," she panted weakly, trying to pull free of Cyril's grip. "Valann—my brother—he's there, he made the fire—"

"Whoever bought us time to get away, I'm grateful,"

Cyril panted. "And I'm not going to waste that by walking back into their arrows. They only let us get that far into the forest so they could trap us there. And you need a healer. You've got an arrow in your leg."

"But you," Ria protested, despite her weakness still astounded. "Your back—the arrow—"

"I didn't trust your elvan friends as firmly as you did," Cyril said grimly, shifting Ria so that her arm looped over his shoulders and he could bear a greater share of her weight. Now Ria could feel the reason the arrow had not harmed him—under his tunic she could feel the unmistakable hardness of Cyril's hard practice armor, and under that the thickness of his padding.

Ria heard the whistle of the arrows, but they were out of range now; for a moment Ria wondered if the elves would come out of the forest to pursue them and finish them off, but apparently they did not consider their quarry worthy of that effort, and finally the sounds of arrows faded behind them as they stumbled onward.

"Can we stop a moment?" Ria gasped. Little lights, like fireflies, were dancing before her eyes. "Just a moment?"

Cyril glanced back at the forest, then nodded, gently easing Ria to the ground. "All right. Just a moment. I'll light the lantern and have a look at your leg. Didn't the history say something about poi—"

The world went gray for a moment; when vision returned, Cyril had already lit the lantern and was bent over Ria's lower leg. Ria risked a glance herself and sighed with relief; there was no arrow protruding from her calf, only bloody wounds on both sides.

"I cut off the point and pulled both pieces out while you were unconscious," Cyril said, his own voice a little unsteady as he tied a strip of cloth tightly around the wounds. "I don't know if that was the right thing to do or not. The bleeding seems to have gotten worse. Can you pull the arrow out of my armor? I can feel the point through the padding, and I'd hate for it to push on through, especially if it's poisoned."

"I'll try," Ria said humbly, but tug as she might at the wooden shaft, she could not budge the barbed point.

"All right, nothing else to do but leave it," Cyril said at last. "I can't take the time to take my tunic and the armor off here, and I can't carry it and the packs and you, too. Come on, I'll help you as much as I can."

Cyril pulled Ria's arm over his shoulder once more and pushed himself to his feet; Ria tried to stand herself and gasped as the world faded again. This time she barely noticed when Cyril lifted her and stumbled onward toward the city; at some point she was dimly aware of some shouting, the light of torches and shocked faces all around her, Lady Rivkah's among them. She was safe—at the cost of losing her brother just when she'd finally found him, and at the cost of the freedom she'd sought so desperately.

Valann, Ria thought hopelessly, and let darkness and despair take her.

"That was an incredibly foolish thing to do," Lady Rivkah said, her face white with anger, her lips a tight white line. "I can't begin to tell you how foolish. If I hadn't had experience with the poison the Blue-eyes use on their arrows, or if they'd changed that poison in the last sixteen years, you might well have died. If you weren't so ill, I'd— well, I don't know what I'd do."

Ria rolled her head up to face the ceiling so that she didn't have to look at Lady Rivkah, the only act of defiance she could muster the strength for. Jenji was crouched on the pillow at her other side; he chittered softly and nuzzled her cheek, but Ria was not comforted. Her leg, massively swollen, throbbed so hotly that Ria thought she would vomit, and the scrape on her cheek, smeared with ointment, burned furiously.

Lady Rivkah laid her hand on Ria's forehead, and her fingers were comfortingly cool.

"None of us who were wounded before were affected so quickly or so strongly," Lady Rivkah said quietly. "It must be your mixture of human and elvan blood. I know so little about elvan healing, too. Many of the journals I kept before the invasion were destroyed in the battle, but at least this was a very simple antidote. And I *know* it was the same poison; Cyril brought me the arrow point, and the one from his armor was poisoned with it, too. For a while we were afraid—well, never mind. You're healing, but it's very slow. You may be sick for some days, but you will mend, in time."

Ria did not smile, but she felt a tiny flash of satisfaction. At least the wedding would be postponed; at least she'd gained that much for all her trouble and pain.

Lady Rivkah sighed again, and Ria was surprised to feel her hand trembling against Ria's forehead.

"I'll let you rest for now," she said softly. "I'll send you a sleeping potion and see if you can swallow some broth." She withdrew her hand, and a moment later Ria heard the chamber door close softly. Jenji curled up beside her cheek and settled there, giving the thrumming sound he made when contented.

Ria herself was far from contented; the turmoil in her mind was almost greater than the pain in her leg. Why had the elves tried to kill her? She was one of them! How could they have meant her harm, even death?

Ah, but had they? She'd fired arrows aplenty in practice, and even with her small strength, a sharp arrow fired from a good bow could penetrate leather armor far stouter than the old practice cuirass Cyril had worn. And if the Blue-eyes' night vision was as good as her own—and surely it was, if they were out in force with bows in the middle of the night—why had they missed so many times? And why hadn't they gone even a little bit beyond the edge of the forest to finish what they'd started? It would be plain to their night vision that no one else was there to fight them.

There was only one possible answer; they were not intending to kill the intruders, only to frighten and drive them away, out of the forest. Had they meant no more harm than that to the humans who had approached the forest, too? Why, then, the poison on the arrows? No; more likely the presence of an elf had confused them, because Lord Sharl had made it plain that they killed, or at least tried to kill, any human who came too near the forest.

Ah, that was it! Ria could have groaned with frustration. Of course; they'd only attacked her at all because there was a human with her! No wonder they'd been confused. Perhaps their arrows had all been aimed at Cyril; perhaps she'd only been hit because she was so close to him. Ah, gods, how could she not have foreseen that? In their eyes, the enemy had followed her right into the forest!

But why, then, had her brother—if indeed it was he, as Ria felt almost certain—intervened? Perhaps—ah, of course, he didn't want Ria driven from the forest at all! If Cyril hadn't dragged her away, he'd have come for her! Why else would he have been there at the edge of the forest, when Lord Sharl and Lady Rivkah said his clan lived near the center of the forest, so far away? No, he'd come all that distance deliberately, looking for her, and now he'd be fleeing back into the forest ahead of Blue-eyes' arrows. Now Ria *did* groan, and a few bitter tears trickled down her face. How close she'd come to success, and how violently it had been torn away from her!

And now what would she do? She'd be weak and sick for some time, if Lady Rivkah was right, and probably lame for even longer. Illness might postpone the wedding for a time, but Ria doubted if the High Lord and Lady would care if Ria limped under her wedding gown. The injury would keep her from another attempt at flight, and in any event, Ria had no doubt at all that she'd be guarded like treasure before the ceremony. Anyway, how could she get away without Cyril's help? And she was very, very sure she could expect no more help from her foster brother.

There was a gentle tap at the door. Ria thought about answering, telling whoever it was to go away, then just sighed. It wasn't worth the strength it would take to call out. Let them come, whoever it was. Nothing could make her more miserable than she felt already, anyway.

Cyril peeped in the door, a tray in his hands.

"Mother said I could bring this in to you," he said.

"Some broth and a potion for the pain in your leg. Want to try to swallow some of it?"

"Why not?" Ria croaked weakly. Neither the broth nor the potion appealed to her, but her throat was achingly dry, and anything that could stop her leg throbbing so wretchedly could only be an improvement.

Cyril laid the tray on the small table beside the bed. He had to stuff cushions behind Ria's back before she could sit up, Jenji chittering indignantly all the while at losing his position on the pillow. Cyril gave Ria the broth sip by sip, carefully.

"How does your leg feel?" Cyril asked, eyeing the swollen lump in the covers dubiously.

"It hurts," Ria admitted, trying to sound as if she didn't care. "Lady Rivkah said it would take a long time to heal."

"Some adventure," Cyril said ruefully. "All that trouble and we didn't even see an elf—not really."

Ria didn't answer. That was a complicated issue, and she didn't really want to think about it all again. She certainly didn't want to have to try to explain it to Cyril, not when she didn't understand it herself.

"I'm sorry you got hurt," Cyril said after a moment. "And for your sake, I suppose I'm sorry it didn't work out with the elves. But it may be for the best, anyway. At least you know that somebody in the forest means you well— your brother, if you think that's who it was. Father took troops out to the edge of the forest almost as soon as we got back. I went with them. There were a few arrows fired from the forest, but nobody came out. I called out, too. I thought maybe if it *was* really your brother—" He shrugged. "Nobody answered. I'm sorry. I tried for a long time."

"Thank you." She was surprised and gratified by the effort; it was a kindly thought on Cyril's part. But of course her brother wouldn't come out of the forest, even if he was still there to hear Cyril calling, after he'd seen Cyril dragging her away.

"I'd like to have met your brother." Cyril chuckled.

"However much trouble we're both in now because of trying to find him."

Ria closed her eyes. A tear slipped down her cheek before she could stop it.

Cyril put the bowl down and reached over to wipe the tear away gently.

"You know, I wish Mother and Father had just left us to ourselves," he said with a sigh. "If we'd had the chance to choose, we might've decided we *wanted* to marry each other without all this fuss."

Ria half-smiled. She doubted it—she wasn't much interested in marrying *anybody,* much less Cyril—but anything was possible.

"You know," Cyril said slowly, "betrothal or no, I don't think they can marry us if we *both* refuse, can they?"

Ria rolled her head over to look at him warily. Cyril met her eyes directly.

"What do you mean?" she said.

"What I mean," Cyril said, a faint twinkle returning to his eyes, "is, let's make believe we never were betrothed at all." He took Ria's hand. "Would you do me the honor of becoming my wife?"

"Oh, Cyril—" Ria began disgustedly.

"No, don't answer me right now." Cyril patted her hand. "Think of it as a kind of bargain if you want. Just listen for a moment. If you decide to marry me, I won't try to make you be someone you're not. I won't make you wear fancy gowns and sit in boring council meetings—unless you decide to do it yourself. I will need an heir, though." He grinned ruefully. "But that can wait a while, too. And if you can get any of the elves to welcome you, you can go see them whenever you want." He patted her hand again, and now Ria could see a strange expression, maybe envy, in his eyes. "Just as long as you come back. Who knows, maybe that's what we need to bring the elves and humans together, a kind of go-between."

Ria didn't know what to say. She bit her lip, feeling new tears welling up in her eyes.

"And if you decide you still don't want to marry me, I'll

refuse, too, no matter how much trouble it makes for both of us," Cyril said, straightening resolutely. "But give it some thought, a few days, maybe. And if you need to try to talk to the elves again before you decide, I'll help you."

"I'll think about it," Ria said, too stunned and confused to say anything else.

"For a few days, you probably won't have much else to do," Cyril said, grinning again. "But in the meantime, try to finish this potion. It might make you sleep for a while, at least."

"All right." Ria let Cyril give her the potion as he had the broth, sip by sip, and then some deliciously cold water to ease her parched throat. When Cyril started to take the cup away, however, Ria managed to squeeze his fingers a little and smile at him.

"Thank you," she said. "You're a good friend. And a good foster brother."

"I'd make a good husband, too," Cyril said, his eyes twinkling. "Sleep well."

The potion was already making Ria drowsy, but she was able to watch Cyril leave. She hadn't expected such generosity from him, or that he would come up with so remarkable a suggestion. Both of them refuse, indeed! Would Cyril really take such an unthinkable stand against his parents—against everything he'd been raised to believe was his duty—or was it just a ploy to get her to agree to marry him? And would Lord Sharl and Lady Rivkah listen if he did defy them? Following that thought came a somewhat amusing vision of them both before the priest, bound in chains and gagged.

Ria chuckled weakly, letting the potion carry her away on a wave of sleep. How delightful that after she had known him for sixteen years, Cyril could still surprise her. He'd make Allanmere a fine High Lord, except that he could never look a proper noble with that mischievous twinkle in his eyes, and he looked so ridiculous in finery . . .

The room had faded from around her, and once again her brother's face was before her. His dark eyes were fixed on hers, and his lips moved as if he was speaking, but Ria could hear no words. Slowly his face faded, too, as if growing more distant, but somehow Ria could still feel him, some faint knowledge of his presence.

Ria smiled and slept.

VI

Valann

"Little fool!" Valann gasped, ducking behind a tree with Lahti. "What could she have been thinking?"

"You are certain it was her?" Lahti was panting too, her brown hair limp and stringy with grime and sweat, her eyes darkly ringed with exhaustion. She nocked another arrow, peered around the tree, and loosed the arrow. A cry testified to the accuracy of her shot.

"Have the arrows stopped burning?" Val asked anxiously.

"Almost." Lahti turned, and he saw the worry in her eyes, too. "You shouldn't have done that, even for your sister. You shouldn't have shot fire at the forest. It's forbidden to put fire to living wood and outside a firepit."

"I knew they'd stop to put it out, giving her time enough to get away," Val said grimly. He pulled Lahti to the next clump of trees. "There's been enough rain. It wouldn't have burned long in any wise."

"It'll burn long in the memory of the Blue-eyes," Lahti said, troubled. "It will redouble their hostility."

"We're almost at their border," Val assured her. "Only a short distance and we'll cross into Hawk's Eye's lands."

"And what then?" Lahti asked anxiously. "What if they've heard the disturbance and—Valann! Above!"

Val leaped aside just in time to avoid the Blue-eyes who dropped like a ripe fruit from the tree, barely drawing his knife quickly enough to parry the blindingly fast attack. Val squinted through the darkness at his opponent, and his heart sank as he saw the tall, beaded coil of a braid at the top of his opponent's head—this was a matriarch, a woman of great age and doubtless great experience with her dagger. He was stronger than most elves he knew, and his reach was very good because of his height, but his opponent was much faster, and he could never hope to match her centuries-honed skill.

The Blue-eyes woman darted in, and Val hurriedly retreated with a burning line of blood flowing down his forearm. He ducked behind a tree, hoping to dodge the Blue-eyes woman long enough for Lahti to—

The Blue-eyes woman grunted and fell with no grace at all. Lahti gazed down at her dispassionately, then tossed aside the branch with which she had clubbed the older woman.

"Hurry," she said. "Before others come."

They ran with almost reckless speed through the darkness, Val letting Lahti, with her superior night vision, lead the way. Fortunately it was not long before he saw the stones marked with glowing runes that indicated the boundary between Blue-eyes and Hawk's Eye's lands. For a moment Val thought fearfully that the Blue-eyes might have set up an ambush at the boundary; then they were across, and safe.

"Stop," Lahti said as soon as they were well beyond arrow range. "Let me tend your arm in case the knife was poisoned. I can't carry you back to Inner Heart if you're weakened."

The scratch was deeper than Val had thought, but after sniffing the wound and tasting his blood, Lahti announced with relief that it was not poisoned. She bound up the cut with a poultice of hastily gathered herbs to keep it from festering, but did not waste what strength she had left on healing the cut. They still needed to get far enough away that if any Hawk's Eye patrol had been alerted by the noise, they would not stumble across Val and Lahti.

"Stop," Lahti said again, this time a note of desperation in her voice. She sniffed the air, her ears twitching as they strained to sort through the forest's night sounds. "Can you smell it? Can you feel it?"

Val sniffed the night breeze, opened all his senses, inner and outer, as he had been taught. Yes. Eyes watched, ears listened from somewhere nearby—was it those bushes, that tree? Had they fled from the wolf and into the bear's den?

"Are you cowards to hide like a snake in its burrow, then strike us down from afar with arrows and spears?" Val called defiantly. He felt Lahti move slowly beside him, turning so the green band at her arm was more visible. Surely they could smell the scent on her despite the sweat and grime they'd both accumulated. "Come down and fight knife to knife with me if you must fight."

"Name yourself and your clan." The hissed voice came from a nearby thicket, but look as he might, Val could see no one there.

"I am Valann, son-by-love of Rowan, Eldest of Inner Heart," Val said. "With me is my mate Lahti, daughter of Kella of the Moon Lakes."

"She is no Moon Lake," a female challenged. "She has the height of a Redoak. And you look no elf at all."

"Inner Heart, Moon Lake, Owl Clan, and Redoak all danced in my mother's High Circle," Lahti said evenly. "And Valann's mother by blood was Chyrie of the Wilding Clan, she who saved your lives and your lands by raising the forest against your enemies. We mean no harm to Hawk's Eye and wish only permission to pass safely from these lands."

A male elf stepped from the thicket, bow in hand and arrow nocked and ready.

"That is for our Eldest to decide," he said. "You will

come with us to see him." Other elves stepped from bushes, or jumped down from the trees.

Val glanced at Lahti, who nodded.

"We have no choice," she said.

The elf who had spoken lowered his bow. Val was not too distracted by relief to notice with some envy the Hawk's Eye warriors' unusual and rather elegant appearance—they were middling in height, neither as tall as the Inner Hearts nor as short as the Moon Lakes. Their skin was almost as dark as the Inner Hearts', and their hair was black, although with occasional odd streaks of a brilliant gold-red shade, and their eyes were almost the same tawny gold as Val remembered Chyrie's to be. As if to accentuate their exotic appearance, or perhaps for its practical value in night patrols, the Hawk's Eye warriors wore leathers stained almost true black, with hoods they could raise to cover the fiery streaks in their hair. With those hoods raised, the warriors would be near invisible in the darkness.

The warrior stepped forward and surveyed Val, then Lahti, with those odd eyes. At last he nodded briefly.

"So long as you cooperate and do not attempt to escape, you will be treated as honored guests, and need fear no harm," he said. "I am Twilight. It would be a long walk to our village, and you appear exhausted. Spark will summon deer to bear us back to the Eldest. Rest for now."

Lahti all but sagged to the ground; Val sat down wearily beside her. Lahti said nothing, only leaned quietly against Val's shoulder, clasping his hand. Val held her close and waited. They were alive, at least, and the Hawk's Eyes offered them no immediate harm. And no matter what they did with him, they'd never harm Lahti, not while she wore the green band of fertility. That was enough hope to sustain him for now.

Twilight squatted down beside them, holding out his wineskin and a leaf-wrapped parcel.

"We have a little cold roast squirrel from our meal, and roasted nuts," he said. "You may have it. A ripened woman must maintain her strength." His voice was tinged with disapproval, and Val knew he was being courteous not to vent his anger that a ripe female had been brought into such a dangerous situation in the first place.

"I thank you for your kindness," Val said quietly. He took the wineskin and the parcel and handed them to Lahti. Lahti accepted them, giving Valann a troubled glance, and Val knew, too, that for the first time their ploy with the green band and the scent troubled her. Fertility and reproduction were sacred to the Mother Forest; what offense might they be committing by their pretense? They'd meant the disguise only as long-distance protection, never anticipating they would have to deal closely with other elves.

There was nothing to do for it now, though, but continue the lie. Lahti ate the squirrel and the nuts—true to Twilight's word, there was only a little—but shared the wine with Val. By the time they were finished, Spark, whoever he or she was, had apparently summoned the deer, for Twilight immediately led them to the waiting animals. Judging from the strong resemblance between the young female elf awaiting them there and their guide, Val surmised that Spark was Twilight's younger sister, but there was no telling; many clans, especially the very small ones, had such resemblances throughout the clan.

Despite their politeness, it was apparent that the Hawk's Eyes still considered Val and Lahti prisoners; Twilight rode with Lahti, and while Valann was too large to share a deer, Spark rode very close beside him. It hardly mattered, however; Val knew that even should he and Lahti have inclination and opportunity to flee on their deer, Spark was apparently a beast-speaker and they were not; the deer would answer to her and return, or simply throw their riders and abandon them. And, Valann would admit, he and Lahti were simply far too exhausted to even attempt an escape.

It might have been a long walk to the Hawk's Eye village, but mounted on the deer it was a short enough ride. Val was surprised to see how tiny the Hawk's Eye village was—hardly more than a dozen huts grouped around a single firepit, and nothing nearly as large as Rowan's speaking hut, either. But then, he reminded himself, probably many clans were no larger than this; the only village he had ever known was Inner Heart, likely the largest village in the forest. At least the Hawk's Eyes he'd seen seemed fit and well fed, not scruffy and half-starved like the Swiftfoots.

What seemed to be the entire Hawk's Eye clan approached to greet them, not thronging joyfully around Val and Lahti, calling out and reaching to touch them as his own people might have done, but gathering silently, not murmuring even to each other, only staring wide-eyed at the visitors, neither welcome nor hostility apparent in their expressions.

Twilight slid from his deer and helped Lahti down, then nodded reassuringly to them and disappeared into one of the huts. He reemerged a few moments later.

"Our Eldest, Silence, will see you," Twilight said, the faintest note of surprise in his voice. "Spark and I will witness to your honorable behavior and our assurances of fair treatment to you."

"We thank you," Val said, for lack of anything else to say. Obviously these Hawk's Eyes were a formal sort of clan, far more bound by ritual than the boisterous Inner Hearts. Rowan would have been there to meet any prisoner brought in by a patrol, not sitting in a hut and waiting for prisoners to be brought before her. Hurriedly Val slid the curled boar's-tusk bracelet from his wrist, nodding approvingly as Lahti lifted her horn bead necklace over her head. He handed her the bracelet.

Spark held aside the leather flap covering the opening to the Eldest's hut; Val had to stoop slightly to fit comfortably through the lower doorway. The hut inside was lit dimly by a fire burned down to embers.

Sitting on the opposite side of the fire was an elf whose very appearance made Valann stop where he was, so that Lahti nearly collided with his back. Rowan was the most ancient elf Val had ever seen, but this creature must have been old while Rowan's mother was still a child. His limbs were stick-thin and twisted with age; one leg ended in a stump midway down to the knee, and his fingers were so stiffly gnarled that they curled at the ends of his wrists like claws. His eyes were white and blind, his long coiled braid was equally white, and his pale face was deeply seamed and wrinkled. Still there was something about him that seemed alive, alive, alive—Valann shivered as he remembered the expression he had seen in Chyrie's eyes. Yes, this creature, like his mother, lived very near indeed to the Mother Forest.

"Enter, young ones, and sit," the ancient one said, his voice a mere whisper. "Partake of the warmth of my fire, the nourishment of my food, and be welcomed as one of my children."

Valann and Lahti exchanged glances. Val had heard the traditional greeting of food and fire a thousand times in his life, but never spoken in such words. Was this perhaps a much more ancient form?

"We are honored to share your food and fire, Grandfather," Lahti said hesitantly. "May joy and friendship be our contribution. We are—"

"Lahti, daughter of Kella of Moon Lake, and Valann, who names himself son-by-love of Rowan, Eldest of that Inner Heart," Silence whispered, barely nodding. "But no matter at what breast he suckled in his infancy, his blood-mother's name is greater still. At the heart of the world is the beating of her heart. She too listens to the many voices. You are welcome here in her name, whatever mixture of seed made you what you are."

Again Valann felt a chill sweep through him, and he was glad to sit down on the thick furs that cushioned the earthen floor of the hut. Silence lifted a hand, and Spark entered the hut, Twilight beside her carrying a bowl and a cup. Twilight handed both to Lahti; to Valann's surprise, the bowl contained only a few roasted nuts and the cup only a few sips of wine.

Lahti glanced confusedly at Valann, but she picked up one of the nuts and ate it, sipping a little wine from the cup before passing it to Valann. Val, who had not had the benefit even of the bit of food that had been given to Lahti earlier, finished the scant repast, embarrassed when his stomach impolitely growled its discontent.

"Thank you, Grandfather," Lahti murmured. She extended the necklace and bracelet she'd been holding. "We bring these gifts for the Eldest of the Hawk's Eyes, in thanks for the honor of our welcome." Then she glanced helplessly at Valann. Silence could neither see the gifts nor reach out to accept them. At last, she awkwardly laid them at his feet.

The seamed old face creased with a smile.

"We must observe the appropriate rituals, of course," Silence whispered. "You have shared my food and fire. You are one with Hawk's Eye. My people will give you a hut to rest yourself, and water to wash your bodies, and food and drink to still the growling beast I hear." Valann flushed miserably. "Tomorrow when you wake, return to Inner Heart. We will give you trail food for the journey and gifts for your Eldest. Say to Rowan, Eldest of Inner Heart, that Hawk's Eye is of one blood with Inner Heart. Her people shall have safe passage through our lands, and those who walk in friendship with them shall come to no harm at our hand."

"Grandfather—" Valann began, but Silence raised a clawed hand again, and Val fell silent.

"Talk is for humans, and of talk there has been enough," Silence rasped. "That was always Rowan's failing—she believed too much in the power of words. Learn to speak with your heart, elvan child." He sighed and lay back on the furs, closing his eyes.

Valann and Lahti exchanged puzzled glances once more, but clearly their audience was at an end; they rose and followed Twilight and Spark silently out of the hut. Val almost sighed with relief, however, when they were outside; somehow the night seemed much safer in its very ordinariness.

Twilight vanished abruptly into the darkness without even a farewell; Spark, however, led Val and Lahti to one of the huts, hesitating outside, glancing at Lahti.

"We have twenty-two males," she murmured, speaking for the first time. "Do you wish to choose among them?"

"Choose—" Lahti shook her head blankly.

"For the sacred dance," Spark said, indicating the band around Lahti's arm. "To fill your womb with life."

Lahti's eyes widened in realization, and she flushed.

"No," she said hurriedly. "My mate is the one I have chosen."

Spark nodded, although her furtive glance at Valann held some puzzlement.

"If there is anything else you need, call," Spark murmured, "and someone will come." Then she, too, was gone.

Val shrugged and ducked into the hut. A brighter, newer fire was burning here, and platters of meat, fruits, stew, and greens were laid beside the fire to keep warm. Apparently this was someone's home, for what were likely personal belongings had been hastily shoved to the back of the hut in baskets. Several buckets of water had been placed just inside the doorway, together with a bowl of rendered-fat soap, and a stack of what turned out to be Hawk's Eye-style leather clothing beside them.

Tired and hungry as he was, the simple act of washing away the sweat and dirt of days of travel was the most wonderful sensation Val could have imagined. He unbraided his black hair and washed it too, the marvelous sensation of cleanliness seeming to lift nights' worth of exhaustion from him. He'd not bother to try the new clothing until morning; at the moment he was far more interested in the food awaiting them, and the thick, soft-looking pallet of furs that served as a bed.

When Lahti came to sit beside him at the fire, however, Valann almost forgot his hunger. She, too, had scrubbed herself from head to toe and was enjoying the warmth of the fire on her clean bare skin. Without the odors of her perspiration, the soiled leather of her clothing, and the travel dirt they had both accumulated, the musky scent Dusk had given Lahti was even more apparent. Val shivered and hurriedly turned to the food, hoping his hunger and the strong aromas of the richly spiced meat would distract him. However odd the Hawk's Eyes might seem in their behavior, they apparently liked to savor a well-prepared meal as much as any other elf. He fancied, however, that Lahti gave him a small smile of amusement as she reached for the wineskin.

"You never told me," Lahti said as she sampled the contents of a bowl of sap-sugared nuts, "how it was you were so certain that that was your sister we almost gave our lives to save. There were two, and so far away, and hidden in the thicket."

"An elf who would blunder openly into Blue-eyes' territory, coming into it from the open lands near the city and bringing a human with her?" Val scoffed. "Who had not the faintest notion of cover or quiet movement? Who else could it have been?"

"Ah." Lahti raised an eyebrow. "Do you know, I thought my night vision the better of yours, and yet we were so far away I couldn't have been certain whether the small one was an elf or a human child, perhaps."

Val tried to remember. It *had* been dark, and there were so many Blue-eyes; had he actually seen Ria in all the confusion?

"But we were going because Dusk warned that she was approaching," Val said at last. "And she did approach the forest."

"Yes, Dusk's vision," Lahti agreed. "I should have realized that. I was only surprised that you seemed so certain so quickly."

Val hesitated.

"I've sometimes dreamed of her," he said slowly. "Sometimes I could almost touch her, it seemed. Dusk once told me that spending so many months side by side in the womb, sharing our mother's heartbeat, that our spirits grew closely as well, and sometimes perhaps they touch in the spirit world."

"As Dusk's spirit journeys to seek his visions," Lahti said, nodding. "I wonder if she felt your presence as well."

Val said nothing; he had not thought of that. Had his

sister seen his face in dreams, reached out vainly to touch
him as he'd reached for her, woken and ached at her fail-
ure? Val shook his head; such things were Dusk's realm,
not his. He would be well content to let the Gifted One
puzzle out the spirit world. Val had quite enough to concern himself in this place at this very moment, the Mother
Forest knew!

The food was excellent, and the wine was the finest Val
had ever tasted, but he might as well have been eating dust
and dry leaves. Clean and comfortable for the first time in
days, his hunger and thirst finally satisfied, his weariness
seemed to vanish as if by magic, and he found himself
glancing sideways at Lahti, helplessly watching the golden
firelight dance over the gentle swell of her small new
breasts and flicker over the smooth, dark strands of her
hair.

"Does the food not please you?" Lahti asked, smiling
mischievously as she popped a berry into her mouth.

"It was good enough," Valann said quickly. "But I can
eat no more of it."

"Is there something else you want?" Lahti asked, and
Val fancied he could hear almost a chuckle in her voice.
"We could call for Spark."

"I don't need anything from Spark," Val said, a little
more sharply than he intended. He wondered irritably why
none of the clan's women had offered to share his pallet
for the night. It would have been unthinkable to deny any
guest of Inner Heart that most basic courtesy. Was it because of his part human blood, or just—

He glanced at Lahti again and sighed. Of course. Why
would the Hawk's Eyes offer him a bed partner when his
ripe mate needed him? Val sighed again and crawled over
to the pallet, pulling a fur over him despite the warm hut.

"Are you ill?" Lahti asked, concern in her voice, but one
eyebrow arched knowingly.

"I'm only tired," Val said gruffly. "It's been many days
since we slept well."

"Of course," Lahti said apologetically, putting down the
bowl of berries. "I'll bank the fire."

Val grunted and turned away so he would not have to watch the soft glow of the fire on Lahti's skin as she carefully piled ashes over the glowing logs, but he could not help but feel her warmth and smell her scent as she curled up against him on the furs. He pulled as far away from her as the pile of furs allowed, but a moment later he froze as Lahti's warm hand touched his shoulder. Then there was nothing to do but roll over and face her. To Val's utter disgust, she was still smiling that secret little smile.

"For days you've wanted my warmth beside you, and now you hide under the furs and pull away from me," Lahti mocked gently. "Did you like me better when I was smudged and dirty and clothed in smelly leathers?"

"Well, you might have spared me Dusk's scent tonight," Val retorted crossly. "No Hawk's Eyes are going to invade our tent this night while we sleep."

"I know." Lahti propped herself on his chest, to Val's utter agony, all the worse for her smile. "And that's why I applied none of the salve he gave me."

Val scowled.

"But I can smell it."

Lahti raised one eyebrow.

"The salve is in my pack, and our packs are between you and the wall, where the Hawk's Eyes placed them," she said mildly. "I would have had to pass you or walk through the fire to reach them."

Utter shock, followed by incredible joy, paralyzed Valann as he realized what Lahti was saying; then he rolled over, pulling her close.

"But when?" he asked incredulously.

"I'm not certain," Lahti chuckled. "This is all very new to me, and I was always so tired and hungry, and stiff and sore, too, from sleeping on the ground every night. I thought I was becoming ill, perhaps. I've never ripened before, you know, to recognize the feeling."

"But—" Sudden leaden despair swept away Val's delight as if it had never been. "We must return to Inner Heart immediately. You haven't taken your passage to adulthood."

"No." Lahti shook her head, her eyes warm. "I haven't. But by the time we journey all the way back to Inner Heart, my time of ripeness will be past."

"If you ripen once, you'll ripen again," Val said, trying to tell himself that a few more days were nothing after months of waiting. The thought felt like a lie.

"Some women ripen only once," Lahti said softly. "But perhaps I'll ripen again, many decades from now. Perhaps half a century."

The thought passed between them in a lightning flicker of understanding—Lahti might ripen five decades from now, but would Valann in fact be alive then? Humans lived such pitifully short lives, and Val was partly, at least, human. He had grown so quickly. He might well be dead, or past his years of siring a child, before Lahti ripened again.

Emotions warred in Val's heart—pride that she wanted his child so badly despite his mixed blood, enough to risk the Mother Forest's disfavor by coupling with him before she had passed her trials of adulthood; fear for the consequences to Lahti; desire, oh, yes, desire and love, too; and a sort of dismay—*What if I don't give her a child, and she has made this terrible choice for nothing?*

"You should return to Inner Heart and take your trials of passage," he said reluctantly. "It's forbidden that I should touch you while you are still a child." Yet he could well understand why she might choose to ignore that law; what elvan woman would pass by a chance to bear a child?

"And if I choose otherwise?" Lahti asked, her eyes sparkling.

"Then—then you should do as Spark suggested, and choose among Hawk's Eye males for your High Circle, to give you the best chance of bearing a child," Val said, forcing the words out.

"Indeed I will not," Lahti said indignantly, pulling back a little. "You'd have me dance the High Circle for my very first coupling, and with these strangers?"

"No. Oh, no." Val gave in and pulled her close again, burying his face in the softness of her hair as he had longed to do so many times. By the Mother Forest, she was so tiny, so slender, her small breasts and barely swelling hips so unformed that, although she was almost a decade his elder, she seemed very much a child still. Had Doeanna felt this sense of awe at the trust that had been placed in her? No; more likely she'd felt mildly amused and perhaps vaguely curious at the odd creature she'd been asked to initiate into the pleasures of coupling: a half-human oddity who'd gone from child to man in hardly more than a decade and a half, too tall and too broad, with hair springing from his face and body in places where it ought not to be.

"Are you certain?" he whispered, pausing to look into Lahti's eyes soberly.

Lahti laughed and reached down to touch him.

"*You* are, and no doubt of it," she said, her eyes twinkling. "Do you remember what Silence said? Learn to speak with your heart, and to listen with it, too." She took Val's hand and laid it over her heart. "Can you hear my heart calling to you?"

Val laughed and laid his head on her breast, turning to kiss the soft flesh.

"Indeed I do," he said joyfully. "And I pledge the Mother Forest Herself can hear mine answer."

VII

Ria

• "But I'm sick of my room," Ria complained, shifting carefully so that her leg lay more comfortably on the cushions.

"That's too bad." Lady Rivkah did not look overly sympathetic. "Unfortunately, bed rest is one of the results of having a poisoned arrow shot into your leg."

"Now that the poison's gone, it could be healed," Ria said sullenly.

"Yes, it probably could." Lady Rivkah laid the tray of salves on the bedside table and began unwrapping the dressing. "I think, however, that a little discomfort and forced bed rest is appropriate enough punishment for all the worry you caused us, and with you confined to your bed, I don't have to make sure there's always a guard outside your door. You'll be on your feet again in a day or two, anyway."

Ria ground her teeth but resolutely did not wince as Lady Rivkah carefully cleaned the wounds and reapplied the salves and dressings.

"You know, Sharl wants contact with the elves just as

much as you do," Lady Rivkah said mildly, tying fresh bandages into place. "I don't doubt that we would have taken you to the forest as soon as we found a safe place to enter it and some elves who would wait long enough to find out who we were before shooting, in the hope that if the elves wouldn't talk to us, at least they'd talk to you."

Ria said nothing. She was sure they probably *would* have taken her to the forest—after she was safely married to Cyril, and under heavy guard, and with Lady Rivkah ready to cast a spell to track her, if necessary.

"If you'd paid any attention to the historical accounts," Lady Rivkah continued, "you'd have known that the Blue-eyes have been a hostile clan since long before the invasion. You might even have supposed that since they were so fierce and hostile, they might have expanded their territory in the sixteen years since the invasion, and since the border lands were often abandoned by other clans. You might have picked a safer spot to try to enter the forest."

"I thought I'd use the road," Ria said sullenly. "The same road you used."

Lady Rivkah nodded.

"That wasn't a bad idea," she admitted. "It might have worked at one time. But Sharl has had the guards in the city looking for that road for years. They haven't found it, and I imagine their poking around the edge of the forest hasn't made the Blue-eyes any more hospitable." She laid the jars of ointments neatly back on the tray. "Sharl and I agree that at this point our best course of action is to wait. Perhaps the elves will attempt to make contact with us. At least the Blue-eyes will have time to settle down a bit, and perhaps we can manage to learn the full extent of their territory so we can avoid it."

Ria scowled and said nothing. Lord Sharl and Lady Rivkah could spare the time to wait; nobody was forcing *them* to marry against their will.

"I don't have to be a thought-seer to know what that scowl is for," Lady Rivkah said, shaking her head. "Ria, I can't understand this attitude you're taking. We're not marrying you to some brutal monster; this is our son Cyril, and you've been friends all your life. It might make some sense if you'd found someone else, but we know you haven't. Sharl and I have been hoping you'd eventually start showing a little maturity and responsibility. I think it's disgraceful that we even have to think about steps such as confining you to your rooms and stationing guards to watch you. But if you insist on acting like a child, you'll be treated like one."

Ria fought hard to swallow an angry retort; she had nothing to gain by making her foster mother more annoyed than she already was, and nothing to say that would change Lady Rivkah's mind.

"Perhaps your mother *did* make a mistake in giving you to us," Lady Rivkah said unexpectedly. "I can't imagine what mistake Sharl and I made in your raising to cause you to be so selfish. Ria, your mother's folk lived centuries upon centuries, and you likely will, too. Is it so terribly much to ask that you spend a few decades of your life to give Allanmere a High Lady and an heir?"

"So when is the wedding?" Ria asked, trying to keep her voice level.

"Sharl had suggested month's end," Lady Rivkah said, and Ria's heart sank. That was less than two weeks away. "But Cyril suggested that Allanmere has never had a mid-summer festival, and that that would be a good occasion for a combined celebration. I think he's right. That will give Lord Emaril's supply ship time to reach Allanmere, and that's a cause for celebration by itself."

This time Ria found herself stifling a smile of triumph. Midsummer—almost a month away! Cyril must have truly meant what he'd said to her, and he was buying her time to think.

When Lady Rivkah had gone, Ria took the crutch from its place beside her bed and clumsily swung herself upright, hobbling slowly over to the window ledge where she could look out. Now the jumble of masonry and the tantalizing nearness of the forest seemed mocking in their false prom-ise of hope. The forest might as well be leagues away for all she could reach it; even if her injured leg would bear her well enough to attempt the long walk and the climb over the wall, the guards would be watching for her, if indeed there weren't any stationed outside her door! Cyril had promised to help, but somehow it felt wrong to ask him to find a way to smuggle her out—too much as if she was agreeing to some implicit bargain she wasn't certain she was prepared to honor.

Ria suddenly yelped as her leg twinged painfully; looking down, she saw Jenji sitting on her foot, pawing at her ankle for attention. Ria hurriedly reached down and scooped up the chirrit before he could do any further damage.

"Mage's familiar," Ria grumbled. "What good does that do me if I'm no mage? It'd be nice if you could manage to give me a little magic."

Jenji chittered agreeably, jumping to his favorite perch on Ria's shoulder. Ria wondered idly if her don't-see-me was actually magic or not; it seemed different, somehow, from the spells Lady Rivkah or Yvarden cast. Lady Rivkah had, of course, tested Ria when she was much younger, and if Ria had shown enough magical ability, she'd have been taught magic along with Cyril. Ria certainly didn't cast any spells, not even gestures or chants. And she had no idea how to use a familiar anyway. But—but perhaps Cyril would.

Ria limped back to the bed and pulled the bell cord. There was *no* chance she was going to open that door and see if there were guards standing outside. It would be too humiliating if there were.

The maid told Ria that Cyril was at his studies, but that she'd see that he knew that Ria wished to see him. There was a bit of a smirk on the maid's face when she delivered this announcement, and Ria wondered how much amusement the servants were enjoying at her expense thanks to her aborted escape attempt, recapture, and subsequent confinement. Ria privately resolved that that particular maid was first in line for a particularly nasty prank when Ria was up to running speed again. Then there was nothing to do but go back to bed and fume privately until Cyril came.

It was, in fact, suppertime before Cyril arrived, when he brought his supper and Ria's on a tray.

"Marliss said you asked for me," he said cheerfully. "So I thought I'd spare myself supper with my parents and the inevitable wedding plans."

"Lady Rivkah said you were the one who suggested putting the wedding back to midsummer," Ria said shyly. "Thank you."

Cyril shrugged a little uncomfortably.

"Well, it *is* a better time," he said. "Besides, how do you think I'd look if the only way I could get you to marry me is to have you dragged before the priest while you're too crippled to get away?"

Ria poked disinterestedly at her fish baked in nut milk.

"Cyril, do you know any healing spells?" she asked.

"Well—" Cyril hesitated. "I have Mother's grimoire, and there are healing spells in it. I just haven't gotten that far in my studies. Why? Mother said your leg was healing well."

"Well, it could be healed by now," Ria said crossly. "And it *hurts*. And I can hardly walk. I know your mother's angry with me, but I think it's cruel to leave me unhealed just so she doesn't have to worry that I'll run away. If you have the spell, you can do it, can't you?"

"Ria, it's just not that simple," Cyril protested. "Some spells don't involve controlling as much magical force. Others are far more complex. I don't know how difficult the healing spell is, and I won't know until I try it, not unless I ask another mage. And my mother's the expert on healing spells."

"What if it's too complex, and you do something wrong?" Ria asked cautiously.

"The spell might just not work," Cyril said. "That's if I'm lucky. Otherwise it could go wrong, do something I didn't mean to do. I wouldn't want that to happen, especially not on a healing spell on a person."

Ria shivered. Even getting away from her wedding wasn't worth being lamed for life.

"What about if you had a familiar?" Ria suggested.

Cyril started to shrug, then glanced at Jenji, his eyebrows raising.

"It's not the same thing," he said slowly. "I've studied the theory of familiars, and a properly trained familiar can channel some of the magical energies, freeing the mage to handle the rest. But that's when a mage has been working with a familiar for a long time, maybe years. Still—"

"Still?" Ria prompted.

"Chirrits are intelligent," Cyril said thoughtfully. "Mother used to say that her teacher's chirrit could speak a little. If Jenji's intelligent enough, it could work. But it still requires a preliminary spell initiating mental contact between the mage and the familiar, and another spell to set up the magical lattice for the framework of—"

"Huh?" Ria asked blankly.

"Sorry." Cyril shrugged. "Anyway, working with a familiar takes two spells I also haven't used. I know those spells are simple enough, though, because Yvarden's talked about getting me a familiar. Mother wouldn't have it. She calls them a poor mage's crutch, despite the fact that her own teacher used one."

"Well, I'm not offering you my chirrit to be your familiar," Ria said hurriedly. "I just thought you might—well, borrow him."

Cyril was silent for a moment, considering, but Ria could tell he was tempted. At last he shook his head slowly.

"I'll give it a try," he said. "I'll need to study the spells, filch all the stuff I'll need. Then I'll try to link up with Jenji. If all that works, *then* I'll try the healing spell."

Ria was disappointed. "When?"

"Maybe tomorrow night," Cyril said after another moment's thought. "Yvarden will be working with the stonemasons rebuilding the wall tomorrow, so I'm to study on my own. She didn't say *what* I had to study in particular. While she's gone I can get the supplies I need. And depending on how difficult it is to set up a lattice between

Jenji and me, I may not be able to do the healing spell until the next night."

Ria stifled her disappointment. She'd hoped irrationally that Cyril could heal her that very moment, or at worst that night. But it wasn't Cyril's fault; he *was* only an apprentice mage, after all, and after what he'd told her, she'd much prefer him to take his time and do the spell properly.

As intrigued as Cyril might be by the possibilities of the use of a familiar, however temporary, he was not distracted from other concerns.

"Have you thought about what I said?" he asked with poorly feigned casualness.

Ria sighed. This was the very last discussion in the world she wanted to have now.

"About marrying you?" she asked.

Cyril nodded, his cheeks flaming.

"Cyril, I—" Ria stopped, disturbed by the expression on Cyril's face. Once again she didn't know what to say. Her first impulse was to tell Cyril frankly that she didn't have the least interest in marrying him now or ever, but that would hurt him, and besides, in that case would he still be willing to help her? That sounded horribly selfish even to her; and a second guilty thought followed that one. She'd promised to consider Cyril's proposal seriously, and she hadn't, not really. She didn't *want* to consider it. Everyone's blind assumption that Ria would marry Cyril, whether she liked it or not, made Ria want to refuse just as blindly. And how was she supposed to pretend they hadn't been betrothed, that a forced marriage wasn't looming just ahead of her, when everything and everyone around her conspired to remind her?

"I guess I need more time to think," Ria said reluctantly, expecting Cyril's disappointment, or even anger. To her surprise, however, Cyril smiled with evident relief.

"Do you know, I guess I was afraid you'd just say no," he said, turning back to his dinner. "I might, if I were you, being kept in here like a prisoner. I almost didn't even ask."

Cyril's honesty made Ria feel even more ashamed of her selfishness.

"Look, I can't promise I'll want to marry you," Ria said shyly, "but I promise I won't say no until I've thought about it. *Really* thought about it."

"I'm glad." Cyril smiled again. "Ria, would you mind if —well, if I kissed you?"

Ria grimaced.

"Do you have to?"

"Come on," Cyril coaxed. "Aren't you even a little curious about what it's like?"

"Well—all right," Ria said reluctantly. "Just this once, though."

"All right."

Cyril leaned forward and Ria held her breath, bracing herself, eyes closed tightly. A long moment later, she opened her eyes cautiously. To her outrage, Cyril was holding his hand over his mouth, barely choking back laughter.

"Well?" she demanded.

"I'm sorry, but you should see your face," Cyril gasped. "You looked like someone punched you in the vitals or you bit into a sour apple."

Anger almost obliterated Ria's embarrassment, and she might have in fact punched Cyril if the maneuver would not have required bending her injured leg in a painfully awkward position.

"The next time you ever ask me for anything," Ria said between clenched teeth, "I'm going to tell you what you can—"

She was interrupted as Cyril, no longer laughing, leaned forward and kissed her gently. Ria was so startled that it was over before she clearly realized what had happened.

"I'm sorry," Cyril said sincerely. "I won't laugh at you anymore. It was just—the way you clenched up your face—" A chuckle made its way out of his throat despite his efforts, but he quickly choked it back down. "So how did you like it?"

Ria scowled at that one brief chuckle.

"What's to like? It wasn't anything much."

"Well, it's generally nicer if the woman isn't trying to talk at the same time," Cyril said, grinning, his voice perilously unsteady.

"Oh?" Ria raised an eyebrow. "I suppose you've kissed a lot of women, so you know all about it?"

Cyril flushed crimson and took a good swig of wine to cover his mistake.

"Well, if you'll shut up for just a moment—"

This time Ria was anticipating Cyril's action, but made no effort to move toward him as he leaned over the bed. His lips were warm and gentle on hers, and Ria thought it wasn't as disagreeable and awkward as she'd supposed it would be; when Cyril tilted his head slightly to one side, everything pretty well matched up all right. Still, she couldn't imagine what the appeal was. Maybe it was something only humans enjoyed, something unnatural to elves.

"Well?" Cyril demanded at last.

"Well what?" Ria retorted. Somehow she was vaguely embarrassed and self-conscious, much as if she'd stepped unaware into a pile of dung and everyone knew it but her.

"Well, wasn't it nice?" Cyril asked insistently. "Didn't it make you feel—well, anything?"

"Of course it did," Ria said defensively, bristling again slightly. She *did* feel something, not what Cyril expected, but *something*, mostly annoyance at Cyril for putting her in such a position.

"Does it make you feel like you'd want to do it again?" Cyril suggested.

Ria thought about it.

"No," she said at last. "It makes me feel like my food's getting cold and I'd rather be eating it than playing silly games with our mouths."

Cyril sighed and sat back, poking at his food irritably. Ria sighed, too. Somehow she'd said something wrong, although she'd told him nothing but the truth.

"Look, whatever makes people want to kiss," Ria said awkwardly, "I doubt if it's an aching leg and an empty stomach. I mean, maybe we can try again some other time. All right?"

Cyril looked up, and Ria was relieved when he grinned again.

"All right," he said. "That's only fair, isn't it?"

"Maybe tomorrow I can go with you to the library," Ria said, suddenly daring.

This time Cyril's eyebrows shot up in surprise.

"You? In the library? I thought books and scrolls bored you."

"They do." Ria sighed. "But this room is even more boring. And I can't *do* anything if I can't walk. In the library, at least you'll be there for company. Lord Sharl and Lady Rivkah were always wanting me to look at the city plans and so on anyway, and it's a *different* room."

Cyril grinned and shrugged.

"I don't see why Mother and Father would refuse," he said. "You can hardly run away from the library, and you might as well be sitting there as here. I'll talk to Mother so she won't just think this is some kind of scheme of yours." He hesitated. "Is it?"

Ria sighed again.

"Cyril, I just *told* you. I'm bored. Is that odd? I don't like sitting here with nothing to do but think about how much my leg hurts. Is that a scheme? Where am I going to go from the library, hobbling on one leg and a crutch? Your parents can put guards outside the doorway if they think I'm going to run away. I'm not going to jump out of a window four or five man-heights above the ground, or fly away, am I?"

"All right, all right," Cyril said mildly. "I'll talk to Mother about it this evening and then come for you in the morning."

Despite Cyril's accommodating attitude, Ria was glad when he was gone. His behavior was just too puzzling. For years he'd ignored her, if not avoided her, and now she couldn't seem to be rid of him. Was this a male thing, a human thing, or just a Cyril thing? There was just no understanding him.

It would have been nice, too, if she could talk to someone about it. But there was no one. The servants loved her, but they thought *she* was the strange one. Once Ria had been able to talk to Lady Rivkah or Lord Sharl when life puzzled her, although they rarely seemed to understand her, but since the announcement of the wedding she couldn't imagine confiding in them. Besides, they were both angry with her now, anyway. When she was very young she and Cyril shared secrets as they played games and pranks and filched tidbits from the kitchen, but that time was long past, and besides, they'd never talked about anything too—well, too serious.

Her brother Valann would have understood her. He'd had the upbringing she should have had, among the elves. He'd understand what she felt—and what she didn't feel, too. He'd understand *her.* She wouldn't be some strange oddity, a usually annoying, at best amusing "savage little beast" of no use to anyone except for the alliances she might bring and the children she might bear. Lady Rivkah had told her that human magical lore held that twins shared a special bond of the souls, and hadn't Ria seen him many times in her dreams? To Ria's brother, whose heart had beat in rhythm with her own in their mother's womb for months, she might have some value simply as herself.

Jenji thrummed his humming purr and burrowed under Ria's hair to nuzzle at her neck comfortingly, as if sensing her thoughts. *Mage's familiar.* Perhaps he had. Ria's mother had been a beast-speaker; perhaps Jenji was an elf-speaker?

Ria pulled Jenji down into her arms so she could trace the tufted tips of his ears with her fingertip and gaze into the dark eyes that seemed so uncannily intelligent. Jenji *was* more intelligent than any animal she'd known; he'd taken on his own to perching on the windowsill, his long, fluffy tail curled up over his head for balance, to let his droppings fall out the window. Bored, Ria had quickly found that "training" Jenji was more a simple matter of showing him once what she wanted.

Mage's familiar.

Was her don't-see-me magic? Could Jenji help her use it as he might be able to help a mage? But how could he? Ria couldn't cast the spell Cyril had mentioned to link the familiar to her; in fact, Ria couldn't cast any spell at all. Even when she made herself unseen she cast no spell—or did she? Lady Rivkah no longer needed incantations, braziers, and the like. Perhaps Ria was in fact using magic—elvan magic, magic of a different kind. But there was no way to tell Jenji what she wanted.

Ria placed Jenji on the covers, blocking him with her hand when he tried to scamper back toward her. "Stay." Jenji chittered unhappily, but stayed where he was when she took her hand away.

Ria closed her eyes and concentrated hard on making herself small, insignificant, unseen, just another wrinkle in the covers in the middle of the bed. She opened her eyes and saw Jenji crouching where she'd put him, gazing directly into her eyes, thrumming excitedly, shifting eagerly from paw to paw. Obviously she wasn't invisible to *him.* Either that, or he was indeed a magic-spotter and could sense her in some way that was not precisely ordinary sight. If only Ria shared her mother's ability to speak to the minds of beasts. Better yet, if only Ria could speak to the mind of her brother!

Frustrated, Ria let her concentration slip away, scooped up Jenji, and curled herself into a small ball under the covers. Her leg throbbed painfully, and Ria sat up again, growling to herself as she reached for the bell cord. To her relief, the maid who answered the bell was Lizette, Ria's favorite among the servants, a kind-hearted matron who had traveled to Allanmere with them.

"My leg hurts," Ria told Lizette. "Would you ask Lady Rivkah if I could have a sleeping potion?" She sighed plaintively. "Although she'll probably say no."

"Poor little creetur," Lizette sighed, patting Ria's cheek with a soap-roughened hand. "She might indeed, she's that angry." Her eyes twinkled. "Say you so, I'll just ask Yvarden instead? The High Lady's that busy, she shouldn't be fretted, eh?" She hurried away, returning quickly with a tray.

"Oh, Lizette, thank you," Ria said relievedly, gulping

down the potion and then sipping more slowly the hot broth Lizette had thoughtfully brought to take away the bitter flavor of the potion. Yvarden, like Lizette, had been a kindly, if secret, champion of Ria's almost since her birth. Ria was as tired of sleeping as she was of lying in bed and staring at the walls of her room, but at least this way the time would pass more quickly.

"Not a word, pet, not a word," Lizette said, chuckling. "Sleep 'ee sound and mend fast."

The hot broth in her belly and the sleeping potion conspired to carry Ria away in warm arms. Ria welcomed sleep, thinking again about her brother. How nice it would be if she could talk to him, tell him all her troubles. And what would he have to tell her? What secrets had he learned in his sixteen years among the elves? He'd have so much to teach her, if only she could—if only—

Ria drifted on the surface of a warm wave of drowsiness as she'd often floated in the pond near Emaril's keep, neither entirely awake or asleep. It seemed that somehow she was not alone, that a comforting, familiar presence was nearby, almost close enough to touch. Instinctively Ria tried to reach out to that presence as she might have lazily stroked her way across that same pond, felt the desired presence even closer, closer, but never quite close enough.

(Valann!) she tried to call, fighting the potion now as it pulled her down into deep sleep, away from the familiar presence.

(Come to the forest. Come home. Come soon.)

Another wave of sleep, too strong to fight. For some undefinable time she surrendered weakly, then again half woke, struggling to recall that brief moment of contact, fighting until she was —

—folded in warm arms, small hands stroking boldly over skin that shivered with pleasure, lips opening under lips, fire that raced along nerves that sang with delight, the exquisite friction of warm skin on warm skin—

Ria stretched and moaned as unfamiliar sensations coursed through her body, sighing as—

—thighs parted only to clasp muscled hips, hesitant

hands explored more feverishly, muscles tensed in pleasure almost too great to bear—

Ria bolted upright in her bed, suddenly wide awake, arms wrapped around her slender body as though to hold something in. Great gods, she'd had odd dreams from time to time, but nothing the likes of *that!* Her cheeks were inexplicably flaming, her skin still stippled with gooseflesh, her body filled with a strange sort of hunger. Was this an effect of the sleeping potion, or could this be something caused by Cyril's kiss? For a moment Ria considered calling a maid to fetch Cyril, but a sudden reluctance seized her. If one kiss had put such odd feelings in her head, what might that kiss have done to Cyril? What if it made him want to kiss her again, or do something else, something like—well, like she'd dreamed of?

Ria shivered again.

Would that be so bad?

Ria shook her head and curled back down into the covers. Those feelings she had dreamed seemed somehow too big for her. Sex was for women with breasts and rounded hips, women who bled every month, not for skinny younglings like her—

Unless, a nagging thought whispered, *elves are different. Maybe elves don't grow like human women. Maybe elves just stay like this forever.* Lady Rivkah had often marveled at how small and childlike Chyrie and her mate Valann had seemed.

How was Ria to know? Who was she to ask?

The elves, of course.

Ria set her mouth firmly and carried that thought down into thankfully dreamless sleep.

VIII

Valann

Dusk shook his head again, touching Lahti's belly as if he could not believe what his healing sense felt there. Lahti smiled and clasped Valann's hand. It would be moon cycles before her belly began to swell, but she had assured Valann that she could feel the first faint changes in her body that indicated that new life was growing there, and by the time they'd made their way back to Inner Heart, Val could detect the slight change in her scent as her time of ripeness ended.

"That the two of you could be so foolish shames everyone who has taught you," Rowan scolded. "I can't imagine what inspired the two of you to act so irresponsibly."

Valann laid his arm comfortingly around Lahti's shoulders, pulling her close.

"It was Lahti's choice," he said stoutly. "It was my choice. I could no more have refused her than I could have forced her against her wish."

"And you," Rowan said, turning to Lahti, "did you spare any thought to what the clan would say when they learned what you'd done? To couple when you have not yet been

146

judged and accepted by the Mother Forest is strictly forbidden, and to conceive a child doubly so, and for very good reason indeed. And now you cannot take your passage, not with a child in your womb who might be harmed by the passage trials and potions. If you'd danced the High Circle and one of the Hawk's Eyes had been the man to sow the seed, he couldn't be blamed for his part in your foolishness—he'd have no way to know you hadn't yet taken your passage. But Valann knew better."

"I wanted a child of Valann's seed," Lahti said staunchly, although there was a slight quaver in her voice. "I couldn't bear to waste my time of ripeness. I might never have had another. And I didn't want my first coupling to be with a stranger. It's not Valann's fault. He tried to dissuade me despite his desire. I'll bear the consequences of my decision."

"And did you spare any thought for the consequences to your child?" Rowan persisted. "Do you know why such a mating is forbidden? It's said that a child born to a mother or father not judged spirit-whole by the Mother Forest will be born awry. Was that, too, a chance you didn't hesitate to take?"

"It's possible that our child might be born awry," Valann said adamantly. "It's possible that any child might be born awry. Many women who have long since made their passage into adulthood have suffered such misfortune. Every elf who bears a child or fathers one faces such a chance."

"I'm to blame," Dusk said suddenly, laying his hand on Rowan's arm. "If I hadn't helped Lahti pursue Valann, she'd have been here when she began to ripen. If I had thought to examine her, I might have sensed the change in her body. Those failures are mine, not Lahti's. What woman would miss her chance to bear a child when such a chance might never come again, and what man would refuse her? Words—even laws—are small beside that desire." He turned to Lahti. "I have taught you. I have touched your spirit many times. There's no doubt in my heart that the Mother Forest will accept you. I'll speak to the clan as your teacher and its Gifted One."

"And I'll speak to them as well," Rowan relented, sighing. "But, Lahti, you know that each member of our clan will make his or her own judgment, and you know full well how some of them will react. It would have been easier, perhaps, if you'd chosen another instead of—" She hesitated, glancing at Val.

"Instead of Chyrie's half-human whelp whom many of our women would never choose for their High Circles," Val finished bitterly. "Many of the elders fear what would happen if I sired children of my mixed blood. Would my offspring be strange creatures like me, no true elf, gifted in ways not of our kind, or even born awry because of the mixing of the bloods? That's what they think, even if they don't say it aloud."

Rowan shook her head, but not in denial.

"What you say is true," she said regretfully. "Unfortunately those fears will only add, Lahti, to the clan's displeasure at your choice. Until your child is born and shown to be born whole, it may likely be that—" She stopped, gesturing awkwardly.

"That I will be shunned by my clan and my kin," Lahti said quietly. "Valann and I spoke of it on our journey home from the Hawk's Eye's lands."

"Lahti will share my hut, even though we're not mated," Val said quietly. The thought of their own people treating Lahti in such a way infuriated him. He'd been subtly set apart by some of his clan all his life, but no matter how he'd hated it, it was understandable: He was different, undeniably so. But Lahti was one of their own in every way. "My hut is already at the farthest edge of the village. I'm a good hunter, as is Lahti. If the other hunters will no longer hunt with me, we'll still not lack for meat."

Rowan made a dismissive gesture.

"Valann, you're being foolish. No elf in this clan, no matter how great her anger, would allow a mother with child to want for food or any other comfort, nor fail to protect them from danger. I spoke only of unkind words."

"She won't have to hear them for now at least," Valann said quickly. "We came only to tell you what happened at the west edge of the forest and to learn if Lahti had conceived. I'm prepared to start west again immediately, and Lahti with me. She'll be safe enough in the Hawk's Eyes' care."

"Valann, I've considered your suggestions since you returned," Rowan said slowly. "I don't agree that we should send you as an envoy to the city, not now. After the Blue-eyes attacked your sister, the humans' anger will be great and their guards will be more than ready to shoot their arrows at anyone who comes near the city, especially if they're seen coming out of the forest. I doubt you could safely come close enough to the city for the guards to even notice your human appearance, and who could fault them for that? With regard to the attack on your sister and her companion, you acted properly, and I'm more grateful than I can say for the message of friendship you bring from the Hawk's Eyes, but there's nothing more to be done for now."

"How can you say that?" Lahti protested. "We saw Ria injured, perhaps badly, by a Blue-eyes arrow. How can we not send envoys to the city to show our concern and learn how she's fared?"

"You are both so young," Dusk murmured, his eyes fastened on some distant spot. "Before the invasion, the humans of the city were as much enemies to us as we were to them. Even when we made our peace with the lord of the city, even when we showed ourselves their friends, their allies in battle, there were those in the city who bore us nothing but ill will. Now that the lord's daughter-by-love has been injured by elves, we dare expect no friendship from them. Now we must wait for the humans to come to us in their own time. And in any wise Lahti, with child, could not risk such a dangerous journey through other territories; you both know that."

Valann started to protest that no elf in the forest, not even Blue-eyes, would ever harm a woman with child, but Dusk anticipated his thought and silenced him with a raised hand.

"Look at Lahti and you can't see that she's with child,"

he said gently. "Smell her and the scent of ripeness is gone, and the scent of a childbearing woman hasn't yet developed. She could wear the green band of fertility and the blue band of pregnancy, but one hasty arrow fired before the elf saw those bands might end her life and her child's. It's one thing to take that risk with a child who might one day be a fertile woman, but another entirely to risk the life of a fertile woman carrying a child."

Rowan nodded sternly in agreement.

"There's no more to be said," she said. "Valann, I've been lenient with you on this matter. I encouraged you to walk into danger because of Dusk's vision, and it's well that you were able to save your sister from harm and perhaps death, but there's nothing more to be gained by endangering yourself and Lahti further, not now. I am your Eldest and I have spoken."

Val glowered, but Lahti shook her head at him, and he bit back his protest.

"Thank you, Grandmother," Lahti said quietly, but Val was too angry for the customary pleasantries, and he rose to follow Lahti from the hut.

"Valann. Wait." Rowan's voice was sympathetic, but Val could hear that it was still the Eldest of Inner Heart speaking to him, and, grinding his teeth, he turned around.

"Dusk and I will speak now to the adults of the clan on Lahti's behalf," Rowan said gently. "Please, Valann, it's your right to be present, as it is Lahti's despite her childhood, but for Lahti's sake, I'd ask that you both stay away."

Hot anger flared—how could Rowan expect Lahti not to speak for herself, or him to stand by her side and support her?—immediately subsiding into confusion. Rowan was his mother in all but blood. Dusk had been Lahti's mentor for years. They had no reason to want Lahti to suffer, and Rowan, as Eldest, had every reason to want harmony and goodwill within the clan. They'd argue as fiercely in Lahti's behalf as Val and Lahti themselves could. And in the end, what would Lahti's presence gain but to force her to listen to angry words that would hurt her? And what would Val's presence do but make everyone even angrier if Val lost his temper, which he was bound to do?

"All right," Val said quietly. "We'll move Lahti's belongings to my hut."

Val conveyed Rowan's words to Lahti, and Lahti was no happier than he expected she would be; to his surprise, however, unlike Val, she was only tiredly grateful that she would not have to stand before the adults of the clan and face their anger—or worse, their disgust.

"Why should I speak to them?" Lahti said, shrugging. "There's nothing more to be said. I knew the consequences when I made my decision, and I'd choose the same again." She smiled at Val, her eyes regaining some of their sparkle. "Would you?"

Val chuckled, sweeping Lahti into his arms and tickling her neck with the short growth of his beard until she laughed helplessly.

"I swear by the Mother Forest I would, and in my hut, I'll gladly prove it again and again," he murmured into her ear.

"Stop, Val," Lahti gasped when she regained her breath. "You should be thinking of your sister, or have you forgotten her, when only a short time ago her safety was your greatest worry?"

That sobered Val; he'd all but forgotten her indeed in his concern for Lahti. This time he could not help but doubt Rowan's wisdom, and said as much. Inner Heart had waited sixteen years and no one had come to them; what was to be gained by more waiting? The humans did not have Dusk's vision to urge them to action. They would never allow Ria near the forest now, not after she'd been hurt. And even if Ria was to come to them, how could she make her way past the border clans, especially the fierce Blue-eyes, and find her way safely to Inner Heart when she'd never been in the forest? No, she'd need help, help that Rowan had forbidden him to give.

It was a simple matter to claim Lahti's few belongings from the small woven-switch bower Lahti had been using since Val had left the child-pack, preferring the treetops to the hide tents Val had used. By the time they finished this errand and reached the edge of the village, although Lahti had said nothing while Val spoke, her twinkling eyes and serene face made Val realize that while she hadn't argued with Rowan's pronouncement, she probably had no thought of obeying it.

When they reached Val's hut, however, Val realized that Rowan and Dusk had already anticipated their rebellion; a small owl, one that Dusk worked with frequently, was perched above the door flap of the hut and eyeing them sternly. Val scowled, but followed Lahti into the hut without speaking.

"It's no matter," Lahti murmured when Val had lowered the door flap and tied it securely closed. "We're both weary and need time to rest after our journey."

"What of my sister?" Val demanded. "You were the one to remind me of her. How does she rest? I've heard that Blue-eyes often poison their arrows."

"It's taken us three days to return from the western edge of the forest on the deer Silence summoned for us," Lahti said patiently. "Even if we set out to return this moment, without Dusk to summon deer for us, we'd have to go on foot, and it would take days more. Even if we walked directly to the city and were accepted in without trouble, by the time we arrived we would be too late to do your sister any good. The Blue-eyes' poison is simple and slow. The human healers will be able to help your sister."

"Then she may be dead already," Val said softly. The thought made him feel suddenly cold inside, terribly alone. By the Mother Forest, how close he'd come to her! Only a few dozen paces more and he'd have been bringing her home to Inner Heart. He sighed bitterly. Yes, only a few dozen paces had stood between him and his sister—that, and a dozen angry Blue-eyes and their weapons.

"If your spirit is close enough to your sister's to feel her presence, you would have felt her death," Lahti said with certainty. "We'll find a way to go to her. Dusk said that you would meet, did he not?"

"No," Val said with a sigh. "He said that I was walking to

meet her with a gift, not that I *would* meet her. But I had no gift for her."

"Then there's a second journey that we must make," Lahti said patiently. "And you can give her no gift unless you meet, and she cannot accept your gift if she's dead."

"What makes you believe I'd feel her death?" Val asked warily. "I felt her presence, but only then. I've never known what's befallen her before."

"Dusk's often told me what he learned of the other clans," Lahti told him. "He said some of the clans had a silent speech, the gift of hearing another's thoughts as a beast-speaker can hear the thoughts of a beast. Your mother's people, the Wilding Clan, had that silent speech. As her children, you and Ria may share that gift."

"Then why can't I feel her now, know what's happened to her?" Val asked, shaking his head.

"There could be many reasons," Lahti reassured him. "Your gift and Ria's may be weaker because your blood isn't pure. You've never trained your gift, and any of our gifts are weak until they're trained and practiced, just as your bow arm was weak and clumsy at first. And especially, she's likely much too far away. I can't heal without touching, and you can't make fire from far away, either. Likely you need to be closer to her, as you were in the Blue-eyes' territory, before your spirits can touch, especially when your gift is unused and weak as it likely is now."

"But sometimes I've seen her in my dreams," Val protested. "And she was likely even farther away then." He scowled. "But those were only dreams."

"Your spirit journeys away from your body in dreams," Lahti said, nodding. "I'd guess that as close in spirit as you and Ria must be, being born at one birth, your spirits are drawn together in dreams." She met Val's eyes. "You saw her in your passage dream, didn't you, more clearly than before?"

Val hesitated instinctively. It was forbidden to discuss passage dreams with—no. Lahti *was* an adult. He had to believe that.

"I saw her," he admitted. "And my mother."

"Sometimes such gifts are wakened, or trained, by dreaming potions," Lahti said, nodding, "because such potions free the spirit for longer journeys."

Val sat up suddenly.

"Do you think if I had another dreaming potion, that I could speak to her in my thoughts? Even only learn whether she's alive?" he asked anxiously.

"Val," Lahti said reprovingly. "You know Dusk will never give you the potion."

Val was silent for a long moment.

"Could you make the potion?" he asked. "You've been learning from Dusk for years now."

"I could make the potion," Lahti said thoughtfully. "But I don't have all the herbs and roots and such for it. And this is the wrong time of year to gather some of them." She looked into Val's eyes and relented. "Dusk has all the ingredients. I could go to Rowan's hut and get them; I'm sure he's still talking to the other adults at the firepit. But Dusk'll be terribly angry if he finds out, and his owl is just outside the hut, watching for us to try to leave the village."

"I'll lure the bird away," Val said quickly, "if you can fetch whatever you'll need back here."

Lahti hesitated, then nodded.

"The potion didn't do you any harm before," she said slowly. "And that was when you were weakened by fasting and by your passage trials. I suppose it's safe enough for you to take again."

There was little time for a plan, not if Lahti was to get to Rowan and Dusk's hut and back before the conference around the fire was over. Val simply stepped outside the door, scowled at the owl, and slipped into the undergrowth; as he'd expected, the owl followed, fluttering from branch to branch to watch him. Having nowhere better to go, Val began working his way around the edge of the village just far enough away that any elves still in their huts wouldn't hear him.

When he reached the point nearest the firepit, Val was both anxious and relieved to see that apparently there was still a discussion taking place around the fire. Rowan was standing, her sharp gestures indicating that she was upset, if not angry. Occasionally a sharp tone reached him, hers or someone else's, but he was too far away to make out the words. He considered creeping closer to hear what was being said, but Dusk might at any time look through the eyes of his owl and know. Val sighed and continued onward, not hurrying, until he'd made an entire circuit of the whole Inner Heart village; then he stalled a little longer by backtracking a bit to use the privy pits.

By this time, Lahti had had ample opportunity for her secret errand to Rowan's tent, so Val strolled back to their hut more directly. As he crossed the small section of the village between the privy pits and his hut, he noticed that some of the adults were trickling back to their huts from the firepit. Only a few saw him, but of those few Val was dismayed to see that there was more than one angry scowl directed toward him, and one elf, Garad, a kinsman of Rowan's, turned aside so his path would not cross Valann's.

A hot surge of anger almost froze Val in his tracks. If this was how *he* was treated—and very little of the fault rested with him; no male elf could really be expected to refuse a ripe female who asked for his seed—how much worse could Lahti expect? For a moment he stood there shaking with anger, longing more than anything to seize Garad and hit him again and again with his fists until that superior, disapproving expression on his face was obliterated by blood and bruises; then he painfully choked down his fury and continued on his way. Fighting with Garad would accomplish nothing but turning even more of the clan against him and Lahti. He quickly decided he'd say nothing to Lahti of what he'd seen of the clan's reaction. She'd learn the full extent of the clan's disapproval soon enough—all too soon, to his way of thinking. Let her have a little peace and contentment while she could.

When Val slipped back through the door flap to his hut, Lahti was pouring a thick liquid from a bowl into a wooden cup.

"The potion's ready," she said, motioning to him to sit on the furs beside her.

"So quickly?" Val asked, surprised.

Lahti smiled sheepishly.

"I took the bowl with me and mixed the ingredients there in Rowan and Dusk's hut," she admitted. "I wanted to be certain I used exactly the proper proportions, and I thought if I carried jars and pouches out of the hut, Dusk would surely miss them. So I brought it back mixed and ready except for the honey and wine to dissolve it in. I didn't think you'd wish to delay, worrying about your sister. Are you ready?"

The last of Val's anger faded in a warm wash of love. Lahti was still weary from their journey; she'd not had so much as time for a bath, and the joy of her ripening and pregnancy had been marred by the certain disapproval of the clan. Yet she'd set all that aside in her concern for him, and her sympathy for his worry for his sister. Yes, he'd have to persuade her to be his mate. This was the woman he wanted to spend his life with, the Mother Forest knew!

"I'm ready," he said, reaching over to caress Lahti's cheek.

"Then drink, and sleep on the furs so there's no danger you'll tumble from your sling bed," Lahti said, smiling warmly, clasping his hand against her cheek. "I'm not giving you enough of the potion for a full night's dreaming, but a smaller portion, such as Dusk takes to seek his visions. I'll watch over you while you sleep."

"There's no need for that," he said gently. "You should bathe and sleep yourself. I spent the entire night lying alone on an altar under this potion with no ill effects. Even sleeping, I'm sure you would wake if you heard me in any distress."

Lahti smiled but said nothing, and Val sighed; she'd do as she pleased, say what he might. But, then, would he love her so if it weren't for that occasionally annoying stubbornness?

Val swallowed the potion. The thick, syrupy liquid had been disagreeable before, when he'd fasted for days and almost *anything* would have tasted good; now, however, he found the taste almost unbearable. He finished every drop, however, gladly accepting the cup of broth Lahti gave him to wash away the bittersweet taste.

This time, likely because he'd not been fasting and weakened by the trials, the potion took longer to affect him. Val had plenty of time to undress and settle himself comfortably on the furs before drowsiness began to wash over him in slow, warm waves. His last awareness was of Lahti sitting at his side, silhouetted fetchingly against the firelight, her hand warm and gentle against his forehead. Then he let the potion draw him gently downward.

This time, too, he knew better what to expect, and he was less afraid as he sank deep into the earth, toward that hot, pulsing center of life. He'd made this journey before unharmed, and this time he'd need no guide to find his way; there'd be no aimless wandering through the chaos. Almost as soon as he pictured the still pool at the center of his mind, he was there. Was this the same place Dusk came to seek his visions?

He concentrated on Ria's face as he'd seen it in his few precious dreaming encounters, trying to fix it in his mind. Where was she? Was she well? Was she, perhaps, thinking of him? It was late, and she'd likely be sleeping; perhaps her spirit would be wandering, too, in dreams.

Val called to her in his thoughts, as he'd called for help during his passage, trying to picture Ria's face before him. He grew frustrated as nothing happened. Was he doing this wrong? But what else could he do? He was here, he was calling, wasn't he? If only someone had thought to teach him! If only he'd asked to learn!

He turned to the still pool before him. He'd seen Chyrie's reflection there before. Perhaps—he tried to picture Ria's face reflected there in the water, her blue-green eyes, still hazy with sleep, meeting his—

Something seemed to flex weakly within him, like a muscle long disused, then more strongly, and suddenly Val felt a presence near, a familiar presence and yet unfamiliar—

Startled.

(WHO COMES HERE?)

Val was rocked with the force of that question, as he might have been rocked by a blast of sudden fierce wind, as he might be nearly swept away by a deep creek fast and full in flood. Was it one voice or many? He had the strangest feeling that there were two voices—one male, one female—so interwoven as to be almost indistinguishable from each other, with some tremendous force behind them that almost overshadowed both.

For a moment Val was too terrified to answer, but he forced himself to stand firm. He'd been here before, hadn't he? Grimly he remembered the sound of Blue-eyes' arrows whistling toward his sister, and anger washed away the fear. This time, perhaps because of his anger, whatever flexed deep within him felt more strong and sure.

(I am Valann, son of Chyrie, and I seek my sister's spirit,) Val thought boldly. (I won't return until I find her.)

Vast surprise, so powerful that Val was almost thrown back into chaos. For a moment it seemed that the entire universe around him rocked with the force of that astonishment. Then confusion almost as great as the surprise, as if the voice he'd heard had suddenly split in two and was arguing with itself.

(RIA?) Image of a tiny baby, delicate face framed in black curls, great blue-green eyes sparkling. Sudden pain, longing that tore through Val's heart.

(HERE?) Dizzying flashes of the Heartwood as if seen through a thousand different eyes, spinning across the length and width of the forest and back again so that for a moment Val's mind refused to accept it all. (WHERE? HOW?)

For a moment Val was too bewildered to realize that the questions were directed at him. A blast of worry/confusion/impatience rocked him again, and before he recovered something swept through him with the force of a forest stream in spring flood, washing his memories up to light.

The battle with the Blue-eyes, Val as frightened as he was furious, utterly certain that those arrows were whistling death at his own sister.

(HOW COULD WE NOT SEE HER? HOW COULD WE NOT KNOW?)

The same battle, but from a different perspective, as if he looked down from a tree through eyes unaccustomed to darkness, roused from drowsy sleep by screams.

Sleepy forest denizens fleeing in confusion as arrows whistled, as shouts echoed through what had been quiet forest.

Nighttime creatures fleeing too, terrified, as burning arrows dazzled their eyes. Fire, the universal fear. Brief confusing image of two forms stumbling from the forest, too fleeting for comprehension over all the fear, confusion, need for flight. Then the sounds decreasing, the forest slowly regaining its equilibrium. The intruders were gone.

(RIA.) Great sadness. Sense of irrevocable loss.

(She's near, in the city,) Val thought desperately. Could this strange duality be his mother? By the Mother Forest, what had she become? Ah, yes. By the Mother Forest indeed. (I want to go to her. Help me find her.)

Sudden change of perspective, perhaps a memory—soaring, flying, leaving the forest, sudden frightening great sky around him, so open, so naked and vulnerable, and ahead, the great stone city—

(NO!!)

Fleeting images of stone closing in around him, the earth shattering beneath him, fire, pain, death—

(NO!!)

Sudden wrenching twist, wresting him from the vision. He was standing beside the pool again. Silence.

(Please,) Val thought again, more urgently. (I want to go to her in the city. Help me find her.)

(NO.) Brief flashing vision of the city, shudder of fear. (NO. NOT THERE. BRING HER HERE TO YOU. TO US.)

(How?) Val repeated. (Show me how.)

Brief flash of impatience. Abruptly a giant hand seemed to seize him and fling him outward into chaos. Terrified, Val felt a part of himself flailing desperately for purchase, for some anchor, but there was nothing to hold, no point of familiarity—

There! Eagerly, almost desperately, Val seized on that one solid awareness within all the confusion. Then the sense of recognition.

(Ria!)

Drowsy fog, only vague awareness, as if she only half noticed him, as if she hadn't the strength to respond. Was she ill, or was her skill that much weaker than his own?

(Come to me,) he thought as strongly as he could. (Come to the forest, come home, come soon.)

Vague understanding, some sense of agreement and longing, but without any clear response. Slowly she faded away again. Either she was too weak to contact him clearly or he was too unskilled. He could feel, too, that the effects of the potion were fading. Well, he'd done what he could. She'd come, or she wouldn't.

Slowly he awakened. The hut was almost dark, the fire burned low, but Lahti was still beside him. She smiled and caressed his cheek when he turned his head to look at her.

"You dreamed only a few hours this time," she said. "Did you find your sister's spirit?"

"I'm not certain," Val admitted, sighing. "I believe I did, but I'm not sure she knew it. At least I know she lives."

Lahti patted his hand.

"She lives, and she's but a short journey away, closer than she's been in sixteen years," she said encouragingly. "Now that you know, we needn't rush away at the first opportunity. We'll have time to make a plan to slip away when Dusk and his winged messengers become a little less vigilant."

Val found her reasoning less than perfect, but there was no use in saying it. Neither did he tell Lahti that in one respect he had to agree with Rowan: He no longer had any intention of taking Lahti with him, not if he had to creep away from Inner Heart against Rowan's wishes. Rowan and Dusk would surely know where he was going, and they'd send word to Hawk's Eye by way of one of Dusk's birds. If the Hawk's Eyes found Val and Lahti in their territory, they'd capture Lahti and likely Valann, too—oh, most respectfully, of course—and take them back to Inner Heart. And even if Val and Lahti could slip unseen through Hawk's Eye's lands, Val could scarcely take Lahti to the human city. Unlike the elves, humans placed no special value on fertility and pregnancy; Rowan had told him as much, and that meant that Lahti's pregnancy would not keep her from harm in the human city. The prospect of taking her with him into hostile territories when Lahti was still a child had been almost unthinkable; he certainly would not risk taking her into much greater danger now that she was pregnant. But there was no use in saying that, either; Lahti would only argue, or say nothing and find a way to follow him as she had before. No, this time he would have to find a way not only to elude Dusk's watchers, but Lahti as well.

"Perhaps you're right," he said, sighing again. "But I'm relieved to learn that my sister's alive."

Lahti lay down comfortably on the furs beside him.

"Isn't that a fine cause for celebration?" she smiled.

"But even better than that," Val said deliberately, "is the child you'll bear. What greater cause of celebration could there be?"

Lahti laughed with delight and came eagerly to his arms.

IX

RIA

• By midday Ria was rather less hopeful than she'd been the night before. Under the guise of studying Allanmere's history, she'd perused the maps made of the forest area during the invasion. According to those maps, the road to the center of the forest should have been just where Ria had looked for it. The territory Lord Sharl and Lady Rivkah had approached on the south side of the forest should have belonged to the Brightwater clan, too, and not the Blue-eyes. Obviously a great deal had changed in the forest in sixteen years. There was no knowing where it might be safe to enter the forest, where Ria might encounter elves who might help her, or at least not try to shoot her full of arrows before she could even tell them what she wanted.

Of course, that might have happened simply because of Cyril's presence. She couldn't risk a similar misunderstanding; this time she'd have to slip away without his help and knowledge, or he'd certainly insist on accompanying her. No, all she could hope was that he was mage enough to cast a healing spell so she could walk, and the rest would be up to her.

Of more interest were the accounts kept by Lord Sharl and Lady Rivkah of their experiences with the elves—in the forest, and among the elves who had stayed in the city during the invasion. Lady Rivkah had taught both Cyril and Ria all of the elvan customs and rituals that she'd learned, and she'd told them both wonderful stories of what she'd seen in the forest, but the notes told the stories Lady Rivkah *hadn't* shared—stories of elves dancing naked by the firelight or running naked through the rain, coupling out in the open in broad daylight or in groups in their huts. It appeared that the elves were very interested indeed in reproduction—including all of its preliminaries. Ria chuckled. Just the sort of thing Lady Rivkah *wouldn't* have told two curious children.

At the same time, however, Ria felt a vague sense of disappointment. So the elves *were* just as concerned with coupling and kissing and other such odd behavior as the humans were. She'd somehow hoped that her elvan kin would behave more sensibly. Apparently that was not the case. Why, then, was Ria different? Was it because of her odd mixture of bloods?

"What are you reading?" Cyril asked idly, glancing up from the grimoire he was studying.

"Just some old histories," Ria said, hurriedly shutting the book. She felt warmth flood into her cheeks. It was hard even to meet his eyes this morning after last night's dream. "Why?"

"You were laughing," Cyril said, raising an eyebrow. "I thought it might be something interesting."

"No, not very," Ria said with forced casualness, placing the book back on the shelf where she'd found it. Somehow she didn't want Cyril reading what she'd read about the elves. Who knew what kind of ideas those passages might put into his head? "What about you? Are you finding what you wanted?"

"Mmm-hmmm. Come and look, if you want."

Ria limped over with the aid of the crutch Lady Rivkah

had given her and looked. She'd expected a magical grimoire to be more elegant-looking, perhaps more—well, mysterious. It was only a large book, however, with a scuffed and battered leather cover, with neat writing covering the parchment. Interspersed with the script were a few arcane diagrams and sketches, and less identifiable symbols.

"That's it?" Ria asked disappointedly. She pointed to an odd-looking pattern of converging lines and curves. Trying to follow the intricate patterns with her eyes made her feel vaguely dizzy. "What's that?"

"That's the lattice structure of magical energies," Cyril said. "It's not as complicated as I was afraid it would be. I'll show you a really tough one." He leafed back a few pages and pointed. "Look at this one."

Ria glanced at the pattern and gasped, hurriedly grasping the edge of the table as the world seemed to spin dizzily. Her stomach heaved, and for a moment she thought she might vomit; when her vision cleared, Cyril had closed the book and risen to his feet, supporting her with one strong arm around her waist.

"What's the matter?" he asked worriedly. "Here, sit down."

"I don't know." Ria was only too glad to let Cyril help her down to the stool he had previously occupied. "I just looked at that thing and it—it made me sick to look at it."

"Oh?" Cyril's eyebrows lifted. "You must have a little magic in you yourself, even if it's not enough for magery, or it wouldn't have affected you. I always thought you might have a little of the gift, the way you seem to disappear sometimes, but if Mother had thought you had enough to train, she'd have—well, sorry, I didn't know. Anyway, the healing spell's simple enough. I'd try it even without a familiar if I could practice first on some of the livestock. I'll try linking up with Jenji tonight, and if that works well, I'll have the materials for the healing spell with me." He glanced down at Ria's bandaged leg. "Still want to trust me with it?"

"If you knew how this hurts," Ria said wryly, "you

wouldn't ask. I can usually get potions for the pain, but then all I do is sleep all the time. Which your mother would probably like, but I'm just—"

"—too stubborn to sit still and quietly take her punishment," Cyril said. "I can't say I would, either. All right. Ready for me to help you back to your room? It's almost time for dinner."

"You don't have to," Ria said hastily. There were a good many stairs between the library and her room, and Ria had stifled several yelps of pain hobbling to the library that morning; tired now, she had no confidence in her ability to make the trip again. She wanted Cyril to go on without her, so he wouldn't witness the indignity of Ria having to call a servant and ask him to carry her back.

"I don't mind." Cyril handed Ria the book, then looped her arm around his shoulders; before Ria realized what he was doing, he'd slid his free hand under her knees and lifted her from the chair. "Oof. You're heavier than I thought."

"It's not me," Ria protested, embarrassed. "It's this book that weighs almost as much as I do."

Cyril kindly refrained from any further criticism, although he was wheezing unflatteringly by the time he reached Ria's room. Whether because of his own embarrassment at the effort it took him to carry the tiny Ria (plus the weighty book) or because of his eagerness to start his preparation for the spells, Cyril left quickly, and Ria was once again alone with Jenji and her thoughts. She hoped to nap until Cyril returned—the pain and exertion after days of bed rest had all but exhausted her—but she'd hardly more than settled herself when Lizette appeared with her dinner and insisted on sitting and watching Ria eat every bite; then Lady Rivkah intruded to tend Ria's leg. The High Lady appeared to be in a more sympathetic mood this afternoon, and to Ria's surprise she was wearing her plain tunic and trousers instead of her surcoat.

"You were wanting to see the market," Lady Rivkah said as she smoothed the wrinkles out of the bandage around Ria's leg. "You've been so miserable here in your room, I thought you might enjoy a ride through the rebuilt parts of the city. I've arranged a cart, if you aren't too tired after your morning in the library."

As tired as she'd been, and as angry as she'd been at Lady Rivkah, the prospect of going *outside,* even for a moment, was the most wonderful idea Ria had ever heard.

"I'd like that," Ria said eagerly. Then she stopped. "But why a cart? Won't a carriage be better?"

"Because we haven't gotten a carriage made yet," Lady Rivkah said matter-of-factly, patting Ria's shoulder, "and likely won't for some time, not when there are so many more important things to be done. Some of the roads are still too blocked for a carriage to get through, besides, but a small cart should be fine. Sharl's been all around the city, but I've hardly had a chance for a good look myself, so if you don't mind a simple, probably bumpy cart and me for your driver, we'll go now."

Ria was out of the bed so quickly that her leg's quick change of position from horizontal to vertical brought tears of pain to her eyes. Lady Rivkah kindly refrained from laughing at her charge's discomfort, and spared her foster daughter's pride, too, by helping Ria down the stairs to the front hall herself, where a narrow pony cart had been pulled up almost to the door. Ria settled herself as comfortably as possible, fuming at the delay while Lady Rivkah tucked pillows under her legs. Jenji took his favorite perch on Ria's shoulder, dancing from paw to paw in his excitement at being outside. It was wonderful just to breathe the fresh air and feel the warm sun on her skin, but she wanted to get as far from the keep as she could, if only for a few hours.

The cart ride was as bumpy as Lady Rivkah had predicted, and Ria was quickly glad for the cushioning pillows; she was soon forced to transfer Jenji to her lap to avoid being constantly throttled by the chirrit's tail around her neck. To Ria's disappointment, Lady Rivkah avoided the eastern section of the city nearest the forest—that would have been a good opportunity to look for probable escape routes—because the eastern and southern sections were still in the poorest condition.

"What are all those buildings?" Ria asked, pointing to the large open area at the northeast end of the city. There were only a few structures there, and only two had been rebuilt.

"Those were temples," Lady Rivkah told her. "There are only the two active now, devoted to the gods Urex and Vittmar the Weeper."

"Why put them all the way over there by themselves?" Ria wondered.

"That was Sharl's idea," Lady Rivkah said. "He believes that because of all the merchants and traders who will come through Allanmere, many priests will want to build temples here, and he planned a whole section of the city for them to use. Someday there may be dozens of temples in our city, and the influx of worshippers will help increase trade, too."

Ria was relatively uninterested in temples, as she was in what Lady Rivkah told her would one day be houses for the nobility just south of the keep. There'd be a whole district for merchants and their shops directly to the east, but for now only the market was in good enough condition for daily use.

The market itself held only a few stalls and carts, and a few vendors selling their wares out of baskets, but Ria was excited, having never been allowed to visit Cielman's market where, according to Lord Sharl, thieves and other unsavory types were all too common.

"It's such a large area," Ria marveled. "How will anybody ever fill it up?"

"Well, there are only a few merchants here now, and of course it's too early in the year for most of the farmers to bring their crops in to sell," Lady Rivkah told her. "But if ships start docking at our city, there'll be goods sold here from northern and southern ports, and brought in by caravan from the east, too. Someday this market will be completely full, Sharl says, of merchants selling goods we can't even imagine now."

A number of the peasants in the market turned to stare as the cart passed through, and Ria was surprised and dismayed to see how many of those stares seemed hostile, even disgusted, when they were directed at her.

"What's the matter with them?" Ria whispered, nudging Lady Rivkah. "Why are they looking at me like that? I don't even know them."

Lady Rivkah did not answer, but her lips firmed into a thin white line and she turned the cart around immediately —not, however, before an old man nearby muttered something and spat in Ria's direction. Ria gasped, as stunned as if she'd been struck, Jenji chattered indignantly and bared his tiny sharp teeth, and Lady Rivkah quickly urged the pony to a faster pace out of the market.

"What?" Lady Rivkah asked as soon as they'd gotten some distance away. "What did he say? I couldn't make it out."

"He said, 'Filthy swine-humping elves,'" Ria said in a small voice. "Why did he say that? I've never done anything to him. I'm not dirty and I've never—never done *that,* not with a pig or anything else!" Waves of hurt and confusion nearly dizzied her.

Lady Rivkah's lips pinched even thinner and her brows drew down in the scowl that had always sent Ria scurrying out of the High Lady's way. When she spoke, her voice was tight and controlled.

"There are a few in the city like that—angry folk who have had a loved one hurt or killed by the elves, probably when they went too close to the forest, or who have simply believed every rumor they've heard about the elves and how they live. Thank the gods there aren't many who feel that way. But there are many beliefs to be unlearned, by us and by the elves, too, before the two will ever understand each other. That man and others like him, Ria, that's why Allanmere needs you as its High Lady, or one day that hatred will destroy us more surely than any barbarian invasion will."

She shook her head resolutely.

"I shouldn't have taken you into the city alone, not until

Sharl's announced the wedding," she said with a sigh. "Don't bother yourself about it right now, Ria. By the time of the wedding, hopefully folk like that will have gotten used to the idea of an elvan High Lady and you won't have any trouble."

Ria said nothing. She hadn't wanted to be High Lady before; knowing that some of the people of Allanmere would hate her, even though she'd done nothing to earn their hatred, certainly didn't make the idea any more attractive.

Lady Rivkah was angry and silent all the way back to the keep, and Ria was glad to return to her room and rest. At least there'd be time to nap after all her exertion and think for a bit before Cyril came, something she hadn't had a chance to do since she'd talked to her foster brother this morning.

Cyril's announcement that he might be able to heal her leg that very night was welcome, but at the same time it caused certain problems she hadn't thought about before. If Lady Rivkah or some other healer was tending her leg every night, that meant that Ria would have to leave that night if she wanted to get a few hours' lead before someone noticed she was gone. There'd be no chance to stockpile food or supplies, and she'd have to hope that her don't-see-me would keep the guards from observing her. Ria was far from sure she could do it, but there was nothing to do but try, and precious little to lose by trying. She'd never be permitted anywhere near the forest before she was married to Cyril.

At the same time, the prospect of sneaking away without even telling Cyril made her feel rather ashamed, as if she was somehow betraying him. Well, she *was*, there was no denying it, and after all his kindness and help, too. But if she tried to take Cyril with her, his presence might ruin her chance of a welcome among the elves, just as it had before, and he'd certainly insist on accompanying her if he knew— if, in fact, he didn't try to stop her from going at all. And it wasn't just herself she was thinking of, Ria reminded herself sternly. Cyril might have been seriously hurt, even killed, by the Blue-eyes; certainly they'd be far more willing to kill a human than they would Ria. So she simply had to leave him behind. What other choice was there?

Cyril was some time in coming, and when he arrived, he slipped furtively through her door carrying a large box of bottles, vials, and pouches, and on top of that, the heavy grimoire.

"I was afraid someone would see me," he said, sighing with relief as he laid down his burden and locked the door. "Mother and Father have invited probably every single person of noble birth in Allanmere to sup and discuss the midsummer festival and the wedding. I'd have had to attend, but I told them that if they weren't bringing you, I wouldn't go, either."

"Thanks," Ria said awkwardly. Again guilt twinged, liberally mixed with anger at Lady Rivkah, who hadn't even mentioned the event to her. But then, in all fairness, Ria had to admit that she'd always dodged formal suppers whenever she could.

"I was glad of the excuse," Cyril admitted, giving Ria a wry grin. "All those nobles, and you not even there to make it less boring? Yech. Guess I'd better get used to it, though, hadn't I?" He started setting out the jars and pouches he'd brought.

Another twinge of guilt as Cyril considerately said *I* instead of making the assumption of *we*.

"Cyril," Ria said uncomfortably, "did you really mean all those things you said about if I married you?"

Cyril glanced up from his preparations.

"Yes," he said, meeting her eyes. "Did you think I was lying to you, trying to trick you?"

"No, no," Ria said hastily. "I just—well, after all the fuss everybody's made about this wedding, it's hard to believe that *someone* cares what I want."

"Well, I do," Cyril said quietly. "And I'm going to prove it to you, too." He glanced at the page in the grimoire. "There. I think I'm just about ready. I'll light the brazier, and then I'll be ready for Jenji."

Ria wanted to ask what he meant by "proof," but Cyril

was already chanting as he struck flint and steel to light the brazier, and who knew what might happen if she interrupted him? She reached to her shoulder for Jenji, but he had already scampered down the pillows and was crouched almost touching Cyril, shifting from paw to paw in excitement.

Pungent smoke drifted up from the brazier, and the flames shifted from orange to blue, then purple. Cyril chanted on, reading from the grimoire, his fingertip marking his passage through the strange words; at last he reached out to touch Jenji. The chirrit scampered over to meet his hand as if understanding what was happening, giving his little trilling purr of happiness.

Ria gasped. *Something*—was it a mist, a kind of glowing light?—was rising from Cyril's skin. She couldn't quite focus on it, much like the flickering shadows she sometimes saw from the corners of her eyes that vanished when she turned to face them directly. She looked slightly to the side; now she could see it almost clearly, a purplish sort of glowing stuff flowing down Cyril's arm to Jenji. A similar glow, pale bluish in color, seemed to rise from the chirrit and flow back to Cyril; the two colors meshed and flowed together where Cyril and Jenji touched. Gradually Cyril's glow assumed a more bluish shade, even as Jenji's glow took on a purplish tinge, so that the two colors matched. Cyril chanted a few more words, and gradually the glow faded.

"Is that all?" Ria asked a little hesitantly when Cyril stopped and sat back on the bed.

"That's all," Cyril said. He shook his head. "It's—it's strange. I can feel him inside me somehow." He shook his head again as if to clear it. "I'm not sure I like it."

Ria grimaced. How often she'd wished *she* could do that.

"Well, I've got a working lattice," Cyril said at last. "Let's try the healing spell so I can dissolve it. No use my getting too attached to using a familiar. Mother would never let me have it, even if Jenji wasn't your pet instead of mine. Why don't you unwrap your leg while I start the spell?"

First Cyril had to set up a clean brazier and kindle a new fire; then he had to assemble the proper herbs and powders and begin his chant, this time with Jenji on his shoulder. It took Ria almost that long to unwrap the bandages, gingerly peel away Lady Rivkah's dressing, and wipe away some of the gooey ointment so Cyril could see the entrance and exit wounds clearly. They hadn't healed much, and her calf was still swollen and achingly tender.

Cyril raised his hands, still chanting, and Ria could see out of the corner of her eye the same sort of glow she'd seen before, but this time much stronger. Cyril laid one hand very gently on each side of Ria's calf, and Ria hissed between clenched teeth as a tight, painful heat shot through her leg, following the path of the arrow. Hurriedly she grabbed a pillow and stuffed the corner into her mouth, biting down hard to stifle a scream that might bring the servants running or, worse, distract Cyril. The tight pain seemed to last forever, but gradually it eased, and Ria took the pillow out of her mouth, sighing with relief as the pain seemed to flow out of her leg. The swelling was subsiding under Cyril's hands even as she watched, and the red, inflamed appearance with it; when he took his hands away, Ria was delighted to see the pale pink of newly healed skin instead of the raw wounds.

Cyril chanted for a few more moments; then at last he stopped, and Jenji scampered down from his shoulder to resume his usual place curled against Ria's side. Cyril slumped, and Ria hurriedly scooted aside so there was room for him to sit back against the pillows.

"Whew!" he said weakly after a few long moments. "I've never tried anything that powerful. Mother always made it look so simple. It wasn't as bad as I thought, though. Now I can see why so many mages have familiars. Mother's right; it would be easy to start depending on that extra help."

"But you did it, though," Ria said excitedly. "Look, my leg's healed."

Cyril looked.

"It certainly is," he agreed. "But remember when

Mother's healed our injuries before. It'll probably still be a little sore for a few days."

"I know that," Ria said impatiently. "But still it's good enough to—" She stopped.

"Good enough to what?" Cyril rolled over to look into her eyes.

"Good enough to walk on," Ria finished lamely.

"Good enough to get you to the forest," Cyril corrected. "That's it, isn't it? Good enough to get you to the forest right now, before Mother finds out that your leg's healed. And this time you wanted to go without me."

There was nothing she could say. Ria cleared her throat uncomfortably, not meeting Cyril's eyes.

"I figured it out as soon as you asked me," he said, quietly closing the pouches and jars.

"But you still did the spell," Ria said hesitantly.

Cyril glanced at her, grinning a little crookedly.

"I said I'd prove to you that I meant what I said," he said. He reached into the box he'd brought and pulled out a small pack. "There's enough food in here for a few days. I hid your practice armor out by the stables. It might stop an arrow if the elves shoot at you again, or then again, it might not. Maybe if I'm not with you it won't have to." He shrugged. "Tomorrow I'll pick up your meals at the kitchen and say I'm bringing them to you. You've kept to yourself so much lately, none of the servants would disturb you. With any luck no one will notice you're gone until Mother or Yvarden stops in to change your dressings tomorrow night."

Ria squirmed uncomfortably. She was beginning to wish she'd never asked Cyril for his help. Even if everything went as she wished, was it worth the guilt she felt?

"Cyril," she said, steeling herself, "I—I'm not in love with you."

To her surprise, Cyril only grinned, raising one eyebrow.

"You think I didn't know that?" he said, chuckling. "I'm not quite that stupid. I'm not in love with you either."

"You're not?" Ria sighed with relief, although she felt a

brief pang of something suspiciously akin to disappointment.

"Of course not," Cyril said, chuckling again. "I suppose
I've never really thought of myself as your brother, though
—you're too different from me, from all of us."

"If you don't love me," Ria said hesitantly, "why are you
wanting to marry me? Is it like your parents, alliances and
politics?"

"I think those are important," Cyril said slowly, "but not
important enough to force you to marry me against your
will and then probably hate me all your life, not after all
those years we were friends. I've got to marry, though, and
I'd rather it be you than anyone else I've met. I've got
plans for Allanmere too, and I think that if you ever
wanted to share the rulership of the city with me, you'd be
a fine High Lady; but even if you didn't, you'd stay out of it
and not hinder me, not get sneaky and ambitious and ma-
nipulative like some of the noble ladies I've known."

He grinned again.

"Besides, I didn't say I don't love you; I'm just not *in
love* with you. I love you as a special friend. Maybe the
other will come in time. I just know it'll never happen for
you—or for me—as long as we have no choice. So I want
us to have a choice, for my sake as much as yours. Is that
so strange?"

"I suppose not," Ria said finally. "I just don't want to—
to owe you anything."

"I don't want you to owe me anything." Cyril reached
down and pulled his Heir's signet from his finger. "Here,
you take this with you. It doesn't mean anything. Just to
remind you that I'm back here thinking about you. All
right?"

Ria slid the ring onto her finger. It was hopelessly large
and loose. At last she pushed it over the knuckle of her
thumb, where it fit comfortably.

"All right," she said. "I'll take the ring. But your parents
are going to roast you over a slow fire for giving it to me."

"What, as if I won't be in trouble enough for healing
your leg and helping you sneak away again?" Cyril said,

grinning. "They'd probably throw me in the dungeon as it is, if they had one."

"I guess you're right," Ria said, glancing at Cyril shyly. Something had just passed between them, some understanding that she did not completely comprehend; somehow the rules had changed.

"Well, you'd best be going, then, to get a good start," Cyril told her. "All the servants are going to be busy in the dining hall for another hour at least, and most of the guards are stationed at the gate tonight to meet the guests, instead of on the wall; you shouldn't have any trouble slipping away. Better go out the window and down the debris."

"All right." Suddenly Ria felt inexplicably reluctant; her escape had somehow become something else, something engineered by Cyril rather than her in a way that made her uncomfortable. But she could spend days questioning his motives, and by the time she figured them out she'd be married.

"All right," she said again. She took the small pack and stood. Her leg was slightly sore and stiff, but it felt wonderful compared to the pain of the last few days.

"I'll—I'll try to come back soon," she said. The words tasted like a lie. "Unless they catch me, and then I'll be back very, very soon."

Cyril smiled.

"No promises," he said. "Just take care." He held her hand for a moment, then released it to stroke Jenji gently. "And take care of this little fellow. I rather enjoyed working with him."

She pulled her warmest cloak and her soft boots on, then turned back and, before she quite realized what she was going to do, leaned forward and kissed Cyril briefly. The sensation was not really unpleasant, and Cyril's smile made Ria feel a little better. She turned away hurriedly before he said anything else, something that might make her feel even more ambivalent. She climbed onto the windowsill, then quickly, without looking back, slid out to the ledge, and freedom.

The ledge was narrow by human standards, but it might

as well have been a broad road to Ria's tiny feet. Despite her still-stiff leg, she scampered along hurriedly until she reached the highest point of the tumbled stone blocks below, where she could safely lower herself to the topmost block and carefully work her way down stone by stone to the ground. Only when she'd safely reached the ground and could take shelter behind one of the blocks did Ria remember to check anxiously along the wall for guards; however, Cyril had been right. There were only a few guards patrolling the wall at infrequent intervals; most of them had been moved to the gate at the front of the grounds.

Without Cyril's big feet and slower climbing pace to hinder her, Ria was up one side of the wall and down the other with amazing speed, and from there it was only a short scramble to one of the abandoned huts. She took almost the same route to the outer wall that she and Cyril had used before, although she planned to climb over the outer wall instead of passing through a gap, just to be safe, in case Lord Sharl and Lady Rivkah had ordered extra guards by the breaches. This time Ria planned to approach the wall at the northern edge of the city nearest the swamp, where the remote location meant fewer guards. She could use the edge of the swamp for cover between the city and the forest, and as she needed to enter the forest much farther north than she had previously, the change in her route made sense.

To Ria's disgust, however, there were plenty of guards on the outer wall, either because of her prior escape from the city or because of the elvan attack on Cyril and herself. Ria stared at the guards from her hiding place and frowned. There'd be no sneaking past them through one of the wall gaps, and they'd quickly see her climbing the wall, too. Well, Cyril had taken a chance and stretched his magical abilities successfully; she'd simply have to do the same.

Ria pulled Jenji out of her tunic and cradled him in her hands, looking into his dark eyes.

"I need your help," she murmured, hoping he somehow understood. "Please help me."

She was so anxious that it was hard to concentrate, hard to think herself small and silent and unnoticeable, but if Jenji's excitement was a measure, she succeeded at last. He gladly settled himself on her shoulder when Ria placed him there, thrumming eagerly in her ear, but Ria dared not distract herself with wondering whether or not he might be helping her hold her invisibility. There was nothing to do but try. If only tonight had been as dark and cloudy as during her previous attempt!

There was no hope of climbing the wall, not and concentrate on her invisibility at the same time, so Ria had to work her way south again to one of the many gaps in the wall. To her surprise and relief, none of the wall guards raised a cry, although ordinarily she would have been plainly visible walking slowly along the wall in the moonlight.

Her intense, prolonged concentration made Ria feel dreamy and somehow detached. Slowly she picked her way through the gap in the wall; slowly she waded through the moat and crept along at a snail's pace over the open ground between the city and the forest, expecting at any moment to hear a cry from the wall. Now her head was starting to ache, and her jaw, too, from the way she'd been clenching her teeth.

No cry came, and at last Ria was far enough away that she was certain they would not see her. She gratefully let her don't-see-me drop and sighed with relief. Jenji gave a disappointed little chirp, but nuzzled Ria's neck forgivingly nonetheless.

Ria sighed again, squared her shoulders, and turned to face the forest, and freedom.

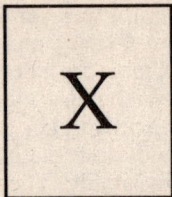

X

VALANN

Lahti settled easily into his hut, apparently willing to put their conversation with Rowan and Dusk and the prospect of the anger of her clan out of her mind for the present. Val, less serene, wondered how soon the clan would make its displeasure known. He himself had felt and resented the slight distance between himself and the other elves of the clan, and even so, the other elves had always treated him kindly enough, until last night when Garad had stepped aside to avoid him. Lahti had never known how it felt to be set apart from her own people. He silently vowed he would do everything in his power to keep her from feeling that pain. By unspoken agreement they spent their morning together in the hut, avoiding the rest of the clan.

By midday, however, the hut had grown warm in the late spring heat, and Val was already growing tired of the dim light and unchanging view. It was Lahti, however, who finally suggested that there was no point in hiding.

"We'll visit my mother," she decided. "She may need

meat. Her hut's only a short distance away. Then we can go hunting, if you like, or go to the waterfall to bathe."

Val had to concur. They couldn't cower in the hut forever like a mouse in its burrow; soon enough they'd be snapping at each other out of restlessness alone.

When they reached Kella's hut, however, they found that the door flap was tied closed, and there was no answer when Lahti scratched at the door and called out. A covered basket lay outside the door; Lahti lifted the cover and all the color drained from her face. Quietly she replaced the cover and picked up the basket, turning away from the hut.

"What is it?" Val asked softly, though he could guess well enough.

"Those belongings I'd left with her," Lahti said dully. "A few carvings that I made when I was very young, such as that. And the bracelet I gave her this year at the Planting of the Seed."

A single tear slid down Lahti's cheek, and the sight of it pierced Val's heart like a spear. He clenched his fists until his knuckles were white, shaking with anger.

"If this is your mother's love for her daughter, may the Mother Forest blight her loins so she never bears another," Val growled.

Lahti gasped and turned wide, shocked eyes to him.

"You mustn't say such a thing!" she said, horrified. "You mustn't even *think* such a thing! Such a wish is—is—unthinkable, an offense against the Mother Forest."

"I don't care," Val snarled. "I don't care." He raised his voice, almost shouting. "Perhaps we'd be better living among the humans! How could they show less kindness and compassion than our own folk?"

"Valann, stop it," Lahti hissed, pulling him back toward their tent. "You've lost yourself in your anger. Stop before you bring more trouble on us."

Retreating like a mouse back into its den. Almost Val pulled free of Lahti and stormed to the very center of the village. By the Mother Forest, he'd fight every elf in the clan if they'd dare cross him! At last, however, Lahti managed to coax him inside.

"You mustn't be so angry," Lahti told him. "Rowan told us this would happen. We knew it already."

"Tomorrow I'll begin building a new hut, far outside the village," Val growled. "Then we won't have to so much as see these vine-rotted folk at all, not until they finally decide we're fit to be treated as clan members and kin."

"Build your hut where you like, and I'll live in it with you," Lahti said warmly. "But, Valann, you mustn't carry hatred and anger with you wherever you go. It twists the spirit. Our kinfolk aren't wronging me. They're only waiting to see the consequences of the choice I made. They don't hate either of us; they're only afraid that because I've done something forbidden, I'll bring the Mother Forest's disfavor upon them. Once our child is born whole and perfect, and once I take my passage, it'll all be well again."

Val said nothing, only shaking his head sullenly. He thought he'd known these folk whom he called his own people; he'd been wrong, horribly wrong. How could anything be well again now?

"Valann, stop brooding," Lahti said gently. She chuckled. "Here we are together in your hut where you've always wanted me, free to couple whenever we wish, and me bearing your child, and all you can do is scowl. Come and hold me."

Val could not possibly sulk while Lahti pulled off her tunic and made herself comfortable on the furs; it was impossible even to think of his anger with the clan with Lahti's soft skin burning against his. After their play, however, perhaps to distract him further, Lahti broached a thought Val had never even considered.

"Your mother carried a human's seed, and she bore two children," Lahti said thoughtfully, leaning on Val's chest. "And you yourself carry some human blood. Do you think I might bear two children, too?"

Val raised an eyebrow.

"How am I to answer that?" he asked, shrugging. "That question is better posed to Dusk. From what Rowan told me, my mother was forced by a human shortly after she coupled with her mate. Dusk says that dangerous magic was used on her while she was with child also. Either of those might be the cause. Or perhaps Ria and I were sent by the Mother Forest to sow the seeds to unite elf and human in friendship against the coming storm of war, as Rowan believes," he added sourly.

"Don't you want such friendship?" Lahti asked curiously. "Don't you think these humans are better our friends than our enemies?"

"I think they'd be better far away from us," Val said, shrugging. "And calling them friends won't make them so, even when they're the ones who say it. Remember Minda? She went to the human city just before the invasion, heavy with child, and humans at the gate shouted angry words at her and threw clumps of dirt."

"But they didn't shoot arrows," Lahti reminded him.

Val shook his head, rolling over to topple Lahti from his chest.

"Humans," he growled. "Why must every conversation begin and end with humans?"

"Because your sister is with them," Lahti said simply. "But we won't speak of it if it angers you. Come and sleep."

"I'm too restless to sleep," Val said with a sigh. "I'll walk a little first."

"Oh, Val, you're not going to try to listen to what they're saying around the firepit?" Lahti sighed. "You know they'll still be gossiping about us. It'll only make them angrier, and you, too."

"I'll stay away from the firepit," Val promised. In truth it hadn't occurred to him to go there; what he wanted to do was assess the best route to sneak out of the village later, while walking off some of his anger so he could sleep.

He fancied that Lahti gave him a sharp look as he pulled his clothes back on and stepped out through the door, but it hardly mattered. He could scarcely creep away tonight without her knowledge; he carried nothing but his knife, and Dusk's four-footed or winged sentries were likely watching every step he took.

The thought brought a wave of fury that made his hands shake. Rowan and Dusk had always said that Valann was one of the Mother Forest's most special children, destined for great deeds, and that the Mother Forest demanded much of such children. But hadn't it been enough that he'd had to prove himself again and again in order to make his place in the clan? Hadn't it been enough that he'd had to fight for his very birthright of passage into adulthood? Now Lahti was suffering with him, and he was as good as a prisoner in his own home!

Defiantly Val strode out of the village into the forest, down to the waterfall and pool where the elves often went to bathe. A slight rustling in the trees above him kept pace, and Val had a sense of something moving in the undergrowth, too. Apparently Dusk had half the creatures in the forest tracking him!

The water looked cool and inviting, but Val merely sat down on a mossy rock overlooking the water and watched the rippling reflection of the moon. His own reflection scowled back from the water—not human, not elf. A prisoner, indeed. Val growled with frustration and threw a pebble into the pool, shattering his reflection.

Suddenly he sat upright, his ears straining. Something had changed subtly. Was it a wisp of strange scent on the wind, too slight for his nose to detect clearly? Had a new note joined the familiar night forest sounds, something his straining ears could not quite hear? Val crouched on the stone, hand on the hilt of his knife, every sense alert. Something was near, something was here, something that was a part of this place, that somehow made Val suddenly seem an intruder. Val squinted again into the darkness all around him. Nothing.

Val glanced down at the water again and gasped. His reflection no longer stood alone on the rock. A tiny figure stood beside him, almost touching him, tawny gold eyes gazing into his in the reflection.

For a moment Val was utterly confused. Had he slipped

somehow back into his passage vision, to the memory of the still pool he'd found at the center of his spirit? Was this a kind of waking dream such as Dusk had? If he turned away, would the reflection vanish as his dream had vanished?

Valann's entire body froze as he felt a warm touch on his hand. In the reflection, he saw small brown fingers, each digit twining with green vines, clasping his own. He realized he was trembling. The pressure on his fingers strengthened, a warm and comforting grasp. The tiny fingers clasping his were rough and callused.

Slowly he turned, afraid to look, afraid to breathe. His eyes skimmed up slender brown legs twined thickly with green vine designs, over a slight body clothed in a tattered leather tunic, and up to the delicately contoured face, framed in tumbled short curls, that he remembered from his dream. Warm gold eyes met his squarely.

Val's heart pounded so fiercely that he feared for it. He clung to the small hand clasping his own as if by that touch alone he could be certain that this, too, was no dream. Small, callused fingers reached up to gently caress his cheek, and then without either of them seeming to move, he was kneeling on the rock and she was holding him while he shook, while his tears soaked into the soft leather of her tunic. She said nothing, only held him close, but somehow she comforted him. Somehow without words he knew that she loved him, that she had always loved him, that often she'd watched him through her own eyes and through the eyes of the beasts around him, that she had ached to know him as fiercely and with as much frustration as he had longed to understand why she had given him to Rowan.

At last Val drew back, and Chyrie took his hand again, drawing him to his feet. She glanced up into the trees; a rustling sound answered her glance, and a small hawk, another of the birds Dusk commonly worked with, swooped down to land carefully on Chyrie's outstretched arm. Chyrie gazed sternly at the hawk, and it launched itself again, flapping away into the trees. Chyrie smiled reassuringly at Valann, then led him out of the clearing away from

the village, back into the forest where a stag and a doe
were waiting.

"Where are we—" Val began, but Chyrie silenced him
with a finger pressed to his lips. She shook her head and
gestured Val toward the stag.

Val hesitated and glanced back toward the village, thinking of Lahti. He didn't want to leave her alone, especially
now, and he couldn't deceive himself into believing she'd
understand, but when might a chance like this come again?
There was no choice to make, not really. Hopefully he
wouldn't be gone long. He climbed quietly onto the stag;
he had to hurry as the animal was already following the
doe upon which Chyrie rode. They had not traveled more
than an hour before Val realized where they were going:
His mother was taking him back to the Forest Altars. But
why?

The ride to the Forest Altars took a little longer than Val
would have expected, as Chyrie did not lead them directly
there, but rather followed a circuitous route. Several times
Val heard noises behind them and turned to look, only to
see other deer crossing and recrossing their track after
they had passed. Did these deer too serve Chyrie? Were
they concealing the tracks of Valann and Chyrie's passage?
Val was awed. Silence's ability to instruct the deer they'd
rode to bear Val and Lahti all the way back to Inner Heart,
a journey of three days on the straight route, had awed Val,
but Chyrie dwarfed even that feat if she could command
several deer at once. He began to believe that Chyrie had
indeed eluded Dusk's vigilance, perhaps even rendered it
impossible for the others to track him.

Chyrie led Valann to the far side of the grove, to one of
the more remote Altars. Chyrie slid from the doe's back,
and the doe wandered over to browse at a nearby bush; as
soon as Val stepped away from the stag, however, it vanished into the forest.

Chyrie took Val's hand and led him into a thicket just
outside the stone-marked boundaries of the grove. There,
to Val's surprise, he found a small camp had been prepared, sleeping furs laid ready. There was no firepit, but a

baked-clay firepot stood handy, and a pile of dry wood had been placed next to it. There was no meat, but small baskets of greens, tubers, and what were probably last autumn's nuts lay nearby. There was a larger wrapped bundle there, too, and Chyrie picked this up.

Valann turned back to Chyrie and again started to speak, only to be silenced again as Chyrie shook her head warningly. She pointed to the campsite sternly, and her meaning was clear: Val was to stay there. Val sighed but nodded his understanding and sat down on the sleeping furs to show that he would obey. Chyrie touched his cheek again and smiled, then vanished from the thicket with her bundle. Val waited a few long moments, then peeked out through the bushes. Chyrie was nowhere in sight, and the doe was gone as well.

Val sighed again and settled back down in his small camp. Judging from the obviously unused state of the camp, Chyrie had prepared it for him; judging from the amount of food laid ready for his use, he would likely be there for some time, too. Apparently Chyrie had departed on some extended errand and he was to await her return.

Once more Val could have growled in frustration. He'd left Lahti alone to face the clan's disapproval, only to find himself stranded at the Forest Altars awaiting his mother's return. He'd managed to slip out of Inner Heart, all right, but now he could hardly go west as he'd wished in search of his sister. He lacked his bow and arrows or even a spear, and he could hardly make his way through the forest and approach the human city armed only with a knife. He had no journey food, and hunting in other clans' territories was forbidden—and extremely dangerous, too, if a hostile clan found him doing it. Reaching the western edge of the forest when he was well armed and fully supplied had been a difficult and dangerous journey; without even those small advantages, it would be all but impossible.

And what if he succeeded? He could go off in search of his sister, but at the cost of losing his mother once more. At least he *knew* where his sister Ria was; nobody had ever known where Chyrie lived—many had wondered whether, in fact, the elusive elf was still alive. Val had wondered himself until the night of his passage, and even then he'd never considered searching for her. If Chyrie had wanted to see him, she would have found him; apparently she'd always known where he was. No elf in the forest, however, could find Chyrie if she did not want to be found, and seemingly she'd never wanted to be found.

Until now.

Val ground his teeth and sat back on the furs. This camp and Chyrie's desire that he remain here was his only link with the woman who had given him life, the blood-mother he had never seen. As Lahti had said, he could never reach the human city in time to do his sister any good. Little could be lost by taking this rare chance to know his mother. Ria, too, would have no memory of their mother. If and when Valann met his sister, she would be hungry for that knowledge. She would understand why her brother had waited.

Slight rustling in the bushes. Leaves parted to reveal the bright, slit-pupiled green eyes of a ringtail. Val had heard of the clever tree-dwelling predators but had never seen one; they were shy creatures and usually lived in the more northern part of the forest. This creature, however, appeared to have no fear of him. It stepped confidently into the thicket, and to Val's surprise it approached, rubbing its short muzzle against his leg. He gingerly reached out to stroke its sleek, tawny coat. The ringtail rolled over on its back, clasping Val's finger with one handlike paw. Valann smiled despite himself and scratched its furry belly. The ringtail closed its eyes in ecstasy and purred noisily.

The ringtail remained with Val even when he prepared for sleep, curling its body against his warmth as if appreciating his companionship. Val wondered if his mother looked out through the ringtail's eyes, or if this was merely one of her four-footed friends. There was no way to know.

Val sighed, closed his eyes, and began to wait.

XI

Ria

• Ria cowered under the meager shelter of a bush, shaking and near tears, as she tried to force a little air back into her lungs despite the burning ache in her sides. It seemed that each time she stopped, something roused her to new flight. She couldn't be sure whether those noises were only harmless forest creatures—whatever those might be—or some savage creature hunting her, or hostile elves with bows and spears ready to shed her blood.

She'd thought the wall guards and the Blue-eyes her greatest obstacles. Leaving the city, however, had been the easy part. She'd chosen a spot to enter the forest as far to the north as she could, hoping to avoid the Blue-eyes' territory. She'd approached the forest openly and at a snail's pace, giving the elves plenty of time to express their displeasure if they did not want her to come closer, or their welcome if they did. To Ria's dismay, however, there'd been no reaction at all; not a single elf had made himself or herself known, either to welcome Ria or to drive her away. Perhaps this area of the forest was uninhabited, as

Lord Sharl and Lady Rivkah speculated many areas were, since the invasion had wiped out entire elvan clans and rendered many parts of the forest too damaged and empty of game for habitation.

Ria was no more than a few dozen steps into the forest, however, before confusion and a growing uneasiness replaced her excitement. She'd never imagined such a place. Tall trees and bushes all around her blocked her vision; even in the thin fringe growth only a little starlight filtered through. The sounds and scents that assaulted her sensitive ears and nose were strange and frightening. Despite her fear, Ria had resolutely pushed deeper into the growth, hoping that someone would come to meet her. No one came.

As Ria made her way deeper into the forest, however, she began to sense uneasily that someone or *something* was very much aware of her presence. Suspicious rustlings in the bushes, small noises, the sound of footsteps, and strange, unfamiliar scents were all around her, working their way between her and the edge of the forest, as if driving her inward. Ria had walked faster, then trotted, trying to look in every direction at once, stumbling clumsily over the unfamiliar undergrowth. The sounds had suddenly seemed all around her, and she could no longer tell which direction was which; at last, terrified, she'd panicked and fled those sounds this way and that, fled and fled and fled again, and now she could no longer even begin to guess which way she'd come. She could be drifting into Blue-eyes' territory for all she knew, or she could be wandering in circles. In the forest darkness, with a thousand leaves blocking her view of the stars, there was no way of calculating direction. She'd fairly given up hope of any elves coming to welcome her; if there were elves in this area who meant her no harm, they would have made themselves known.

Her brief time in the forest before had not prepared Ria for this journey. She'd had no time to realize how confusing a place it was, where one tree looked so much like every other tree around it, where too many plants tangled around her feet and too many strange sounds and smells kept her confused and disoriented. She could do nothing but stumble onward, hoping to cross some path or landmark, or perhaps a clearing or a hill from which she might gain a vantage point over her surroundings.

But she was so tired, scratched by branches and brambles, bruised from stumbling into trees and falling, and shaking with fear. Some time after she'd entered the forest, she'd blundered through a patch of short, bristly plants that stung her legs like a swarm of bees despite her stout cloth trousers, and now her legs burned and itched furiously. Insects hummed in the darkness and bit, leaving itching welts. Her newly healed leg was aching furiously now. Surely hours had passed. Jenji had ridden her shoulder until they reached the forest, but the chirrit was as much a stranger to this alien and frightening place as Ria herself, and now he cowered in her tunic, trembling as hard as she.

Rustling in the bushes right behind her. Ria's heart leaped with terror and she bolted from her bush, only to collide with a tall form whose black clothing had blended perfectly into the darkness. Ria glanced up into a dark, exotic face and golden eyes that gazed coolly down at her, and she felt the world begin to dissolve around her as it had when she'd been shot. It was too much; Ria let the world go and slid gratefully into darkness.

Her next awareness was of cool water at her lips and an arm supporting her shoulders. There was no disorientation; Ria remembered her last waking moment and bolted upright, spilling the water down over her front. She'd been hot and sweaty before, but she'd cooled as she lay on the ground, and she shivered as the water soaked her tunic. She turned to face her captor—benefactor?—and was amazed to see, instead of the tall black figure she'd seen before, a slender elvan woman no taller than Ria herself, with tumbled tawny hair as curly as Ria's own black locks, with merry golden eyes now warm and full. Again there was no moment of doubt or disorientation; Ria knew exactly whose hand steadied her shoulder, whose smile warmed her to the depths of her spirit.

"Mother," Ria whispered, and then those arms, twined with vines and flowers and festooned with images of berries and butterflies, were warm and strong around her. There were a thousand things Ria had thought she might say at such a moment, unhappy and angry and resentful things, but somehow they all seemed foolish and needless; everything was said in those warm eyes, in the arms that held her tight, tight, in the heart she could feel pounding as hard as her own, in the hands she could feel shaking against her back. Ria sighed and let her anger flow out of her with her fear, leaving a certain weary peace behind in their wake.

Chyrie sat back and smiled at her daughter, then picked up the cup Ria had knocked out of her hand. She only had to reach a short distance to fill it again, and Ria realized that her mother—or possibly the strange elf she'd seen—had moved her while she was unconscious; they were on the bank of a small stream in a growth of forest so dense that little sunlight trickled down through the leaves. This time Ria accepted the cup gratefully.

When Ria had drunk her fill and washed the sticky tear tracks from her face, Chyrie led her away from the stream to a small camp; she'd simply brushed the leaves from the soil in a circular area, dug a tiny firepit, and spread a few warm skins to sleep on. A clay pot had been set close beside the fire, and Ria could smell simmering vegetables and, to her surprise, meat. She'd thought Chyrie would not hunt, not according to what Lady Rivkah had told her about beast-speakers.

Jenji, smelling the food, chittered and poked his nose out of Ria's tunic. Chyrie gave a hoarse yelp of surprise, the first sound Ria had heard her make, and leaned closer to look. Ria embarrassedly fished the chirrit out of her tunic.

"You had a chirrit once, didn't you?" Ria asked softly. "Lady Rivkah said so; the mage who taught her had it, and he died, so you took it. Her name was Weeka, wasn't it? This is Jenji."

Chyrie started at Ria's words, almost wincing, as if Ria had shouted suddenly in her ear or distracted her from listening to some other conversation on which she'd been concentrating deeply. Chyrie reached out to stroke Jenji with a careful fingertip; Jenji crooned with delight and leaped from Ria's hand to Chyrie's, scampering from Chyrie's shoulder and nuzzling her face. Ria suppressed a sudden surge of irrational jealousy at Jenji's desertion and the sense that some communication passed between the chirrit and the elf—why not? Her mother was a beast-speaker, wasn't she, and Jenji a beast—but she quickly forgot her resentment when she saw Chyrie's rather wistful smile. Yes, it'd been sixteen years, and Weeka had probably not been young; the chirrit must have died some time ago.

Chyrie glanced at Jenji, tilting her head with such a listening air that Ria found herself straining her own ears; then a look of worry crossed Chyrie's face. To Ria's surprise, Chyrie all but pushed her down to the ground, fairly attacking Ria's left trouser leg in her haste to push it up. Ria scowled as she saw the angry red rash stippling her leg; that certainly explained the itching. Then Chyrie was examining the pink scar of Ria's arrow wound with some relief, and Ria understood.

"It's all right," Ria said. "My friend Cyril healed—"

Chyrie was nodding her understanding before the words had left Ria's lips, and Ria fell silent. Did her mother hear Ria's thoughts before the words were formed? Well, if she could hear the thoughts of beasts, why not those of her daughter? She'd been called a beast a time or two. Ria chuckled at the thought, and Chyrie, meeting her eyes, chuckled too as if understanding the joke.

Chyrie rolled Ria's trouser leg back down with a sigh of relief, then turned aside to rake the pot away from the fire with a stick. When the stew had cooled somewhat, they ate it, Ria bringing out some of her journey bread for them to sop up the gravy. She found that some of the dried meat had vanished from her pack; that explained the meat in the stew. Chyrie looked so longingly at the cheese in Ria's pack that Ria laughed and gave it to her.

After they had eaten, Chyrie pulled several pots, jars, and pouches out of a fur bag (where had she gotten the fur? Ria wondered) and ground several substances together to a paste in a small stone bowl. She scraped the paste into a small clay jar and gave it to Ria, indicating in gestures that Ria was to rub the paste over the rash on her legs. Ria obeyed, and the paste alleviated the furious itching of the rash to some extent.

Ria had assumed that her mother would stay with her that night; to Ria's utter surprise, however, Chyrie gave her daughter an apologetic glance and vanished into the darkness when Ria was ready for sleep. Jenji appeared unafraid, however, and Ria was so weary after the day's exertions that despite the unfamiliar forest sounds, the lumpy pallet, and her solitude, she was quickly asleep.

When she woke to Chyrie's touch on her shoulder, it was barely light. Chyrie gave her daughter no time for breakfast, however; two does were waiting at the edge of the camp, and Chyrie had already bundled together everything except the furs Ria was sleeping on. Ria had never so much as touched a living deer, much less ridden one, but she was offered no alternative; Chyrie helped her to mount, then mounted her own doe, and they were off.

Ria had read Lady Rivkah's accounts of elves riding deer through the forest, and it had sounded very exciting, but the reality was somewhat more uncomfortable. Unlike horses, the deer were sure-footed in the forest and did not need to follow the winding elvan trails, pursuing a straighter course directly through the underbrush. The does' hides were tough enough to offer them protection from the swinging branches and raking thorns, but Ria found her cloth leggings less helpful, and the rash on her legs was itching again. The doe's back, too, quickly became very uncomfortable, as there was no way to avoid the hard ridge of the deer's spine without sitting far back on its rump, and Ria quickly wished for the padding of a saddle. Chyrie apparently was not troubled by these discomforts or by the biting insects that had come for deer blood but, it appeared, liked elf blood even better. Ria quickly found herself wishing she'd remained on foot. The travel might have been much slower, but it couldn't have been any more miserable.

As hours passed and Ria slowly grew accustomed to the annoyances of deer-riding, however, she found that there was plenty to distract her. The forest by day was a much less threatening and confusing place than it had seemed by night. The arching canopy of leaves was awesome in its height and thickness, and the rays of green-tinted sunlight filtering through dappled the ground. The trees were not all alike as they'd seemed in the darkness; there seemed to be as many kinds of oddly shaped leaves and rough or smooth bark as there were wildflowers on the plains. There was an endless variety of birdsong to listen to, and so many new and interesting creatures to watch that Ria was dizzied. Chyrie appeared to be on good terms with everything; she amused her daughter as they rode, bringing squirrels or birds to her hand where Ria could look at them closely and even touch them. Despite these distractions, however, Chyrie kept the deer to a quick walk, not stopping even at midday for dinner; Ria finally took some of the preserved food from her pack to eat as she rode. She couldn't imagine why her mother would feel the need to hurry; now that Ria had found Chyrie, and hopefully soon her brother, she didn't much care *where* in the forest they went, or how long it took to get there.

Twice they passed what Ria realized from Lady Rivkah's accounts were clan markers—glowing symbols on large stones. Those symbols gave Ria pause to worry despite Chyrie's apparent familiarity with their route. They were passing, obviously, through several territories, and not really making any special effort to be quiet and inconspicuous; might some of the clans not attack them, as the Blue-eyes had done? Perhaps they'd stayed in the territories of more friendly elves; otherwise, why hadn't the strange dark elf Ria had seen killed her? Or perhaps her mother was using the animals of the forest to look for elvan patrols so they could be avoided.

Ria had her answer when Chyrie's deer ahead of her suddenly came to a stop. Ria glanced up, startled, and then gasped as she found herself gazing into half a dozen pairs of very elvan eyes. She'd never seen any of her people besides her mother (well, and a brief glimpse of the elf in black) in her life, and for a moment she was too surprised to be frightened; then, seeing no spears or arrows immediately pointed in her direction, she was too curious for fear.

These elves were not as exotic-looking as her mother with her brilliant skin designs or the male in black leather she'd seen. In fact, the few elves she'd seen from the eastern cities were more odd-looking with their golden hair and blue eyes and graceful movements and strange clothes. These elves were anything but elegant, dressed in plain leather tunics and trousers, only two wearing low leather boots and the rest barefoot. They were a good bit taller than Ria and Chyrie, almost as tall as Ria's human foster parents, and their sun-browned skin and dusty brown hair and brown-green eyes seemed almost commonplace. Only the pointed tips of their ears and the elvan cast of their features distinguished them from any human peasant.

The elves stood silently, their eyes wide, apparently as surprised by the intruders on their land as Ria was by them; then Ria realized they were staring at her mother, and what she had mistaken for surprise was something closer to awe.

Very slowly, almost timidly, a female stepped forward. She lifted a necklace of animal teeth from around her head and held it out gingerly toward Chyrie.

"You honor us with your presence, Grandmother," she whispered, and Ria had to concentrate hard to understand what the woman was saying. She'd worked hard at her Olvenic all her life, but she'd never heard it spoken by a native of the forest, and the accent in which the young woman spoke it was very strange. Did her brother speak like that?

Chyrie smiled a little sheepishly and accepted the necklace, nodding and hanging it around her own neck. Then one of the males stepped forward also, extending a lumpy hide bag.

"The fruits of our hunt, Grandmother," he said, also whispering. "We'd be greatly honored if you'd accept this meat for yourself and"—he glanced at Ria, his eyes widening—"and your daughter."

He could tell she was Chyrie's daughter just by looking at her? Ria swelled a little with pride as Chyrie accepted the game bag. Obviously her mother was a person of some importance here. But of course she was; hadn't Rowan told Lady Rivkah that Chyrie had turned the whole forest against the invaders, beating the barbarians back in the final battle?

Ria would have liked to see more of the strange elves, perhaps talked with them, but Chyrie was in a hurry to continue onward. They rode all day, stopping well after the sun had set. When Ria finally slid from the doe's back, she almost screamed in pain; she was unaccustomed to riding more than a short while, and that with the comfort of a saddle, and her muscles ached with a hard, fierce pain. Immediately Chyrie was beside her, concern and regret plain in her expression, easing Ria to the ground and massaging her thighs and calves until the cramps eased. Chyrie applied more salve to the itchy rash on Ria's legs, scowling so puzzledly that Ria wondered if her mother had expected the rash to be completely gone. Gesturing sternly to Ria to stay where she was—Ria was only too glad to comply— Chyrie made another small camp, then helped Ria to move to the fur pallet. Ria had learned during the journey to Allanmere how to clean game and set it to roasting, and was proud to be at least that much help as Chyrie built a fire; after what Lord Sharl had said to her on the wall in Allanmere, Ria was determined to be of use to her mother.

Again, without explanation, Chyrie disappeared into the forest, leaving Ria with only Jenji for company; however, she returned only a short time later, her arms full of tubers, greens, and berries for their supper. The little preserved food Ria had eaten that morning and at midday might as well have been nothing; Ria's stomach rumbled plaintively as the food cooked, giving off the most delightful aromas. As soon as the food was ready, Chyrie ate as heartily as her daughter; Ria realized guiltily that Chyrie had had nothing at all to eat that day and was probably even hungrier than Ria herself, and how long might it have been since Chyrie had fresh meat?

After supper Chyrie rooted through her pack and brought out a clay pot of some pungent-smelling salve that she proceeded to rub into Ria's sore thighs; then once more she left Ria alone in the camp. Ria was too tired to fret over this fact, but it puzzled her; was Chyrie keeping watch all night, or did she just not want to sleep near her daughter? At least Jenji showed no inclination to stay with Chyrie instead of her, so that Ria wasn't left completely alone.

The next day was exactly like the one before it, except that Ria was now more accustomed to the long ride. The night's soreness had been completely gone when she awakened, and though she dreaded another day of riding on deerback, there seemed nothing else to do. She was surprised to note that this morning they were riding two different deer, a doe and a stag; she'd thought Chyrie must have special favorites that were more amenable to being ridden, but apparently the beast-speaker simply summoned whatever deer were closest when she needed them. Probably, too, Chyrie preferred to summon fresh mounts after they'd ridden the does so hard the day before; Ria knew enough about deer from hunting them to realize that steady travel over a long day at a quick walk was very unlike even a plains deer's usual behavior, and forest deer likely did not even need the endurance for seasonal travel over long distances.

By evening, they had traveled far enough that Chyrie appeared pleased with their progress and somewhat less anxious. She stopped while there was still a little light in the sky and made their camp beside one of the many small streams that crisscrossed the forest.

This time when Chyrie disappeared into the forest to

gather their supper, Ria was determined to do some of the
providing herself. She didn't have her bow and arrows, or
even hooks and line, but using her chemise as a makeshift
net—it needed washing anyway—she managed to catch
three good-sized fish for their supper. By the time Chyrie
returned, Ria had scaled and cleaned the fish and laid
them proudly on a rock beside the firepit.

Chyrie was delighted by the fish, although Ria was disappointed that her mother did not really seem surprised; in
fact, Chyrie had brought back broad leaves in which she
wrapped them, then covered the whole with a thick layer of
mud from the creek. She poked the muddy bundles into
the fire to cook slowly, and by the time the tubers were
baked to mealy tenderness and the greens had stewed in
their pot, the fish had baked to moist perfection.

After their meal, mother and daughter were glad to
bathe in the stream and wash away the dirt, sweat, and
deer hair collected in their travel. Chyrie showed Ria the
roots that could be pounded between rocks and then sub-
merged in water to make a soapy foam. To Ria's surprise,
Jenji loved the water and swam skillfully, splashing after
water beetles, minnows, and tadpoles and, to Ria's squea-
mish fascination, eating what he caught.

More fascinating, however, was the full extent of the
designs Ria had barely glimpsed at her mother's wrists and
legs, now fully visible in the moonlight. Vines twined and
coiled up the smooth skin of Chyrie's legs to join together
over one hip, then exploded outward in a riot of tendrils
coiling around her torso up to her shoulders, and spilling
down both arms. The emerald leaves sparkled as if with
dew, or were ornamented with multicolored butterflies,
clusters of green or ripe fruit, or budding and blossoming
flowers. It was as if the very essence of every green thing in
the forest had been distilled down and painted on Chyrie's
skin, giving her the uncanny appearance of something part
elf and part plant.

As awesome as the vibrant designs on Chyrie's skin
were, a part of Ria winced to see them. Lady Rivkah had
told her about those designs, that Chyrie's mate had used

needles and dyes to prick them into her skin. It sounded rather like some bizarre form of torture to Ria, no matter how lovely the end result.

As if sensing Ria's thought, Chyrie chuckled and patted her daughter's shoulder, and Ria flushed with embarrassment to realize she'd been staring at her mother's naked body first in awe, then wrinkling her nose and almost cringing. What in the world must Chyrie think of her?

Once more Chyrie disappeared as soon as Ria curled up on the furs to sleep, but as there'd been no trouble the night before, Ria was not frightened. She was fairly certain by now that Chyrie *did* hear her thoughts, maybe every single one; if that was so, her mother would probably get precious little sleep lying there next to her with Ria's every ache, itch, and dream bombarding her. Chyrie was either standing guard or confident enough of their safety to leave Ria alone, or perhaps Chyrie had other guards, furred or feathered in the trees or hidden in the bushes. The thin pallet bed of furs was still hard and lumpy, and Ria's legs were itching again (it might not just be the rash, either; Ria suspected that even if the furs hadn't had any fleas at all in them when they started, after riding on deer for a couple of days, they *would* have fleas by now), but her hard day's ride made it easy enough to ignore those minor discomforts. The sounds of the forest, too, seemed less strange and frightening now, and Ria let that lullaby ease her down into sleep.

In the middle of the night, Ria woke to find that a light rain had started, but was steadily growing heavier. Ria huddled under the furs, wishing irritably for a waterproofing spell and wondering where she was supposed to take shelter in a forest where there wasn't even a tent. She was shivering and almost soaked, Jenji chattering miserably, before Chyrie materialized at her side, scowling with impatience, and led Ria to a thick clump of bushes. Her expression said more clearly than words, *Don't you have sense enough to get in out of the rain?*

Ria stripped off her wet clothes and curled up inside her warm cloak, utterly embarrassed and humiliated. How was she supposed to know how to get along in the forest? She'd never been in one in her life—had hardly even seen trees. Gods, was it true that she'd be nothing but a bother to these people, a mist-witted fool who couldn't survive a day without help? Maybe she should've stayed in the city and married Cyril. At least *he* had some use for her. For a moment Ria knew utter despair. Was there nowhere she truly belonged? Then she shook herself and resolutely wiped away her tears. There was still her brother somewhere in this strange place, and Ria *wouldn't* let the forest become her enemy. It was her home, her people's home. She'd simply have to learn, that was all, just as anybody would have to learn in a place that was new to them. Chyrie had probably been just as frightened and out of place when she'd come to the city.

She'd just have to learn.

Once more in the morning there were two new deer awaiting them, but this time Chyrie apparently did not feel the need to hurry, for she let Ria break her fast on some of the preserved food she'd brought with her before they continued their journey. Neither did Chyrie urge the deer to the quick pace of the prior two days, and instead of the straight course they'd been following eastward through the forest, Chyrie seemed to be circling slightly northward now.

Before midmorning Chyrie slowed the deer even further, and Ria could see why—they were approaching a strange place, possibly the goal of their journey. Ahead of them was a long line of low rocks, each only a couple of man-heights from its neighbor, and each bearing a glowing symbol such as Ria had seen on the territorial markers they'd passed before. Each symbol, however, was different from the others. The line of stones curved gently, and Ria supposed they enclosed the strange-looking space ahead of them.

Inside the line of stones Ria could see a number of old campsites, or at least cleared areas that had the look of frequent use. Interspersed with these campsites were large, roughly hewn slabs of stone perhaps half a man-height in

thickness, their tops smoothly flat. Ria could see that the
nearest such stone slab had several small objects on its
surface—a string of beads, a cup containing some half-
dried purple liquid, a few dried fruits and nuts, and a bird
feather. Other stones appeared to bear similar offerings.
This, then, was the Forest Altars, the holy place Lady
Rivkah had mentioned in her histories, where she and
Lord Sharl had met Chyrie and her mate. But why had
Chyrie brought Ria here?

Chyrie slid from her doe's back, nonchalantly picked up
the dried fruit from the nearest altar, and fed the fruit to
the two deer, apparently untroubled by the idea that she
was stealing someone's offering. Ria dismounted also,
standing awkwardly with her pack and wondering why
they'd come here. Was she expected to worship at these
strange altars, or leave something of hers as an offering,
perhaps?

When the deer had wandered away, Chyrie took Ria's
hand and led her through a circuitous maze of pathways
between the altars and campsites. Once Chyrie paused,
tilting her head as if listening to something, her brow fur-
rowing worriedly; then her face cleared and she chuckled,
leading Ria onward without explanation.

They'd passed almost through the altar-dotted piece of
land when Chyrie paused not far from a thicket of bushes.
A second later a curious creature the size of a large cat
bounded out of the bushes and into Chyrie's arms, its
black-ringed tail swishing excitedly. A moment later, a very
startled elvan face peered out of the same thicket, gold
eyes widening as they fastened on Ria and Chyrie.

The bushes parted and the stranger stepped out, and
Ria stared in puzzlement. The man was a good bit taller
than Chyrie, and though his skin was as brown as hers, the
tips of his ears were rounded, not pointed as Chyrie's and
Ria's own. In fact, except for his tawny gold eyes so much
like Chyrie's and the exotic cast of his features, he looked
very much human, if short for a human male. But there
was something about his face, about the eyes that fastened
so sharply on her, that made Ria shiver with recognition.

She'd seen that face in dreams a thousand times, pictured it in her mind every day—

The stranger stepped forward slowly, hesitantly, and Ria stepped to meet him just as slowly, searching her mind for every scrap of Olvenic she'd ever learned.

"Valann?" she murmured. "You're Valann. My brother."

He took the last step forward and reached out his hand very slowly, his own fingers shaking, as if afraid she would vanish at a touch. Ria felt her own hands trembling, but she reached out, too, closing her eyes with relief as she clasped warm, strong fingers.

"And you are Ria," Valann said, almost whispering. "My sister."

Ria swallowed hard, feeling unexpectedly shy.

"Chyrie brought me," she said. "We came all the way from the western edge on deer, and Chyrie—"

They both turned, and then were silent. Only Ria's packs were there, abandoned on the ground.

Chyrie was gone.

XII

• There was so much to say, and neither had the words to say it, but they tried, babbling in both languages, words over words, interrupting each other and laughing at their own confusion and each other's. The sun traveled from east to west, hours passing like minutes as Ria spoke, then Val, then Ria, then Val. Again and again one or the other would reach out to touch the other as if unable to believe they were both really there, truly meeting at last.

Val wondered at Ria's descriptions of Cielman and Allanmere, pressing her for details of the metal so freely available and the amazing ease with which one human city traded with another, strangers meeting as easily as if they were kinfolk. He scowled in indignant sympathy when Ria told him of her involuntary betrothal to Cyril, shaking his head in admiration when Ria spoke of the invisibility that had allowed her to creep from the city, although Ria was far too excited to demonstrate.

Ria in turn could not hear enough stories about life in Inner Heart, Dusk's visions, Valann's own prowess at hunt-

202

ing and tracking. She was astonished to learn that Valann was all but mated and Lahti with child. The forest seemed like such a strange and rather harsh place to her; that Val had lived in such simple happiness here seemed amazing to her.

But even after the stories, nothing matched the miracle of that very moment, sitting and talking together, brother and sister solid and real to each other's eyes. Again and again one or the other would nod, grinning reminiscently or wincing sympathetically, "Yes, yes, it was just like that—"

At last empty stomachs and parched throats demanded relief, and Val brought out the last of his camp food while Ria emptied her pack. Their makeshift meal was broken frequently by laughter when Ria spit out dried root grubs as soon as she realized what it was she'd eaten, or as Val wrinkled his nose when he sipped the wine Ria had brought from the city. The laughter was as filling and as satisfying as the food. At last, hunger satisfied and words temporarily exhausted, they simply sat and stared at each other, smiling and shaking their heads.

Valann traced the planes of Ria's face wonderingly, gently touching the delicately pointed tips of her ears.

"Your eyes are not of us," he murmured. "So deep, as if sky and leaf bled together. And you so young, so small."

"I'm not so young," Ria said, a little embarrassed. "I'm as old as you. Exactly as old."

To Ria's amazement, Valann reached out and ran his hand over the front of her tunic, feeling her small breasts as casually as Ria might have checked the teeth on a horse.

"No," he said. "You're still only a child, of course. But you will grow in your own time."

They were silent for a long moment, Ria building her courage to ask the one question that still burned in her heart.

"Valann," she said at last, in a very small voice, "Why did she do it? Why did she give us away? Why did she give me to humans who'd take me away from my home, my own people?"

Val was silent for a long moment. He'd asked himself that same question so many times that his mind had worn away at it like a river at its banks.

"Rowan and Dusk always told me that you and I were born for a great destiny, to serve the Mother Forest by bringing elf and human together in peace," Val said slowly. "I can't say with a whole heart that that's not truth. But I believe it isn't the only truth, or even the greatest truth. I've looked into our mother's eyes, I've touched the heart of the Mother Forest, and those were not the things I saw there.

"What happened to our mother, or why, we will likely never know. Her spirit lives in a place within the Mother Forest, and I know that that place is no place where a mother can live and care for her children. I think perhaps she can hardly bear to be near us—or anyone—for long, so many voices clamor for her attention."

Val waved at the forest around them.

"When we were born, the Heartwood was burned and ravished, a hard place to live for many years. Game was scarce; even many of the food plants were gone. Many elves died of hunger or illness. Many others died in the raids and squabbling between clans desperate for land and food. How our mother even survived alone, no one can say. I believe she gave us up because her love for us, her desire for our safety and well-being, was greater than her own need to keep her children."

"But to give me to the humans!" Ria protested.

Val only shrugged, although his heart ached at the thought.

"Besides her own clan, who were dead," he said carefully, "Chyrie knew only Rowan and Dusk and the humans Sharl and Rivkah. I think there were many reasons she gave us as she did. She knew the humans would bring you back home in time, and that you would never know hardship and lack food as the elves did in those early years after the battle. Perhaps she only meant for you to bring your knowledge of humans to the Heartwood when you returned." He sighed. "For me, I've ached and resented and wondered as you've done, but she cannot give us those answers, and anything I tell you is a guess and little more. But you and I have seen the love in our mother's eyes, felt it in her touch. That much we can believe. And perhaps in time—"

He froze, listening, then sniffing the air.

"Someone comes. A strange scent."

Ria sniffed the air, too, but her nose was filled with the unfamiliar forest scents and she could isolate nothing. She strained her ears, and this time, despite the small sounds of the forest, she heard something she *could* recognize.

"Horses," she said, and sighed. There could be no doubt of who the riders were. But how could Lord Sharl and Lady Rivkah possibly have tracked her here?

"Humans?" Val scowled. "But how could they have come here? Other clans would have driven them forth, or killed them."

"Unless Lady Rivkah hid them by magic," Ria corrected exasperatedly. "That's probably how she found me, too."

"Then we too must hide." Between one breath and another Val had seemingly vanished; glancing amazedly around her, Ria finally found him seated on a branch over her head, almost invisible behind the thick foliage, beckoning impatiently. "Hurry!"

Ria stared blankly; she couldn't reach even the lowest branch, and she'd never climbed a tree in her life—there were no convenient cracks for footholds, and she could hardly be expected to shinny up the thick trunk like it was a rope. Instead she hunkered down in the undergrowth at the base of the tree and concentrated, making herself small, insignificant, unseen—she heard Valann's gasp of surprise above her and almost lost her concentration, but recovered it.

It was only a few moments before Ria saw the legs of Lady Rivkah's favorite riding horse, although she did not dare peek upward to see if Lady Rivkah was in the saddle. Her curiosity was satisfied a moment later as Lady Rivkah's boots, then her old leather trousers, appeared beside the horse. To Ria's consternation, dried brown stains on the trouser legs looked suspiciously like blood.

"There's no one here," Ria heard Lord Sharl say, his voice heavy with exhaustion and a note of something very like despair. "Are you sure this is the place?"

"It's where my tracking spell ends," Lady Rivkah replied, her own voice just as leaden. "I don't know what else to do, Sharl. Should we try to go on to Inner Heart?"

"Gods, I don't know what we'll do if anyone else shoots at us," Lord Sharl sighed. "I've used all my crossbow bolts, and your magic is exhausted, don't pretend it isn't. And I don't know how much farther Cyril can ride."

"I can ride." Cyril's voice was weak, so weak it frightened Ria. "But why would she have come here? There's no one here. I thought she was looking for her brother."

Ria hesitated. What was happening? Was Cyril injured? Had they been attacked in the forest? Then why hadn't they turned back to the city? But one thing was certain: If Lord Sharl and Lady Rivkah had gone so far as to risk bringing Cyril into the Heartwood, nothing so simple as hiding or invisibility was going to keep them from finding Ria. Even if Lady Rivkah had exhausted her magic, as soon as she'd regained her strength, she'd use it, and that would be that.

Abruptly Valann dropped from the limb above them, confronting the humans boldly.

"She came seeking her brother, and she has found him," he said. "And who comes seeking her?" He scowled fiercely, his hand resting threateningly on his knife hilt, although he made no move yet to draw the blade.

That was enough. Ria let her don't-see-me drop and stepped out of the bushes.

"They're my foster parents, High Lord Sharl of Allanmere and High Lady Rivkah," she said ruefully. "And their son Cyril."

When she glanced at the humans, however, she was silent in shock. Lord Sharl and Lady Rivkah might have been riding day and night without cease, their plain riding leathers were so soiled and their faces so grimed and drawn with exhaustion. Blood stained their clothing in places, and Lord Sharl's right forearm and wrist were wrapped in bloodstained bandages. Lady Rivkah's head was bandaged, too, and the edge of an ugly bruise showed past the bandages. Cyril, however, had fared the worst. His right shoulder and thigh were bandaged, and there was a frighteningly dark stain on the left side of his tunic.

Slowly Valann took his hand away from his knife hilt.

"There's a camp in those bushes," he said slowly, gesturing. "The boy can rest on the pallet there." He turned to Lady Rivkah. "Rowan told me you were a healer."

"I can use healing magic, yes," Lady Rivkah said tiredly, stepping over to help Cyril down from his horse, "when I haven't exhausted my power fending off hostile elves and concealing us from patrols so they couldn't finish what they'd started. Not to mention using tracking spells to find our way when we were driven away from the trails we'd been following. Are there any healers here?" she added anxiously. "I thought I detected someone approaching from the east, close by."

"Who's coming?" Lord Sharl said quickly, drawing his sword despite his obvious exhaustion. Cyril stumbled over to one of the altars, leaning against it and reaching for his own sword.

"Do not dare draw your weapon in this place," Val hissed, hand again on his knife hilt. He sniffed the air. "Those who come have a right to be here, and you have none." He turned to Ria, grimacing. "Rowan, Eldest of Inner Heart, who has been as my mother from birth, her mate and Inner Heart's Gifted One, Dusk, and my mate Lahti, all riding on deer. I'm surprised only that they didn't track me here sooner."

"Maybe they weren't attacked three times by hostile patrols," Lord Sharl said wryly, "but maybe their mounts rode around in circles like ours did. Maybe deer crossed and recrossed your trail until the gods themselves would've needed signposts to follow."

Ria glanced at Valann, and he nodded almost imperceptibly. Lord Sharl's pursuit explained Chyrie's haste to bring

Ria to her brother; no doubt she'd had deer trampling their back trail to confuse their pursuers.

Ria hurried to Cyril's side and helped him boost himself up onto the flat stone where he could sit more comfortably. Somehow all her anger and resentment at her human family seemed insignificant when she looked at the stained bandages.

"Are you all right?" she asked anxiously. He seemed so weak and pale.

"It's not as bad as it looks," Cyril said gamely, but his grin was pained. "Nothing dangerous, but it looks like I'll be the one limping for a while."

There was an awkward moment of silence as the five of them eyed each other. At last Cyril turned to Val.

"So you're Valann," he said quietly. "Ria's been wondering about you as long as I can remember. I'm glad we were both finally able to meet you." He extended his hand.

Valann stared blankly at the extended hand, but made no effort to take it. Then reluctantly he stepped forward and embraced Cyril carefully, to the human's vast surprise.

"You are the one with whom my sister was to be forced to mate," he said. "She told me you fought for her freedom. For that kindness I honor you as if we were born of the same womb."

"I—thank you," Cyril said awkwardly, forcing himself to return the embrace. "I only wanted Ria to be happy."

"Happy? She's fortunate to be alive, and so are we," Lord Sharl said impatiently, tying his horse to a tree. "Still, if you say Rowan's coming, we may as well wait for her."

"No need to wait," Val said, shrugging. "Rowan is here. I'll bring them." He vanished into the undergrowth with a suddenness that unnerved Ria.

As soon as Valann was gone, Lord Sharl rounded on Ria.

"I hope you realize this little adventure of yours could have gotten you killed, and us with you. I didn't dare bring guards into the Heartwood for fear of provoking every elf in the forest into a massive battle—not that the guards would've been much help against elvan patrols hidden in the bushes and trees and shooting arrows that probably would've pierced the stoutest armor. They'd have killed us if Rivkah hadn't managed to hide us with her magic. Cyril's badly hurt, thanks to you, and if I can't manage to make some kind of treaty with Rowan, it may be even more dangerous getting back out, now that Rivkah's exhausted."

"There will be no danger if you leave passing only through the blighted lands, and I will tell you that road," Rowan said quietly, following Valann into the small clearing, Dusk and Lahti behind her. "Not all clans are so easily fooled by human magic as they were when last you used it to cloak your journey into our forest. Many small noses followed your scent, many ears marked your passage, and carried that message to Dusk. Fortunately we were already bound for the Altars in search of our wayward Valann." She laid her hand on Valann's shoulder. "Strangely enough, there was no trail at all to follow, and not a beast or bird seemed willing to give Dusk any idea of his whereabouts. When Hawk's Eye sent a bird bearing the news that Ria had come to the Heartwood, however, we knew where Chyrie would take her."

"Maybe the patrols had beast-speakers, too. That must be how they found us," Lady Rivkah murmured. "We thought they'd found some way to see through magic."

Dusk chuckled dryly.

"I imagine most of the patrols near the border were seeking Valann, not a band of humans, as he was the last to trespass on their lands, and his exploits no doubt in part explain why you were attacked so fiercely," he said. "But magic notwithstanding, I have no doubt that Valann would have been the more difficult to find, for all the noise your huge riding beasts make and the wide track they leave."

"And you are Ria." Rowan stepped closer to Ria, gently tracing the bones of Ria's cheeks with her fingertip before pulling Ria close in a warm embrace. "There's much of your mother in your face. Welcome among us, little one. Many of us have prayed to the Mother Forest that one day you would come home."

"I'm glad to be here," Ria said, infinitely relieved at her

welcome. "But Cyril's badly hurt, and he's my good friend. Is there someone who can help him?"

"Lahti and I will tend to him," Dusk assured her. "We've both dealt with arrow wounds many times."

Lord Sharl cleared his throat awkwardly.

"Look, I can't say I planned this meeting to happen in this manner, but since it has, I'd like to see something good come of it. It seems to me that I recall Rivkah and myself getting into a good bit of trouble just for being in this place. Is there somewhere else we could go to talk and have my son's injuries tended?"

Val scowled darkly at the interruption, and even Rowan frowned gently—what could possibly be more important than the reunion of kinfolk?—but the Eldest nodded, took Ria's hand, and turned away, leaving the others to follow or not as they chose. Lord Sharl hurriedly grabbed the leads of the horses, pulling Rivkah after him, although the High Lady gave a troubled glance toward Cyril. Cyril waved to her to go on, watching Valann as he leisurely bundled up the sleeping furs and supplies from his makeshift camp in the bushes, then wrinkling his brow in puzzlement as Valann laid the bundle on one of the altars.

"Are you just going to leave it there?" Cyril asked hesitantly.

"They're not mine," Valann said, shrugging. He glanced narrowly at Cyril. "Do you need assistance walking?"

"I think I can manage." Cyril stood upright, holding his side. "As long as we walk slowly."

Val nodded shortly, slowing his pace to match the human's. After a long moment he spoke again.

"Why do you wish to take my sister as your mate?"

Cyril hesitated thoughtfully, then sighed and shrugged back.

"Sometimes I'm not sure I do," he said. "Mother and Father could give you a hundred good political reasons. Mine are a little different, but they sound just as worthless when you say them out loud." He pulled a leaf from a bush as they passed and tore it raggedly in half, holding up the halves. "The two pieces look nothing alike, but they fit together along the edges. I guess it comes down to, for me, a feeling that Ria and I fit together along our jagged edges somewhere. But you said Lahti is your mate, didn't you? I guess you know all about it."

Valann chuckled.

"Lahti and I are not yet actually formally mated," he admitted. "She says it's too soon to decide, but she smiles when she says it, and she lives in my hut as if we were mates. I think she'll agree before our child is born." His smile faded as he remembered the cold, closed faces of the adults as they'd left the firepit on the first night of his return to Inner Heart. Lahti would need him when their child was born, need his support and love more than ever. Hopefully Lahti would agree to the mating quickly, while Valann was certain that their joining would be from love and happiness, not loneliness and need. "There are many reasons for our mating, too, more than I'd expected. I always supposed it a simpler thing."

"Lahti's pregnant?" Cyril raised her eyebrows. "It doesn't show yet."

"Our first coupling was only days ago," Valann said absently. "Lahti had not yet passed into womanhood." He glanced at Cyril sharply. "As my sister has not. She's too young still for coupling. Elvan women seldom leave their childhood until their third decade, and sometimes their fourth."

Cyril's face fell.

"How old is Lahti?" he asked after a long moment.

"Lahti has two decades and five years." Val glanced at Cyril and felt an unwilling sympathy. His own time of waiting for Lahti had been so short, only a few months, and yet so troublesome. How many long years might this human have to wait for Ria?

"But Ria's half of human blood, like you," Cyril protested, "and you've grown into adulthood in sixteen years, haven't you? So won't Ria grow faster, too?"

"Who can say?" Val sighed, shrugging. "She doesn't appear to have been speeded in her growth by her human blood, but all things are possible. But I haven't heard my sister say she wishes to be your mate."

"I know." Cyril glanced at Val rather defensively. "That's between Ria and me."

"Indeed it is between you, and I wonder that you leave it standing there," Val said, chuckling a little. "I'll give Lahti no peace until she agrees to be my mate. You and I, young human male, don't have centuries of leisure to indulge elvan patience. If you are meant to be my sister's mate, make her believe it. And be prepared to find other lovers to fill your arms while my sister is yet a child," Val added sternly.

Cyril flushed but said only, "They'll be wondering where we are. And my father will want me present for the negotiations."

Val only shrugged and led Cyril outside the circle of stones marking the common land of the Altars. Just outside the circle of stones, Rowan and Dusk had sat down on the earth to face Lord Sharl and Lady Rivkah, Lahti beside them. Ria had settled herself rather awkwardly at the base of a tree, carefully behind Rowan and Dusk, as if the elves were a wall to protect her from her foster parents. Elves and humans alike wore expressions of wary stubbornness.

Dusk and Lahti immediately came to help Cyril settle himself comfortably on the ground while they unwrapped the bandages and checked his wounds. To Val's untrained eye, they looked serious, and Ria was obviously alarmed, but Dusk seemed relieved by what he saw. To Val's pride, Dusk allowed Lahti to heal the wounds in shoulder and thigh by herself, after the Gifted One had smelled each wound for any signs of poison or infection and healed the wicked-looking gash in Cyril's side himself.

"You'll be well enough, young one," Dusk said kindly, patting Cyril's shoulder before he returned to Rowan's side. "You'll be weak for a few days from the loss of blood, but the wounds should heal cleanly."

Cyril pulled his tunic back down and glanced at his parents, then at Ria, hesitating. To Val's surprise, he turned and gave Val a rueful half-grin, then went to Ria, extending his hand. Ria hesitated only a moment before taking it, and let Cyril draw her to the circle of humans and elves. They joined neither side, but sat slightly apart between them. Val chuckled to himself and took Lahti's hand, drawing her slightly to the side also so that they faced Cyril and Ria. Lord Sharl spared Cyril only the briefest of scowls before turning his attention back to Rowan.

"I don't understand," Sharl said impatiently. "You were willing enough to make a treaty when Allanmere was last settled."

"I was," Rowan agreed. "And I'm eager to make peace between our two peoples now. But you must realize that circumstances are different in the forest now. I've never spoken for all the clans of the forest, but when we made our alliance just before the war, many clans were willing to listen to me, and perhaps to be guided by what I said. Now I speak only for my own clan, and my words bind no others. I've tried for sixteen years and still have formed no lasting alliance among our own people. It's always been our way that the clans have fought for their territories, and we're not a people to change our ways quickly. I was centuries trying to forge some unity between our clans before the war, and even with the storm of war gathering, many clans still disagreed with my goals and remained apart. After the invasion, they all fell to fighting again, and after a decade and a half they see no reason to stop. Building an alliance again may take centuries more."

"You told us Dusk had a vision of another invasion," Rivkah pressed. "It was the prospect of an invasion that brought the clans together before. Can't you use Dusk's prediction in the same way?"

"I am already attempting to do so, and will continue," Rowan said patiently. "But—your forgiveness, beloved," she said gently aside to Dusk, "—Dusk's visions are neither so clear nor so reliable that even my own clan follows them eagerly and without reservation, and they've seen the truth of his predictions many times. How can I expect more from the other clans, especially when all Dusk has seen is a vague warning of some unknown time in the future? What he foretold might be decades, even centuries ahead of us. That's what the other clans will say, if they believe us at all. If other signs come, if other Gifted Ones have visions of their own, that will help us."

"But there's your own clan," Sharl said slowly. "If your own clan formed a treaty with us, might that not lead the way for other clans to follow? If the Hawk's Eye Clan is sending messages, it seems they have some regard for you."

Dusk shook his head.

"Since the invasion, most of even our people remember humans only with hatred and fear," he said. "Only a very few of them actually saw your city, met your people, and have a firsthand memory of any kindness coming to us from humans. The others remember humans as the invaders, the attackers who burned the forest around us, or at least as trespassers and poachers who once invaded our territories to kill our trees and slaughter our game—and continue to do so, I might add. If it were known that Rowan's clan were dealing with the human rulers of the city, it would hurt Rowan's chances of forming an alliance within the forest, not help."

"Most clans prefer their solitude and have no desire to become part of a larger whole," Lahti said slowly, shaking her head. "If they knew that Rowan was dealing with the human leaders, they might believe Rowan was enlisting the humans' aid in defeating the neighboring clans and seizing their lands, or perhaps bargaining so that if the humans invaded the forest, Inner Heart alone might be spared."

"And there's more still to make me hesitate," Rowan said frankly. "Sixteen years ago you came to our forest and behaved in a disgraceful way toward our people—" She glanced at Ria and Cyril. "I won't elaborate in the presence of children the offenses you committed against the Mother Forest. But you came among us intending to cheat us, to use us to your own ends. Only when you bore our geas could I be assured that we wouldn't be cheated or betrayed. Sixteen years is only a moment here in the forest, but that's not so for a human. Now I no longer know your motivations, and I fear this is yet another attempt to use us for your own ends. I'm not certain you can be trusted to deal fairly with us."

Sharl grimaced.

"I could say the same," he said. "But I suppose I know better. Your folk don't actually *need* anything from us anymore, while the elves control all of the timber and most of the good game in the area—things that we in the city definitely *will* need. Isn't it enough that the elves are bargaining from a position of power?"

"That power you speak of is an empty promise," Rowan said, frowning. "Inner Heart cannot bargain with the lands of the border clans, either to grant humans passage there or for wood or game from those lands, so we have little to offer in trade if we desired it. And the elves of Inner Heart are few and the humans of your city many. We have no way to enforce any treaty we make, and no reason to trust that it would be honored."

"But what if the leaders of Allanmere represented elvan interests as well?" Rivkah asked quietly. "What if one of the rulers of the city, Cyril's wife, was an elf born in the Heartwood—Chyrie's daughter, in fact?"

Rowan glanced at Ria and smiled slightly.

"I don't know you," she said gently. "You weren't raised among us. You are but a child, and your spirit has not yet been tested by the Mother Forest. But you came to the forest of your own accord, alone and without weapons, and Chyrie brought you among us. You have your mother's courage and strength of will, and I see no guile and deceit in your eyes. I believe I could trust you to deal honestly with us. But that's only a beginning, and that is as it should be."

"What do you mean?" Sharl asked suspiciously.

"Once we made an alliance founded on one night's meeting," Dusk told him. "And like a tree whose roots had no time to dig deep, that alliance toppled and died in the passage of a storm. If another storm is indeed coming, these roots must have nourishment and time to dig deep. If it's your idea that Ria should represent our needs, perhaps it would be best that she spend some time among us to discover those needs, to come to understand her own people. If she learns the ways of the Mother Forest and takes her passage when she comes of age, other clans would trust her more easily."

"Now, wait," Lord Sharl said quickly. "Ria has a purpose to serve in the city—convincing its people to trust her as a co-ruler, and through her, to learn tolerance for the elves. She's got a great deal to learn about ruling the city, too. I pray Cyril will have better luck teaching her than I have," he added a little sourly. "At any rate, especially considering the danger of passing through the border lands, it's necessary that Ria stay in the city."

"Whose needs are you considering?" Dusk said gently. "Ria is a child now, but she will in time pass into womanhood in the manner of elvan women. What if she becomes soul-sick? Are you prepared to deal with *that* need?"

"Soul-sick?" Lord Sharl said. He and Lady Rivkah exchanged glances.

"Ria has always been healthy," Lady Rivkah said slowly. "She's never contracted any illness I couldn't deal with easily."

Rowan smiled a little condescendingly.

"That you speak so only shows that while you may have cared adequately for the needs of her body, you have left unanswered the requirements of her heart and her spirit. Where does she run in your city when her blood burns within her and her skin hungers for the spring rain? Where does she hunt in the stone walls when she aches to taste the fresh blood of her own kill? Where does she go to smell spring breezes sweet with flowers and leaves and warm, moist earth? Don't look at me in that dismissive manner," Rowan said sternly, frowning at Lord Sharl. "If humans wish to feed only their bellies, well enough for them; but we starve and die as easily without that food that nourishes our spirit. And as regards the tolerance that Ria might teach your people, there's no small teaching that must be done here in the forest as well. My people must also come to accept her, to learn that despite her years among humans she's still the daughter of Chyrie, if you wish them to believe that she might represent their interests in the city. And it might be best if some of our people visited your city to learn something of humans and their ways, too." She turned to Valann. "Perhaps you and Lahti would wish to go, to travel between the forest and the city with your sister."

Valann glanced at Lahti. He'd been curious enough about the human city. It would be hard to leave the forest, to enter a world he knew nothing about, but what harm could a visit do? They could return to the forest whenever they wished—it would be only a short walk to visit with Hawk's Eyes if they liked, too—and it would be good to have time to know his sister. But better yet, it would take Lahti away from the cold, closed faces and accusing mutters of the clan for a time, and perhaps spare their child some of the troubles Val had faced.

"Would you go?" he asked her quietly, taking her hand.

"To see all the wonders of a human city of stone with you?" Lahti chuckled warmly, squeezing his hand. "Need you ask? And if you were there, who could keep me away?"

"But I've not yet heard Ria say that she desires such a position of rulership, or such a mating, and the choice must be hers," Rowan said calmly. "We make no prisoners of our children as you do your bound beasts."

Suddenly all eyes turned to Ria, who squirmed under the scrutiny.

"Neither of us has agreed to anything yet," Cyril said suddenly, rather sharply. He climbed a little stiffly to his feet, pulling Ria up after him, to her vast surprise. He turned to Ria and spoke more gently. "Can we talk for a moment?"

Ria nodded gratefully, glad to be away from the sudden attention, and followed Cyril a short distance away. When he would have stopped, however, Ria pulled him farther from the group, back into the altar area.

"If I can still hear them," she said practically, "the elves can probably still hear us."

When they were comfortably out of earshot, however, they both hesitated uncomfortably. At last Ria broke the awkward silence.

"Cyril, I'm so sorry you were hurt," she said slowly. "But why did you have to come after me?"

"Well, you seemed so certain you'd be all right in the forest," Cyril said with a sigh. "But Mother and Father were just as certain you were as good as dead, and I suppose I had my doubts, too. I'd have waited—I promised, didn't I? But Mother and Father were getting ready to charge right into the forest after you, and I thought it'd be better if I came, too, so that maybe Mother and Father wouldn't be quite so hard on you when—if they found you. I even thought that maybe if we found you and you *were* all right, maybe I could persuade them to let you stay for a while, at least.

"We got into the forest all right, going in near the swamp where Mother's tracking spell showed you'd gone," Cyril continued. "We got through a whole territory without trouble, judging by the markers—that must've been the Hawk's Eyes Rowan mentioned. But we'd hardly crossed the markers when it seemed like every elf in the forest attacked us, and they chased us deeper into the forest—no chance of getting back out, so all we could do was keep going until we had enough time to stop and let Mother cast a spell to hide us. Even with that protection, we still ran into two more patrols and didn't do much better." He shrugged ruefully. "I guess Dusk was right—horses are hard to conceal in the underbrush. But at least we're alive. I'm just glad you didn't run into any of that trouble while you were alone."

Ria remembered the plain-looking elves who had given her mother the necklace and the food. They'd seemed so friendly. Had they been the ones who'd wounded Cyril?

"I wasn't really alone," Ria confessed. "My mother—Chyrie—met me not long after I entered the forest. She must've been watching for me. Nobody bothered me while

I was with her. Then she disappeared as soon as she brought me to Valann." She sighed sadly at the memory.

"Have you thought about—well, you know," Cyril said awkwardly, not meeting her eyes. "What we talked about before you left."

This time it was Ria's turn to look away.

"Cyril, I really, really like you," she said slowly. "I even love you in a way. When I saw you were hurt—well, I guess I'd rather they'd have hurt me than you. I even missed you when I left, a little. But I don't know if I could—I mean, if we—" She shrugged helplessly. "I just don't know if I could be somebody's wife and have children."

"Valann told me you might be a child for many more years, maybe more than another decade," Cyril said slowly. "I could stand that, I suppose, if you could stand me taking other women to my bed."

Ria grimaced. Cyril thought he was being accommodating, but the whole idea seemed so—so artificial. Wouldn't she be, in truth, just the hanger-on Lord Sharl had told her she might become, with no true marriage to Cyril, no inclination for rulership?

"Then why marry *me*?" Ria asked slowly. "Why not marry some lady you can tumble with and have heirs like you're supposed to?" She hoped almost desperately that Cyril wouldn't lie to her, mouth some ridiculous romantic speech.

Cyril looked at the ground, then sighed and met her eyes again.

"I know you feel like everyone's trying to use you," he said. "And I'm doing it too, aren't I? But you and I are friends, true friends, at least. If I don't marry you, Mother and Father will arrange some other marriage for me, probably to some noble lady who's been schooled from birth for rulership, and I'd be bound for life to a woman whom I might not even like, and we'd spend our lives playing power games against each other. And Mother and Father would still find some way to use you to make an alliance with the elves—or Rowan would."

Ria was silent. She wanted to believe the elves were

above that kind of dealing, but from what Valann had told
her, Rowan had been more than willing to use him—
whether because of his part-human blood or his status as
Chyrie's son—very similarly. And then there'd been the
way everybody's eyes had fastened on her even as Rowan
said the choice was hers. Even if Ria was able to stay in the
forest—and after her miserable time so far, she was rather
less certain that she wanted to—what use might the elves
make of Chyrie's daughter who had spent all her life
among humans and knew their ways so thoroughly? And
more—she was Cyril's friend and foster sister. Rowan
would likely have some use for that relationship, too.

Ria groaned and held her head. Before they'd come to
Allanmere, everything had seemed so simple. Now, even
though Rowan had said the choice was hers, there seemed
to be no choice she could make that left her any chance for
happiness or freedom.

She saw understanding in Cyril's eyes, and Ria wondered whether Cyril had thought through all the same
choices she had. He'd been a prisoner from birth, too, Ria
realized; he'd just decided to make the best of his cage
until he was the one holding the keys.

"There's nowhere to run for either of us," Cyril said
softly. "I suppose the only difference between us in that
respect is that I never had anywhere I could dream of running *to*. But we have one advantage left—our friendship. If
we marry, Mother and Father will abdicate in our favor—
they have to, to get Rowan to deal with the city and make
the alliance they want. They'll still try to use us, but *we'll* be
the High Lord and Lady then. They can advise us—and by
the gods, I hope they do—but we'll make our own decisions. And we, at least, know that we'll never try to use
each other." He shrugged, then grinned the engaging grin
that was so much like his father's. "We care for each other.
We can trust each other. And who knows? Over the years
we might even come to love each other, too."

Ria sighed and rubbed her eyes with the heels of her
hands. How ever did Cyril weave his way through all these
complications? It was just too much for her, too much.

Surely Cyril was prepared for rulership of Allanmere, just as surely as she was not. But she *could* trust him; she knew that much, at least, and friendship was something she *could* understand.

"You promise," she said at last in a small voice, "No itchy gowns and formal dinners and books and embroidery? And you won't object if I spend some time in the forest with my brother?"

"I promise," Cyril said, his voice heavy with relief. "And I'll make Valann and Lahti—or any other elves—welcome at the palace anytime they want to come."

Ria closed her eyes. She was trading her freedom for a power she didn't want and a destiny she'd much rather flee, with only her trust in Cyril to assure she wasn't trading everything for nothing. But she could make the trade herself, or, in one way or another, it would be made for her. She sighed and spoke the words to seal her fate.

"I'll marry you, Cyril."

"As they all want," Cyril said, his eyes twinkling. "But we'll do it for our own reasons. And when we're High Lord and Lady, we'll be no one's tools."

He held out his hand and Ria took it, and quietly they walked back to the clearing where the others were waiting.

"I've agreed to marry Cyril," Ria said quietly.

There was a long moment of silence. Lord Sharl and Lady Rivkah exchanged glances of relief; Rowan and Dusk nodded with satisfaction. Valann gave Ria a rather calculating glance, then grinned; Lahti appeared to have little understanding of and even less interest in the politics of Allanmere's government.

"Then when you and your mate speak for the human clan of Allanmere," Rowan promised, "Inner Heart will bargain with Allanmere, and I will try to persuade Hawk's Eye as well. They're a small clan, but they'll be a valuable ally, living at the edge of the forest nearest the city, and they might have use for weapons and even help defending their territory against the Blue-eyes. Perhaps other clans will agree to bargain with the Allanmeres when they know the daughter of Chyrie, savior of the Heartwood and beloved of the Mother Forest, speaks in part for the Allanmeres."

"And as soon as we can have the wedding, Rivkah and I will turn over the seat of Allanmere to Cyril and Ria," Lord Sharl promised. "If Dusk has the true gift of foresight and there *will* be a second invasion, there's no time to be lost beginning preparations."

"The first thing to do is make sure all the elvan clans are well armed, alliance or not, especially the border clans," Cyril said immediately. "Maybe that will foster goodwill among the clans."

"More likely the border clans will use those same weapons against any human who ventures too near their territory," Lord Sharl corrected with a scowl.

"It would be advantageous if the Inner Hearts could witness your mating ritual," Dusk suggested. "They've never seen Chyrie's daughter."

"We can't hold the ceremony in the forest," Lady Rivkah protested. "It's just as important that the people of Allanmere see the wedding."

"Perhaps we could have two ceremonies, one in the city and one in the forest," Cyril suggested. "If we simply—"

Ria turned her back on the conversation. It made no difference to her whether she was married in the Heartwood or the city, although she was curious to see the Inner Heart village. Somehow the whole issue no longer seemed to concern her. The decision had been made; the details didn't really matter, did they?

To Ria's surprise, Valann and Lahti rose and came to her, Lahti embracing Ria as Rowan had done.

"The human lord Sharl rushed us so, I had no chance to greet you," Lahti said rather reprovingly. Then she smiled radiantly and embraced Ria again; Ria was struck by how much taller than herself Lahti was. "But you who were born of one womb with my beloved Valann, you'll be to me as dear as my own sister."

How odd, to have a sister, of sorts at least, whom she'd never met before. But then, she'd never met her brother before today, too. Ria found she rather liked the idea.

"I'd like to have a sister," she said shyly. "Will you and Valann really visit us at the city?"

"Valann is half of human blood, and our child, too, will share that heritage," Lahti said, folding her hands over her flat belly. "Dusk is right—Val and our child should learn something of these people whose blood they share. And I'm curious, too, to see the city and its people."

"I've had only one day to meet my sister," Val added, taking Ria's hand. "Besides our absent mother, you're my only blood kin. I'm glad to spend my time learning to know you and the world you've lived in. But you must come to the forest, too, and spend time among our clan. They'll welcome you with great joy."

"Oh, I want to," Ria said quickly. She reached down to scratch the itchy rash on her legs. "Not—not now. But soon." She hesitated. "I expect we'll have to go back right away for the wedding, whatever Rowan says. I don't suppose—would you come back with us, stand beside me at our wedding?"

Val and Lahti exchanged glances. Lahti turned and looked back over her shoulder in the direction of Inner Heart, and a fleeting expression of pain crossed her face. When she turned back to Valann, however, she smiled and nodded.

"We would be honored to stand beside you at your mating," Val said, smiling as well.

Ria sighed with relief. She'd been so afraid that from the moment she stepped outside the Heartwood, her life would be nothing but endless politics and meaningless formalities. At least with her brother and Lahti in the palace, there'd be somebody else to talk to when Cyril was too busy, somebody who really didn't care about politics and formalities.

Then she grinned. With Val and Lahti at the palace, life would be anything but ordinary and boring. There'd be stories to tell and to hear, new games to learn and to teach.

"One thing troubles me," Lahti said slowly. "Dusk's vision. He said you were walking to meet your sister, bearing a gift that would give her freedom. What was the gift?"

Val shrugged.

"Who can say?" he said. "Perhaps the gift was our kinship that will return her to the forest, even if only from time to time. Perhaps Dusk was merely wrong. He said Ria was walking unseen toward the forest, but she came with Chyrie."

"No, I did walk unseen," Ria corrected. "All the way from the inside of the city and part way across the open ground between the city and the forest." She was fascinated with the idea of Dusk's vision; Lady Rivkah had told her that true foresight was very rare indeed among mages. But there was nothing Val could give her that would give her freedom, not now.

"But I have nothing to give you," Val said regretfully. "Nothing but my friendship and my love. Our mother whisked me from my hut with only the clothes I wore. My whole clan would have brought you gifts, if we'd known you were here."

The thought of a whole clan prepared to welcome her and celebrate her arrival, High Lady-to-be or not, made Ria feel a little better. Still, she reminded herself, they'd be celebrating not the arrival of Ria, but of Chyrie's daughter. *That* thought was rather less satisfying.

"I would give you freedom if I could," Valann said more soberly, taking Ria's hands. "If this mating is wrong for you, tell me. I'd fight to my last drop of blood to spare you a mating against your choice. I know Rowan would say the same."

But would she? After listening to Cyril, Ria thought perhaps not. Rowan was an elf, yes, but she, too, was a leader, like Lord Sharl and Lady Rivkah, and her people's welfare would certainly would be her first consideration. And there *would* be tremendous advantages to be gained—perhaps not now, but by and by, especially if there were a second invasion—from an alliance and perhaps a trade agreement with the humans. Ideally that meant Ria on the throne of Allanmere. Ria shook her head disgustedly. Gods, were these the things Cyril thought about all the time? How wretched!

"Cyril's been my friend all my life," Ria said slowly. "I don't love him like a wife would love a husband, but maybe someday I will. I know he'll be good to me. If I don't marry him, I think I'd have to come live in the forest, and"—*and it's not my world, not now, with all the strange smells and strange sounds and no roof over my head and lumpy beds and itchy legs, and I don't know anybody here but my mother who I've known only a few days, and my brother who I've just met*— "and I don't think I could do that."

She thought Val might be surprised, but he only nodded slowly.

"Your roots haven't grown here," he said, smiling a little. "How could they? But at least we'll have time to know each other."

"Unless Dusk's vision is true, and invaders burn the forest down around us," Lahti reminded him, frowning a little.

That silenced them both, and Ria felt her fragile happiness begin to fade again. She'd thought so much about her own future, so blindly, as if nothing else mattered. Even Lord Sharl and Lady Rivkah were thinking in terms of trade agreements and profit, when the city *and* the elves might be facing the same kind of invasion that had once devastated both. Cyril had wisely seen past those minor goals when he'd spoken of arming the elves. Yes, he'd be a fine ruler—one whom humans and elves alike could respect.

And maybe one she could respect, too.

A sound behind her made Ria turn; to her surprise, it was Cyril himself.

"I thought you were busy deciding the future of Allanmere and the forest with your mother and father and Rowan and Dusk," Ria said, a little more sharply than she meant to. Yes, she was still a little annoyed that her homecoming to the forest had been turned into diplomatic negotiations, but that was hardly Cyril's fault.

"They think that's what they're doing," Cyril said, grinning that lopsided grin that was so much like his father's. "I didn't bother to correct them."

"What do you mean?" Lahti asked him. "You think they're premature in their plans when another invasion could well destroy the city again, or the forest, or both?"

"Well, there's that, too," Cyril admitted. "But what they don't realize is that *we're* the future of Allanmere and the forest, the four of us, not them; they're the past. They can talk all they like, but in the end it's the four of us who'll shape the future."

Valann raised one eyebrow.

"How can you say that?" he asked. "You and my sister will rule the city, it's true, but Lahti and I are barely out of childhood. Rowan will speak for the Inner Hearts until she dies, and then the next Eldest will take her place. I'll most likely be long dead by then. I'll never speak for the Inner Hearts."

"You don't understand." Cyril took Ria's hand. "Rowan speaks for Inner Heart, yes. But she listens to Inner Heart, too. Dusk's visions, she listens to those, and that influences the decisions she makes. I'm sure she listens to other voices, too. Valann, Lahti—you'll know Allanmere and its people better than any elf in the forest. Valann's the only elf in the forest with some human blood—until your child is born. You're Chyrie's son and Ria's brother. Every elf in the forest knows who you are. Rowan will listen to your voices—she has to. And other clans in the forest, bit by bit, they'll listen to you, too. And it may come to pass that your voice is heard in more places through the forest, heeded by more Eldests, than Rowan's."

Valann looked at Lahti, troubled, but he could not deny what Cyril said. "You must be the one." Rowan had said it. Dusk had said it. *Mother Forest,* he thought, *make me strong enough. If I am indeed Your tool, I beg You, do not break me.*

"We're the ones who will decide the future," Cyril said softly. "You and Lahti will have a child to protect, and Ria and I will have a city to protect. We're the ones with the most to lose. And that's why we'll be the ones to decide."

Lahti took Val's hand, and he could feel her strong fingers trembling slightly.

"Silence was wrong—the words we speak here indeed

have power," she murmured. "What seeds are we planting today?"

"Seeds of kinship and understanding," Val smiled, his free hand clasping Ria's.

"And friendship," Ria added. Cyril's and Valann's warm hands clasping hers made her feel suddenly strong, something more than a confused child. Perhaps a part of something greater. Perhaps not a High Lady—but perhaps the seed of one.

"And peace and prosperity," Lahti said almost like a prayer, reaching for Cyril's hand to complete the circle.

"Seeds of the future," Cyril said, squeezing Ria's hand.

"A great storm is coming," Lahti murmured. "Mother Forest grant that this time the seeds we plant are strong enough to stand against it."

"As long as the four of us stand together, we'll be strong enough," Cyril promised.

Ria looked down at Val's hand clasping her own, his fingers large, hers small, and for a moment she felt the ghost of another touch there. For a moment she could almost see another hand, green vines twining between small, strong brown fingers, resting on theirs.

Ria glanced up, and her eyes met Val's, saw the understanding there. Almost imperceptibly, he nodded.

We'll be strong enough, she thought. *The five of us.*

From very far away, the sound of distant thunder.